LUKE TRAVIS: Every kind of outlaw comes his way. But this time he faces two bands of killers gone out of control . . .

OWEN BRODERICK: The tall, prosperous rancher is hoarding money he's robbed from banks. Now, he's out to save his fortune—and his wife . . .

LUCINDA BRODERICK: Owen's comely young wife is the only survivor of a brutal Indian raid—and the prize of an Indian renegade . . .

TATE DRISCOLL: With his animal cunning and fast gun, the outlaw joins the revenge-crazed Brodericks—looking for a quick killing of his own . . .

NESTOR GILWORTH: In his shaggy buffalo-hide coat the old hunter is a relic from another age in the West. But when the shooting starts he's there—with a gun . . .

CLAW: The ruthless warrior with a withered, twisted hand touches off bloodshed with his raid on the Broderick ranch—and no man takes him alive . . .

WESLEY STILLMAN: The teenage boy is heading west with his parents, until the harsh prairie winter makes him an orphan—fighting for his life . . .

Books by Justin Ladd

Published by POCKET BOOKS

Most Pocket Books are available at special quantity discounts for bulk purchases for sales promotions, premiums or fund raising. Special books or book excerpts can also be created to fit specific needs.

For details write the office of the Vice President of Special Markets, Pocket Books, 1230 Avenue of the Americas, New York, New York 10020.

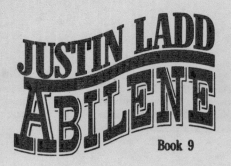

JUSTIN LADD
ABILENE

Book 9

THE
TRACKER

™ **BCI** Created by the producers of
**Wagons West, Stagecoach,
White Indian, and San Francisco.**

Book Creations Inc., Canaan, NY · Lyle Kenyon Engel, Founder

POCKET BOOKS

New York   London   Toronto   Sydney   Tokyo

An *Original* Publication of POCKET BOOKS

 POCKET BOOKS, a division of Simon & Schuster Inc.
1230 Avenue of the Americas, New York, NY 10020

ISBN: 0-671-68151-6

First Pocket Books printing August 1989

10 9 8 7 6 5 4 3 2 1

POCKET and colophon are trademarks of
Simon & Schuster Inc.

Printed in the U.S.A.

THE
TRACKER

Chapter One

———❦———

LUCINDA BRODERICK STOOD IN THE DOORWAY OF THE ranch house, watching as the gathering dusk turned the yard and the Kansas prairie beyond it a deep purple. Winter was coming on quickly, and the air was chilly, but the beauty in the evening light had prompted her to pause for a moment to enjoy the sunset despite the cold.

A covey of quail erupted from the scrubby brush about fifty yards from the rough plank building, the beating of wings loud in the evening shadows. Lucinda stiffened as she saw the startled birds fly up. Their flight meant only one thing. Something—or *someone*—was out there.

Lucinda was tall for a woman, with a lithe, slender figure and wavy blond hair that fell to her shoulders. As she peered out into the twilight, she wished that she had worn a scarf or a bonnet, anything to hide her shining gold hair. Even in this dim light it would draw attention.

Moving slowly and trying not to look alarmed, Lucinda eased back into the house. Behind her, she heard the familiar sounds of the long table being set for dinner—softly murmuring voices, occasional laughter, the patter of running footsteps. The aroma of cooking food drifted deliciously from the kitchen.

All of that is about to come to an abrupt, horrible end, Lucinda thought. She had lived on the frontier for long enough to have developed a sense for trouble. Even before that, when she was still at the parlor house in New Orleans, she had known when violence was about to explode.

"Deborah," Lucinda called in a voice tinged with urgency.

Deborah Broderick walked out of the dining room and came unhurriedly to the younger woman's side. At thirty-two Deborah was ten years older than Lucinda and was rather plain. Dressed in a simple cotton gown, she wore her long brunette hair gathered tidily in a bun. She was married to Max Broderick, brother of Lucinda's husband, Owen, and in a decade of marriage had given Max two children, a boy and a girl. Ranch life had roughened Deborah somewhat, as it did any woman who had to live such an isolated, work-filled existence, but she still managed to smile warmly as she came up to the younger woman. "What is it, Lucinda?" she asked.

Lucinda did not turn to look at her. Keeping her eyes fixed on the flat, brush-dotted terrain beyond the doorway, she said quietly, "Something's out there."

Deborah gasped. "You're sure?"

"I'm sure." Lucinda nodded.

"Did you see anything, any horses?"

Lucinda shook her head. "They're there, though. I saw some quail fly up. Something startled them."

"A coyote, maybe?" Deborah suggested hopefully.

"I don't think so."

"Where are Hollis and Borden?"

"Still out at the barn, as far as I know." Lucinda had seen the two hired hands enter the barn and knew they had gone to feed and bed the horses down for the night.

"Why don't you go get them?"

Lucinda looked at her sister-in-law and for the first time since she had spotted the startled quail expressed the fear that had been lurking in the back of her mind. "I . . . I can't," she stammered.

"Somebody has to. We'll need them if we're going to get through this, Lucinda." Deborah's voice was firm, but Lucinda could hear a hint of fear in it, too. Neither of them had said what she was really thinking, but some words did not have to be spoken. No one had to scream *Indians!* The flight of the startled birds, the heavy silence that had followed it, the very feel of the air . . . that was enough.

Indian raids were a major concern to people living on isolated ranches in this part of Kansas. Abilene, the nearest good-sized town, was many miles to the east. While townspeople occasionally had problems with the Indians, attacks on large settlements were becoming rarer all the time.

During the past decade the Kansas Pacific railroad had pushed across the state all the way to Denver, Colorado, cutting a broad swath through what had once been ancestral Indian lands and hunting grounds. This incursion of the iron horse had enraged the Indians and prompted a series of bitter clashes between white and red men. The Indians had won some battles, but they had lost the war.

Many of the bands of warriors—Sioux and Cheyenne and Arapaho—had been rounded up and sent to the reservations in Indian Territory. But other groups of braves still roamed the prairie, waging a war that had already been lost. These marauding Indians preferred to attack isolated ranches like the one owned by Owen Broderick and his brothers, Max and Al.

The brothers had come here with their wives and children, planning to make a good life for themselves. Now all of that might come to a crashing end in the gloom of an early winter evening.

Lucinda swallowed. Deborah was still waiting for her answer. The older woman was right, of course. With Owen, Max, and Al away from the ranch on a job, the women would need the assistance of the two hired men if they were to have any chance of surviving an Indian raid. She was just wasting time by letting fear rule her common sense.

Raising her chin, Lucinda looked squarely at Deborah. "I'll go get them," she declared and started toward the doorway.

Before she could reach it, a scream tore through the night. The cry of pain came from the barn, and it was followed a split second later by the boom of gunshots.

A piece of crockery shattered with a loud crash as someone in the kitchen dropped it. Deborah grabbed Lucinda's arm, pulled her away from the door and into the front room, and thrust her toward the windows. "Close the shutters!" the older woman commanded. Deborah spun around and headed toward the kitchen, shouting, "Everyone inside! Close up the house! Close up the house!"

Frightened cries burst from the other rooms as Deborah's urgent commands made it clear what they were facing. The loudest, most fearful shrieks came from Constance, Al Broderick's wife. Al was the youngest of the brothers, yet Constance was older than Lucinda, Owen's second wife. Constance lived in mortal dread of Indians. Now she cried helplessly as the others scurried around preparing for the attack that was already starting.

Lucinda slammed the shutters closed on the first of the three windows in the front room. The windows were large and actually had glass in them—an expensive rarity on the frontier. The panes had been carefully brought on wagons from Abilene. Owen had insisted on it. Nothing was too good for his family, he always said, and it was not as if he were spending his own money. But he was cautious, too, and had installed thick shutters on the inside of the windows that would be closed in the event of a raid.

Another pair of shots rang out from the barn, and then a figure burst through the open doors. It was the hired hand called Hollis. Lucinda saw him just as she was shutting and latching the shutters on the second window. In that fleeting glimpse she had seen a bloody stain on Hollis's shirtsleeve. He had his gun in his hand, and by the time Lucinda reached the third and last window, she saw him twist around and fire a shot into the barn as he ran. Then she heard his booted feet pounding right outside the door.

He pushed aside the heavy wooden panel and staggered into the room. Lucinda was ready, the third window shuttered now. She shoved the door closed behind Hollis, reached up to grasp the heavy bar that was fastened to the wall, and swung it down into the sturdy brackets that Owen had designed to catch it. The door was thick enough to stop most bullets, the bar strong enough to withstand heavy impacts. Owen Broderick and his brothers had built this place to last.

And if they were here, Lucinda thought bitterly, *instead of away in Nebraska holding up a bank, we would have a good chance of surviving this Indian raid.* As it was, the odds were against them.

She ran over to Hollis, who was gripping the back of an armchair for support and breathing heavily. Blood dripped from his arm onto the floor. Lucinda glanced at the wound and saw the ragged tear in his forearm through his ripped shirt. Clutching his uninjured arm, she asked, "What happened?"

"Injuns . . . jumped us," Hollis panted. "First I knowed they was around was when one of them red devils grabbed Borden and . . . and cut his throat. There weren't nothin' I could do for him, Miss Lucinda. I let off some shots at 'em and held 'em off long enough for me to light out. One of 'em cut me 'fore I got out of the barn, but I managed to blow a hole in the bastard!" He sagged and grasped the chair harder to hold himself up. "Pardon my language, ma'am," he gasped.

"Don't worry about that, Hollis," she told him, willing her voice to stay calm. "I'm just glad you were able to shoot him. Here, let me see to your arm."

She darted into the dining room, snatched two napkins from the table, and hurried back to Hollis's side. Pushing up the torn sleeve, she mopped the wound with one napkin and swiftly fastened a bandage with the second. As she tied the cloth around his arm, she asked, "Can you make it to the window?"

The hired hand took a deep breath and pulled himself upright. "Yes, ma'am. I surely can."

Lucinda studied him briefly. He was on the high side of middle-aged and wounded on top of it, but there was a fierce determination in his weather-beaten face. "Good," she replied, squeezing his arm in encouragement. "I'll bring you a Winchester."

The front windows commanded a view not only of

the barn but also of the plain where Lucinda had seen the disturbed quail. That was the best spot for Hollis. Owen had built rifle ports into the shutters, and someone handy with a Winchester could do quite a bit of damage from there.

Once Hollis was set, Lucinda became aware of the hubbub in the house. She could hear more shutters slamming and the rattle of rifles being yanked out of their storage racks. The small children were crying. She could not blame them for being afraid.

Taking a deep breath and trying to calm her own racing pulse, Lucinda took stock of their defenses. With Borden dead in the barn and Constance hysterical and useless here in the house, there remained only five able-bodied people to defend the ranch. She could handle a gun, and so could Deborah. Even wounded, Hollis would give a good account of himself, she decided, and her two stepsons, Jack and Frank, had been taught to shoot at an early age. Owen had taken pride in how well the boys could fire a Winchester. They were fifteen and twelve years old respectively, hardly men but no longer children, not out here on the frontier. The other youngsters, Max and Deborah's boy and girl and Al and Constance's three girls, could load and fetch, but that was all they could do.

Too few to defend this place against what may be a horde of savages, Lucinda thought. If this was just a small raiding party, they might have a chance. But if there were more than a dozen Indians, the outlook was grim.

She hurried into the dining room and almost ran into her stepson Frank. The twelve-year-old had a rifle in each hand, and he thrust them at her. As she took them, Lucinda could see how pale his face was in the lantern light.

"Thank you, Frank," she said. "I'll give one of these to Mr. Hollis."

"Okay, Lucinda," he replied. "I'll get another gun and cover one of the windows in here."

She nodded. For an instant, she regretted that Frank and his brother had always called her by her given name, rather than calling her *Mother*. Even in this moment of crisis, Frank did not turn to her for a maternal hug, a sharing of warmth. She had always gotten along well with her husband's sons, but she had never been able to replace their mother.

Lucinda brushed aside the twinge of regret. She had no time to worry about that now—not with all of their lives at stake. She ran back into the front room, handed one of the rifles to Hollis, then hurried to one of the other windows. She worked the lever to make sure there was a round in the chamber, catching the cartridge that was ejected in the maneuver and sliding it back into the loading gate on the side of the weapon. Grasping the little ring on the rifle port in the shutter, she pulled it open and thrust the rifle's octagonal muzzle through it. The opening was barely large enough to accommodate the weapon and give her enough room to aim over the top of the barrel.

There had been no gunshots fired since the brief flurry that had exploded in the barn when Hollis made his escape. Gradually an eerie silence fell over the house. It was quiet outside, and the only sound inside was Constance's soft sobbing. Even the children made no sound now. For long moments Lucinda stood in front of the window, hearing only the pounding of her own pulse in her head.

This is just like the savages, Lucinda thought as she waited. They were just toying with the people in the ranch house, stretching the moments out agonizingly before they launched their attack. The light would be gone soon, and the Indians would move in then, able to dart through the shadows until they were almost at the house before they could be seen.

No matter how it ends, Lucinda knew, *this is going to be the longest night of my life.* But now that all the frenzied preparations had been made, she could do nothing but wait—wait and think about the life that had brought her to this ranch on the Kansas plains.

If Deborah and Constance had any idea what her days had been like in the parlor house, they never mentioned it. When Owen brought her to the ranch from New Orleans, they had welcomed her into the family as best they could. Yet they must have been suspicious. When a man who has been widowed for a year returns from a city like New Orleans with a beautiful blond bride who is much younger than he, there was only one logical conclusion to draw. But Lucinda had never felt that Deborah and Constance looked down on her. Their children had liked her, too, and Jack and Frank had accepted her, even though they had never grown close to her. Max and Al, of course, were taken with her immediately; Lucinda had met very few men who were not struck by her beauty. But neither of them had ever made improper advances toward her or treated her as anything other than a sister-in-law. Owen Broderick was definitely the leader of his family, and his brothers would never cross him.

That was why the Broderick brothers were still robbing banks, even though this ranch, originally intended as a hideout and a safe place to keep their families, had prospered. The ranch had done so well, in fact, that Owen had been forced to hire Hollis and Borden to help out.

During the last couple of years, Owen had stashed over fifty thousand dollars in the carved wooden chest he kept in his study. Once the ranch became a going, profitable concern, it had seemed to Lucinda that Owen's nest egg was large enough to see them through any hard times that might come. But Owen had thought they needed more, and as usual, what Owen thought best was what the Brodericks did.

He had made one concession, though. Lucinda remembered clearly how he had taken her in his brawny arms and bid her farewell, saying after he kissed her, "This will be the last time, 'Cinda. I promise you that."

"I hope so, Owen," she whispered, looking up at his broad, florid face. "I want to start giving you some sons, too."

He grinned then, that carefree smile that had first drawn her attention. "We'll get started on that as soon as I get back," he promised, his pale blue eyes twinkling.

Now they might not ever get a chance to have those sons, Lucinda told herself as she kept staring over the barrel of the Winchester. It was getting harder to see anything outside. Darkness was closing in, and no doubt so were the Indians.

Never enough. Nothing was ever enough for Owen Broderick. He and his brothers had lived a rough-and-tumble early existence as buffalo hunters, and Lucinda was convinced that that life had scarred the man. In the time that she had known him he had always wanted more, whether it was money or land or cattle or love-making. That drive, that ambition, was part of the reason Lucinda loved him.

But that was what had driven the brothers to Nebraska, had caused them to leave their families alone here. Nothing bad had ever happened while the men had been away on other trips, and Owen had probably convinced himself that it never would.

Lucinda closed her eyes for a moment and moved her lips in silent prayer. It had been a long time since she had talked to the Lord, but now she asked Him to keep them all alive through this ordeal. If they made it, she would see to it that Owen never left them alone again.

There was still no movement in the yard as Lucinda opened her eyes, and a ludicrous thought suddenly occurred to her. What if there were only a bare handful of Indians out there? They might have fled after murdering Borden, especially since Hollis had probably killed one of them. There might not be one single Indian within five miles of the place at this very moment. If that was the case, the people inside the house would probably remain tense and terrified all night long . . . and all for nothing.

Lucinda was just about to voice her thoughts to Hollis, who was crouching ten feet away at one of the other windows, when outside an ululating screech shattered the possibility.

Movement flickered in the shadowy yard. Lucinda saw it through the narrow opening of the rifle port and instantly squeezed the trigger of her rifle. The Winchester boomed, shattering Owen's precious window glass, and kicked back against her shoulder. The recoil was painful even though she was braced for it. She had no way of knowing if she had hit anything. All she could do was jack another round into the chamber and wait for the next chance to fire.

Gunshots, mingled with more intimidating howls from the Indians, blasted outside. Lucinda's heart sank. There had to be at least a couple of dozen savages in the attacking band, probably more. Shots rang from the other side of the house as the inhabitants began to return the fire. Lucinda thought she saw something else and triggered again. The acrid bite of gunsmoke stung her nose. Constance let out another wail.

That was the beginning of a nightmare that seemed to have no end. Lucinda doubted that the battle lasted more than half an hour, but time had no meaning now. There was only killing and trying to keep from being killed.

The Indians charged the house again and again, suffering a few wounds in the process but not seeming to lose any men. Then they set fire to the barn, and the hay stored inside went up quickly. At first she thought they had made a mistake by firing the barn, that the illumination would allow the defenders to see the Indians better. But that proved not to be the case. The flames flickered and danced and threw grotesque shadows that only helped hide the Indians as they ran toward the house.

It's only a matter of time, Lucinda thought, *until they set fire to the house itself.* That would be the end. All the people inside could do then would be choose how they wished to die.

But in the meantime, she emptied the Winchester and then turned away from the window to find one of the children, a little girl, holding a fresh rifle for her. The child could barely support the weight of the weapon, but there was a determined look on her face as she lifted it toward Lucinda. Lucinda bent to take it and brushed her lips quickly across the top of the little girl's head. For a moment, her self-control threatened to desert her as the horror of their plight sank in, but then she steeled herself, forcing herself to turn back to the window and start shooting again.

When the end came, it was quick and from an

unexpected source. Instead of setting fire to the house, the Indians turned their attention to the front door. Lucinda caught a glimpse of several warriors running toward the house, carrying a heavy wagon tongue that had been stored in the barn. It was unusual for Indians to make use of a battering ram, but that was undoubtedly what they were planning. Lucinda fired at them, but her shot did not slow them down. A second later the heavy column of hardwood slammed against the door. Involuntarily Lucinda let out a small yelp of fright.

The bar across the entrance withstood the first blow, although the door itself shuddered. Lucinda tried desperately to angle her rifle so that she could fire at the savages just outside, but the rifle port was so narrow that she could not manage it. Twice more the wagon tongue crashed against the door, and at the second blow there was a loud crack as the bar started to give.

Hollis glanced at Lucinda through the haze of gunsmoke that was floating in the room and waved an arm. "Get out of here, Miss Lucinda!" he shouted. "Get into the other part of the house! I'll hold them heathens off!"

Hollis could not stand up to the Indians alone, and Lucinda knew it. Besides, flight would only postpone the inevitable. Better to face death now and go down fighting, she decided. Forcing aside the panic that was tearing at her, she yanked her rifle out of the opening in the shutter and turned toward the doorway just as another blow thundered against it.

This time the bar gave completely. It split in the middle; chunks of wood flew to the sides as the door was smashed open. Lucinda saw a piece of wood coming toward her and flung her gun up to try to block it. The fragment hit the rifle and knocked it out of her hands. She staggered, felt herself falling. The back of her head thudded against the wall. Stars exploded behind her eyes, but their brilliance was fleeting. A wave of blackness suddenly slid over her, and she slumped to the floor.

Lucinda did not completely lose consciousness. A part of her was still aware of what was going on around her, aware of the shouts and the gunshots and the agonized screams that seemed to go on forever. She lay huddled against the wall, waiting for the bullet or the knife thrust that would end her life.

Then, after a timeless interval, she felt rough hands grasping her and pulling her to her feet. A hard, callused palm cracked across her face, jerking her head to the side and forcing her back to reality. She blinked and tried to focus on the figure standing in front of her.

He was a tall man with long raven hair worn in braids and surprisingly handsome features, even streaked with war paint as they were. Broad-shouldered and lean-waisted, he wore the traditional buckskins of the Plains Indians. Lucinda thought he was probably a Sioux; most of the members of that tribe's various lodges were north of here, fighting the white man in Wyoming and Dakota, but some bands of renegades still roamed this far south. The pain in Lucinda's head made her wince and close her eyes for a moment, but when she opened them again, he was still there. The nightmare had not gone away.

Two more braves were holding her up by the arms. One of them started to slide a hand toward her breast, but the warrior standing in front of her made a sharp gesture, stopping the savage from pawing her. Lucinda sagged in their grip, most of her strength gone.

She looked past the warrior and saw Hollis lying on the floor, his clothes covered with blood. He had been shot and then hacked almost to pieces. At least his pain was over, Lucinda thought fuzzily.

Glancing toward the doorway into the dining room, she saw the sprawled bodies of her stepsons. Jack and Frank had evidently tried to meet the Indians' charge after they broke through the door, and the lads had been brutally cut down. Beyond them Lucinda could see Deborah and Constance lying on the dining room floor, both nude, both dead. The Indians had slashed their throats when they were through with them. There was no sign of the children, but the ominous stillness that pervaded the house told Lucinda that they were probably dead also.

She closed her eyes again and shuddered in horror. Undoubtedly the only survivor, she could think of only one reason her life had been spared. The savages wanted to take their time with her, make their pleasure and her torment last as long as possible. She wished she had turned the rifle on herself as soon as they started to break in—

"So, Yellowhair, you fear us," the warrior in front of her abruptly said. "You should. All whites should fear the rightful vengeance of the Sioux. We shall spread blood and death until all of you are driven from our lands!"

Lucinda said nothing. She could make no reply to this man.

"But you . . . you shall not die," he went on. "You will come with us."

Her stomach knotted, and for a moment she thought she would be sick. All her hopes for a quick death fled.

But if they took her with them as a captive, a small

part of her brain told her, she at least had a chance to escape. Better to live, she told herself, even as a slave, with the hope of survival and eventual freedom.

The tall Indian, who was evidently the chief of this band, nodded. "Winter is coming," he went on. "You shall warm my blankets when the snow falls, Yellowhair."

That was what she had expected. She glared at him, trying not to let him see the emotions that were writhing within her. He could kill her, but he would not break her.

A smile suddenly appeared on his face, but his dark eyes glinted cruelly as he stepped closer to her. "Ah, you have spirit," he said as he lifted a hand to caress her cheek. "Claw likes a woman with spirit. They ride well."

Lucinda tried to pull away as she saw the hand he raised toward her. It was twisted and malformed, the fingers grown together. Surely it had been that way since he was born and had no doubt given him his name. But if he was ashamed of his deformity, he gave no hint of it. He ran the hand over her face, laughing as she flinched involuntarily.

"You will learn to enjoy the touch of Claw, Yellowhair," he told her. "You will moan for it in the night." Then his features hardened, and he spat out a guttural command in his native tongue. The braves who were holding her dragged her toward the shattered doorway.

Lucinda had no strength to resist. She let them pull her out into the cold night air. The barn was still burning, although the roof had already collapsed. Lucinda looked away from the barn and saw the large group of horses waiting in front of the house. She felt herself lifted onto one of them. Shivering from the chill, she sat there and watched the Indians loot the house. They stole all the guns and most of the food from the larder. Claw strode imperiously out of the house and stood with arms folded, watching as his braves emerged.

One of them came out carrying the small wooden chest that had been in Owen's study. Lucinda recognized it immediately. Made of rich rosewood, it had elaborate carving on the lid. Brass fittings strengthened the corners, and a heavy lock secured it.

Evidently the chest struck Claw's fancy, because he rapped a command to the warrior who had claimed it. Lucinda could not understand the language, but Claw's intent was clear. Truculently the warrior handed the chest to Claw, who hefted it and studied the lock. He nodded, then gave the chest to another Indian, who brought it to the horse where Lucinda waited. The Sioux rapidly lashed it onto the horse's back, positioning it so that Claw would have room to ride behind her.

Claw issued more orders. Several warriors brought torches from the burning barn and flung the firebrands through the doorway into the house. Within seconds, Lucinda could see the rising glow inside the building as the flames began to spread.

When he was satisfied that the fire had taken hold, Claw walked over to the horse and swung lithely up behind Lucinda. She felt his warmth and smelled his pungent, oily scent as he pressed himself against her. The other renegades were mounting, too, and when they were ready Claw shouted a command and waved his deformed hand in the air. Then he clamped that arm around Lucinda's waist and, with his good hand, grasped the reins and wheeled the horse around. Lucinda lurched back against him as the animal broke into a gallop.

She heard the triumphant whoops as the Indians

raced into the night, felt the cold wind tearing at her face. Claw had not even given her a chance to take a last look at what had been her home, but it did not really matter. There was nothing back there for her now. She clung to the fact that she was still alive and the hope that somehow, some way, Owen Broderick would find her.

A man could see a long way on the Kansas plains. Owen Broderick had learned to be watchful, keeping an eye on both his back trail and the landscape unfolding in front of him. There was a Winchester in his saddleboot, a long-barreled Remington holstered on his hip. He scanned the horizon as he rode, on the lookout for any kind of ambush up ahead or any sign of pursuit behind.

Not that anybody was likely to be chasing them, he thought as he and his brothers rode through the gray, early morning light. They had made a clean getaway from the little town just over the Nebraska line where they had robbed the bank. In and out in a hurry, that was the way to do it, Owen always said. The longer you stayed in a place, the greater were your chances of trouble.

The three of them had successfully used that method for years. No one had ever been hurt. They had swapped lead a few times with the local lawmen as they rode out of town, but none of the bullets had ever hit anything. Owen liked it that way; the money was all he was interested in, not shooting folks.

He was a tall, barrel-chested man, and the heavy coat he wore made him look even bigger. His hair under the flat-crowned brown hat was fair and touched with gray, as was the beard stubble on his strong-jawed face. He had a quick, easy grin, and despite his size, he looked harmless most of the time—until his pale blue eyes turned icy and the grin fell away. Then he was a man to stay away from.

His brothers were riding on either side and a little behind him. Max, the older of the two, was as tall as Owen but lacked his bulk. His brown hair was close-cropped, and his face was broad and pleasant. Owen had always thought that Max would have looked more at home behind a store counter than anywhere else, but he had to give his brother credit. Max was a good man; he took orders and certainly did not lack courage. Owen knew that Max was more than ready to give up bank robbing and settle down to a life of ranching, but Max seldom complained, content to let Owen decide what they should do next.

Al did not always feel the same way. He was the youngest and smallest of the three, having inherited their mother's slender frame and dark curly hair. He had a quick temper, and his impulsiveness would have ruined more than one plan if Owen had not kept a tight rein on him. Still, like his brothers, he was cool in a pinch and as devoted to his wife and family as Owen and Max were to theirs. As they rode over the prairie, he was talking about how much he had missed Constance on this trip.

"Damn, but I'll be glad to get home," he said as they started up a long, gentle rise. "We're not going out again this winter, are we, Owen? A man oughtn't to be out robbing banks when it's this cold."

"Owen said we weren't going back out at all, remember?" Max reminded him. "We're ranchers now, not bank robbers. Isn't that right, Owen?"

"Sure, Max," Owen replied, not really paying that much attention to the conversation. "We'll see how things work out."

"But you said—"

"I said we'll see how things work out."

25

"All right, Owen." Max nodded. "Whatever you say."

Owen knew that when they topped this rise, they would be only a few miles from home. Al was right; it would be good to be back. He had missed Lucinda and the boys.

The three riders crested the slope, and suddenly Owen hauled back on the reins and jerked his mount to a halt. The other two stopped as well, following his lead as they usually did. "What is it, Owen?" Max asked anxiously. "Why'd you stop?"

Owen lifted his arm and pointed with a blunt finger. "Look," he said, his voice hollow.

Max and Al followed his outstretched arm. Their eyes fell on what had brought Owen to an abrupt halt—a thin finger of black smoke curling toward the sky.

"Oh, God, no," Al moaned in a pained whisper.

Max blinked rapidly and shook his head. "That can't be our spread, can it, Owen?" he mumbled hoarsely.

Owen ignored the question. Spurring his horse into motion, he called over his shoulder, "Come on, dammit!"

The three men pushed their tired horses for all they were worth. The few miles that remained between them and the ranch seemed to stretch out and become even longer. But at last they drew up to the place. Most of the ranch house had been destroyed; only two smoking walls and the central chimney remained standing. The barn had been razed. In its place was a smoldering pile of charred rubble.

Owen's face was a tight, grim mask as he raced his horse into the clearing between what was left of the two buildings. He threw himself out of the saddle and ran toward the ruins of the house, shouting, "Lucinda!" The heat from the ashes warmed his face as he approached.

Max and Al were right behind him, looking equally bleak. They reined in, dropped from their horses, and ran after Owen. For once they were more level-headed than their older brother. Catching up to him just as he reached the smoldering pile, the two brothers grabbed his arms and held on tightly as he tried to pull away from them.

"It's too hot, Owen!" Max cried. "There's nothing you can do!"

"They're in there!" Owen raged. "Goddamn it, I know they're in there!"

"I know," Al moaned, tears running down his cheeks. "But we can't do anything for them now. Come on, Owen. Please."

Owen roared, his body taut with fury and frustration. Then abruptly his rigid body sagged, and he stopped struggling. Drawing a deep, ragged breath, he let his brothers lead him away from the smoking ruin. The three men walked slowly toward the corral. Most of it was still standing, but some of the rails had been broken so that whoever had done this could steal the horses.

Leaning against the railing of the corral, Owen Broderick's stunned eyes slid over what had been done to his home. White men would not have been this wantonly destructive. There was no doubt in his mind that Indians had been responsible.

"We'll find them," he said hoarsely. "We'll find the redskinned bastards who did this. And then we'll kill every damned one of them."

Grief etched on their faces, Max and Al nodded their agreement.

By midday the smoldering pile that had been their home had stopped smoking and had cooled enough for the brothers to make their way into the rubble. It was a hideous task, but they had to find the bodies.

As the men began to pick through the wreckage, they discovered that the front room had been gutted, but the fire had not completely destroyed the dining room. Somehow the blaze had gone out and had not engulfed it. Two of its walls were still standing, and while some timbers had fallen, the table had not burned.

Lying next to one of the walls were Frank and Jack. Owen paled as he noticed their bullet-riddled young bodies. Then Al and Max moaned when they found Deborah and Constance beneath the fallen timbers. Their naked, slashed bodies were all too easy to identify. The five youngsters were lined up in a hideous row just outside the kitchen doorway; each of their throats had been cut. Nowhere was there any sign of Lucinda.

As the brothers carried their loved ones' bodies out of the ruins, they grew increasingly more haggard and drawn, but none of them cried. Gently they placed them on the ground and wrapped them in the blankets they carried in their packs on the horses. The tears would come again later. Now there were graves to be dug.

Deborah Broderick and her two children were placed together in one grave that was hacked from the hard, cold ground. Constance and her three daughters went into another. Owen dug the final resting places for his two sons. Sweat streamed off his face as he worked, making the brisk December wind seem even colder. Finally as the sun began to set, the brothers finished their task. They buried what was left of Hollis and Borden, after the body of the latter had been found in the ashes of the barn.

Then they stood before the mounds of earth, hats in hand and heads bowed. Owen tried to say a prayer, but he could not find the words. After a long moment, he vowed, "We'll get the ones who did this. I promise all of you that. They'll pay. By God, they'll pay."

He turned and walked away, and his brothers hurried after him. Max caught his arm and said, "We never found Lucinda, Owen. You know what that probably means."

Owen's head nodded jerkily. "They took her with them. Took her to be a slave and a whore. Lord, I wish they had killed her, too."

"But if she's still alive, maybe we can go after them and get her back," Al pointed out.

"We're going after them, all right." Owen pulled his arm out of Max's grip and turned toward the ruins of the house. "But there's something else I've got to do first."

In the fading light of approaching evening he plunged back into the ashes. His brothers watched him as he went to what had been his study, threw aside the charred timbers, and began to paw through the rubble. Several minutes later, he straightened and stomped out of the wreckage.

"It's not there," he announced flatly. "The lock wouldn't have burned, and those brass fittings would have been left, too. They took it, those sons of bitches."

"What are you talking about, Owen?" Max asked.

"Our money," Owen grated. "I had over fifty grand stashed in that chest I kept in my study, and it's gone." He spun around and started toward the horses. "Come on, we're riding."

"Going after Lucinda?" Al asked as he and Max hurried to catch up to Owen.

"Lucinda . . . and that chest," Owen said as he swung up onto the horse. He slid his rifle from its boot and laid it across the pommel of the saddle. "Those heathens stole my wife and my money. They're going to wish they'd never laid their filthy red fingers on either one."

Chapter Two

———◆———

THE SUN STILL GAVE OFF A LITTLE WARMTH THESE DAYS,
Marshal Luke Travis thought as he strolled along the
boardwalk that edged Texas Street, Abilene's main
thoroughfare. It was early December, and winter had
not yet gripped the Kansas plains. At night the temperature dipped well below freezing, sometimes the
wind blew bitterly, but the days were sunny and not
terribly cold. This Saturday morning was downright
pleasant, but after years of living on the prairie Travis
knew how deceptive that was. The weather could turn
bad without any warning. There was nothing on the
vast, open plains to stop or even slow the blue
northers when they whistled down from Canada.

Texas Street was busy. The one- and two-story
frame buildings that lined the street housed many of
Abilene's thriving businesses—mercantiles, ladies'
dress shops, even a pharmacy—and this morning they

were all doing a booming trade. That was common on Saturday, when folks who lived out of town came in for supplies and a welcome break in the monotonous routine of range life. Travis did not expect any trouble until later in the day. Most of the people bustling around town now were respectable ranchers or farmers and their families. But once dusk set in, cowhands from the outlying spreads would drift into town and head for one of Abilene's numerous saloons. Then things could get out of hand, and Travis and his deputy, Cody Fisher, would be hopping to maintain the peace.

Luke Travis was tall and well-built with the broad shoulders and lean hips of a man equally at home on his feet or in a saddle. Beneath his dark, flat-crowned hat his intelligent eyes surveyed the street, and his thick, sandy hair, streaked with silver, curled from under the brim. A mustache of the same shade drooped over his wide mouth. Strapped around his hips was a shell belt of fine leather, its holster sheathing a worn but carefully cared-for walnut-butted Colt Peacemaker. The pants of Travis's dark suit were tucked into calf-high riding boots. Pinned to his vest was the silver badge of his office.

The people he passed nodded, smiled, and greeted him warmly. He had been Abilene's marshal for quite a while and had taken a town gripped by lawlessness and worked to make it a decent place to live. He had had a great deal of help in cleaning the town up, Travis himself would quickly point out, but the townspeople knew how vital he was to their community.

Today the marshal recognized everyone he saw on Texas Street. A good lawman, he reminded himself, knew who lived in his town. But as he neared the corner of Texas and Cedar streets, Travis noticed a canvas-covered wagon driven by a stranger pulling up to the boardwalk in front of Karatofsky's Great Western Store, Abilene's largest mercantile. It was a typical light wagon, identical to those used by thousands of immigrants on their westward treks, pulled by four mules, and undoubtedly loaded with all the worldly possessions of the family who rode in it.

Perched on the wagon's crude plank seat were a man and woman; the man was handling the mule team's lines. As he hauled on the lines to halt his team, a blond-haired teenaged boy appeared in the canvas's opening behind the couple.

Their son, more than likely, Travis thought. He started across the street to introduce himself to them. These strangers might just be passing through, or they could be planning to stay in Abilene. In either case Travis wanted to welcome them.

The driver was a heavy-set man in his forties with a wide, flushed face and rust-colored burnsides that extended nearly to his chin. He turned, his forehead creased in a frown, and snapped, "Get a move on, Wesley. My God, the way you dawdle sometimes, a person would think you weren't right in the head."

His wife, a round, mousy woman whose brown hair was dangling in wisps from under her bonnet, put a hand on his arm and said, "Now, Edward, you know Wesley tries. He's just not accustomed to traveling yet."

"He damn well better get accustomed to it," the man replied peevishly. "We've still got a long way to go."

Travis could hear the conversation, despite the clopping hoofbeats and rattling wheels of the other wagons, buggies, and buckboards in the street, and he frowned slightly at the man's unpleasantness. He noticed that the youngster had gone to the back of the wagon, scrambled out, and landed awkwardly on the ground. Then the boy hurried to his mother to help her climb down.

The man stayed on the wagon seat. Travis stepped up onto the raised boardwalk in front of the store, which put him roughly at eye level with the driver. Pushing his hat back on his head, he said, "Howdy, folks. Welcome to Abilene."

The man turned to see who had addressed him, his eyes narrow slits in his puffy face. He regarded Travis suspiciously for a moment, then his scowl turned to a jovial grin when his assessing gaze fell on the marshal's badge. "Ah, good day to you, Sheriff," he said heartily.

Travis did not think either the grin or the suddenly cheerful manner was genuine, but he cautioned himself not to make any hasty judgments. "It's Marshal," he corrected the man. "Marshal Luke Travis."

The driver stood up and scrambled off the seat onto the boardwalk. He was even less graceful than his son, but he managed not to fall or break anything. He thrust out a beefy hand toward Travis and said, "Very glad to meet you, Marshal. I'm Edward Stillman."

Travis shook Stillman's hand. Despite the chilly air, the man's palm was clammy. Travis glanced over his shoulder and saw that the woman and the boy had vanished into the store. "Planning to stay around here, Mr. Stillman?" he asked.

Stillman waved a hand. "Oh, no. No offense meant, Marshal. I'm sure this is a fine town, but we're just passing through. We're on our way to California." The man's voice rang with pride.

"I hear California's quite a place," Travis commented with a slow nod. "But you won't make it this year, Mr. Stillman. Winter's coming, and you'd do better to wait it out right here in Abilene."

Stillman's harsh laugh sounded like the braying of

one of his mules. "You must be joking, Marshal," he guffawed.

"Not at all," Travis replied seriously. "Winters can get pretty rough on the plains, Mr. Stillman. They're mighty cold to start with, and a blizzard can blow up before you know it. I know it doesn't look bad now, but a lot of folks have regretted pushing on when they should have stopped and waited for a couple of months."

With both hands Stillman pulled open his coat, hooked his thumbs in his vest, and puffed out his chest. "Nonsense," he declared. "I'm a New Englander, Marshal. I daresay I know more about winter weather than someone who lives out here on the prairie."

Travis had instinctively disliked Stillman from the moment he heard the man speak so harshly to his own son. With each exchange the feeling had grown stronger, until now it peaked as he looked at the smug, arrogant grin on Stillman's face. Travis had immediately pegged Stillman as an Easterner, and Stillman was demonstrating the superior attitude that was typical of many Easterners new to the West. The man thought he knew all there was to know about anything important, and if he was not familiar with it, it must not matter. That sort of thinking could get you killed real quick this side of the Mississippi.

Travis took a deep breath to control his intense dislike. "Just thought I'd warn you," he said lightly. "I have a strong feeling there'll be a cold snap sometime in the next few days."

"I appreciate the concern, I truly do," Stillman replied airily. "I *know* we can't make it all the way to California without having to lay over for the winter. You don't take me for a complete fool, do you, Mr. Travis?"

"No, I guess not," the lawman drawled.

"But I'm certain we can make a great deal more progress before we have to stop. Santa Fe, perhaps."

Travis tried not to snort in contempt. He had been over the Santa Fe Trail more than once, and he knew only too well that Stillman and his family would never make it that far before bad weather set in. *Even so, it's his choice to make, not mine,* Travis reflected. At last he said, "Well, you just do what you think is best, Mr. Stillman."

"I always do, Marshal," Stillman assured him. "I always do."

Travis believed that.

The woman and the boy came out of Karatofsky's, and both men turned toward them. As they walked over to Stillman, he asked sharply, "Well?"

"I gave the clerk the list you drew up, Edward," his wife replied. "He said he could gather the order and load it in the wagon in an hour."

"An hour?" Stillman exclaimed. "That long? My God, don't these yokels have any idea how to go about their business? Why, in my store, I'd never let a customer wait an hour for an order—"

"Is that why your store went out of business, Papa?" the boy interrupted his father with a grin.

Stillman jerked around and raised a hamlike hand. "Why, you young pup!" he blustered. "I'll teach you to talk like that to me!"

The boy flinched and backed away, and the woman quickly grasped Stillman's arm. "Please, Edward," she whispered urgently. "You said you'd try to control your temper."

"But the boy can't talk to me like that!"

"I'm sure he didn't mean anything." The woman turned to her son. Her plain face was pale and anguished. "Did you, Wesley?"

The youngster was still edging away. "Nah, I didn't mean anything," he mumbled quickly. "You know that, Papa. Is it all right if I look around town for a while, since we've got to wait anyway?"

Before Stillman could answer, the boy's mother replied, "I'm sure it's fine. Just don't go too far, Wesley. We want to leave as soon as the supplies are loaded."

Stillman was still fuming at his son's impudence; Wesley's apology had clearly been insincere. Stillman took a deep breath and turned to Travis, who had watched the brief exchange in silence. "I'm sorry, Marshal," he muttered. "The lad has never learned to respect his elders. It's impossible to discipline children properly when *some* people want to coddle them." He glared angrily at his wife.

Travis's jaw tightened. His initial impression had been correct. Edward Stillman was a gold-plated son of a bitch. Travis would have stepped in if the man had been too hard on the boy, even if it was not his place to interfere in family business.

He turned to the woman and said quietly, "I don't believe we've been introduced, ma'am. My name is Luke Travis. I'm Abilene's town marshal." Travis touched the brim of his hat.

Stillman did not let her respond. "My apologies, Marshal," he said gruffly. "I neglected to introduce my wife, Martha. And that young reprobate wandering down the street is our son, Wesley."

"Pleased to meet you, ma'am," Travis said, nodding to Martha Stillman. "Looks like a fine boy you've got there."

"Oh, he is, Marshal," she said quickly; the color appeared to be returning to her cheeks. Her husband cleared his throat disgustedly.

Travis looked back at the Easterner. "Did I hear you

say you used to be in the mercantile business, Mr. Stillman?"

"Yes, indeed. I had the finest store in New Haven, Connecticut. I still would have if I had not been run out of business by some cutthroat competitors." Stillman's voice was bitter.

"Now, Edward, you know those other men were just trying to make a living, too. They did nothing wrong—"

"Women," Stillman cut her off scornfully. "They know nothing of business matters, Marshal. Don't place any credence in what my dear wife says. Women should smile sweetly and keep their mouths closed, don't you think?"

Travis tried not to grin, realizing Stillman might mistake that expression as agreement with his arrogance. Actually the marshal was thinking of what Dr. Aileen Bloom's reaction to this blowhard would be. Aileen was Abilene's leading physician and was as intelligent as she was lovely. Travis was fond of her, but more than that, he respected her opinions, just as he had respected those of his late wife, Sarah. Aileen would have cut Edward Stillman to ribbons in a minute.

"What I think is that I'd better be moving along," Travis said. "Hope your stay in Abilene is pleasant, folks. If I can help you in any way, my office is just down Texas Street."

"Thank you, Marshal, but I'm sure we'll be fine. As I told you, we won't be here long, just until we've taken on our supplies. Then we'll be moving on."

Travis nodded curtly. "You think about what I said about the weather," he advised, then strode down the boardwalk.

He shook his head as he walked. Martha Stillman seemed like a nice woman, and Wesley appeared to be a good youngster, even if he was a little cocky. That probably came from living with a man like his father and having to defend himself all the time.

But if they kept heading west with Edward Stillman at this time of year, the odds were they would wind up dead in no time. The man struck Travis as careless, and that was the most dangerous quality a man could have out on the prairie. There was a vast difference in knowing when a risk was acceptable and when it was just plain foolhardy.

But he had done all he could by warning them. He certainly could not keep them in Abilene until spring if they did not want to stay. Not without putting them in jail, anyway, and he had no reason to do that.

No, like everybody else, Edward Stillman and his family would have to make their own mistakes—and live or die by them.

There was nothing like a Saturday morning in Abilene—especially for a youngster. Lots of folks were in town to make things interesting, and best of all, school was not in session. Michael Hirsch was wide-eyed and eager as he and several of his friends strolled down Texas Street's boardwalk.

Jokes and laughter passed back and forth among the boys. Michael and his friends called hearty greetings to some of their chums from the outlying ranches. Most of the children from the ranches attended school at least part of the time, but seeing somebody in school and running into them on the street were two entirely different things.

Michael Hirsch and his older sister, Agnes, were two of the orphans who had come to Abilene with the Dominican nun named Sister Laurel. The nun had journeyed west from Philadelphia, originally planning to establish an orphanage in Wichita. But circumstances made them stop here, and with the help of Reverend Judah Fisher, the pastor of one of the local churches, Sister Laurel and her charges had settled in Abilene. The spacious parsonage of the Calvary Methodist Church, which sat on a knoll on the banks of Mud Creek just northwest of town, now housed several dozen children.

Michael could not have been happier. Abilene was an exciting place to live, and he was especially friendly with Deputy Cody Fisher, the pastor's younger brother. Cody, whose quick draw rivaled that of any gunslinger, was a figure almost as dashing as the ones Michael read about in dime novels. The boy worshiped him and tried to emulate Cody's good-hearted, impulsive nature. Michael's own enthusiasm and recklessness made him an instinctive leader of the boys his own age.

He and his friends had walked up and down Texas Street five or six times and were wondering how they should spend the rest of their Saturday, when somebody hurried out of a store and banged heavily into him.

"Hey!" Michael exclaimed as he caught his balance. "Watch where you're going!"

The boy glared at him arrogantly, turned, and started to walk away. Without thinking, Michael grabbed the other youngster's coat sleeve and jerked him to a halt.

"I said to watch out," Michael snapped. He saw now that the other boy was both taller and heavier than he. As the stranger swung around to face Michael, his features were set in a menacing scowl. He wore city clothes and shoes, and his shock of blond hair was rumpled and unruly.

"Get your damn hands off me, kid," he growled, still glaring at the orphan.

Michael Hirsch was a stocky, redheaded youth. His freckled face was friendly and open, and he usually got along well with just about everyone. But he felt a flush of anger at the other boy's harsh words. He released the boy's sleeve and said slowly, "All I did was tell you to watch out. And be careful who you're calling kid. You're not that much older than me."

The blond lad's mouth twisted in a sneer. "I'm fourteen. How old are you?"

"Fourteen," Michael answered coolly. He was pleased at the faint look of surprise on the other boy's face.

"Damn, they really grow runts out here on the frontier, don't they? Slow ones, too. You'd better learn to get out of people's way, sonny." The boy's accent, as well as his comment about the frontier, told Michael that he was an Easterner.

Michael's hands slowly clenched into fists. He was well aware that all his friends were watching. They looked to him as their leader and followed his example. He could not let himself be backed down by some Eastern loudmouth. Michael and the other boys already thought of themselves as Westerners, even though they had not lived in Abilene for very long. This challenge could not go unanswered.

"And it's time you learned you can't go running over people and get away with it," Michael growled.

His adversary's mouth had curled into an arrogant grin. "What are you going to do about it?" the boy asked lazily. "You're too puny to fight."

"Puny, am I?" Blood was pounding in Michael's head. "We'll see about that!"

He lunged and hurled a punch at the bigger boy's head.

The blow did not connect. The other youth dodged aside and hooked a fist into Michael's belly, the grin on his face turning into a look of pure glee as he did so. Michael gasped as the blow drove the air from his lungs. He staggered, caught his balance, and lashed out again. He vaguely heard the encouraging whoops and cries of his friends.

Michael's second punch grazed the other boy's shoulder but did no damage. In return, Michael caught a hard right to the chest that rocked him again. He had been in enough fights to recognize that his opponent had a longer reach. There was no way Michael could stand up and trade slugs with him successfully. He would have to handle this differently.

He threw himself forward, dove under a sweeping punch, and smashed into the other boy's midsection. The flying tackle sent both Michael and the blond boy plunging off the boardwalk. Michael landed on top, knocking the breath out of the other boy, and he tried to take advantage of his opportunity. He sat on his opponent's chest and started peppering his face with short, hard blows. His friends on the boardwalk cheered him on. A small crowd was gathering since the fight had also drawn most of the adults in the vicinity. Some of them were calling out encouragement as well.

Suddenly strong hands clamped down on Michael's shoulders and pulled him to the side. He let out a cry of frustration and struggled in the grip of the man who was hauling him to his feet.

"Stop it, Michael!" a stern voice rapped. "Stop this brawling right now!"

The sharp words penetrated the anger that was clouding his brain, and he dropped his arms and unclenched his fists. He looked up into the frowning face of Reverend Judah Fisher. Standing beside the minister, her pale blue eyes snapping their disapproval, was the black-garbed figure of Sister Laurel.

"Michael Hirsch!" the nun demanded. "What is the meaning of this . . . this fighting in the street?"

Michael took a deep breath, glared down at the stranger who had been to blame for the fracas, and said nothing. Adults never seemed to learn that some things were none of their business. A fight between two fellows was one of them.

"It wasn't Michael's fault, Sister," cried one of his friends. "That other kid started the fight."

The blond boy slowly got to his feet. He brushed off his dusty clothes and said in a surly voice, "That's not true. This little son of a bitch threw the first punch."

"There's no need for language like that, son," Judah chided him. "I don't want to hear it again." He turned to Michael. "Is that true? Did you throw the first punch?"

"You bet I did!" Michael exclaimed hotly. "He deserved it. He ran into me, and then he said I was puny!"

"Oh." Judah glanced at the other boy and saw the arrogant glare on his face. "Well, it looked like you were handling yourself all right, Michael, so I wouldn't worry about what he said."

"Reverend!" Sister Laurel cried, her blue eyes wide in shocked surprise. "Regardless of what was said, there's no excuse for brawling."

"You're right, of course, Sister," Judah agreed. But Michael sensed a change in his attitude. Now that Judah had assessed the situation, Michael could tell that the minister was not as upset with him as he had been at first. Judah went on solemnly, "You know that fighting seldom solves anything, Michael. We've tried to teach you and the other lads at the orphanage to use reason—"

"Orphanage!" the blond boy snarled. He looked at

Michael and laughed. "I should have known that a little tramp like you wouldn't have any parents. What happened, they get tired of looking at your ugly face and jump in the river or something?" He laughed again, a cutting mocking jeer.

Michael felt hot tears stinging his eyes, and his chest tightened with anger. He glanced up at Judah and Sister Laurel and saw they were both upset. This newcomer was begging for trouble, and for one exciting moment, Michael thought that the pastor and the nun would give him their blessing to whale the tar out of him.

But then a harsh voice called, "Wesley!" and the blond youth seemed to quail under its angry lash. He turned around and looked at the man striding toward the little gathering.

"I'm right here, Papa," he said quietly.

"I should have known," the man snarled as he came stomping up, his beefy face set in tight, impatient lines. "Should have known I'd find you lollygagging around somewhere. Dammit, I told you to be back at the wagon when we were ready to go. We won't ever make it to California the way you keep slowing us down!"

The man paid no attention to anyone else standing on the boardwalk. Ignoring Judah and Sister Laurel and all the evidence that a fight had just been broken up, he grabbed the boy's arm and jerked it callously. "Come along now!" he growled. "We're wasting time." The man dragged the boy away.

Michael felt disappointed that any possibility of the fight continuing had ended. *Some people deserve to have trouble blow up in their faces,* he thought, *no matter what Judah and Sister Laurel say about turning the other cheek.* Michael had a feeling that Wesley was one of those folks.

He sighed and wiped a sleeve across his nose. "Should've let me whip him," he muttered to no one in particular.

"And what if he had whipped you instead?" Judah asked.

Michael looked up at him and grinned. "He would have darn sure *earned* it!" he insisted.

Shaking his head, Judah put a hand on the youngster's shoulder and led him up onto the boardwalk. Michael's friends crowded around him, slapped him on the back, and congratulated him, just as if he had won the fight.

A few minutes later, after Judah and Sister Laurel had gone on their way, Michael was leaning against a lantern post on the boardwalk as a canvas-topped wagon rolled by. He saw the bewhiskered man who was evidently Wesley's father sitting on the seat and handling the team. Beside him was a mild-looking woman, and sitting behind them, just inside the wagon, was Wesley himself. Michael met the blond boy's cold stare with one of his own, and as the wagon passed, Wesley moved to the rear of it and continued to glare at him through the opening in the back.

The wagon was heading west. The man had said they were bound for California. *Good riddance*, Michael thought. *As far as I'm concerned, California can have Wesley!*

Chapter Three

AS LUKE TRAVIS HAD SAID, THE WEATHER ON THE PLAINS
was highly unpredictable. Saturday continued to be
pleasant, and Saturday night was a bit less chilly than
the previous nights had been. But late on Sunday
afternoon, a low line of blue-black clouds appeared on
the northern horizon and began rolling toward town.
Throughout the weekend there had been virtually no
wind, but as the sun set, the few people who were out
and about felt the cold air suddenly whip around
them, stinging their cheeks and hands. Frigid gusts
blew through the streets, and the temperature
dropped steadily. Folks on the prairie had a simple
term for what was blowing into Abilene tonight—a
blue norther.

By midnight, the wind was howling, and the temperature was plummeting toward zero. Water standing
in buckets and troughs had developed a coat of ice
that was thickening rapidly. Those who could stay

indoors huddled around fireplaces or cast-iron stoves as the wind worked its icy fingers into every crack in the simple plank buildings. Anyone called to be outside hurried about his tasks. Undoubtedly, few of them bothered to glance up and see that the low, scudding clouds had completely obscured the moon and stars. This was not another minor cold snap like those that had swept across the plains during the past few weeks. Winter had at last rolled down from Canada and gripped Abilene.

At daybreak the last of the clouds moved off to the south. The wind began to die down, leaving behind a bitter cold that seemed to hover over the town. When the weak yellow eye of the sun finally edged up over the horizon, its rays cast sparkling reflections off the frost that coated the whole town.

Thurman Simpson despised cold weather. *By God, I hate it,* he thought as he trudged toward the schoolhouse.

The sun had been up for an hour, but the schoolmaster felt no warmth in its glow. Simpson tried to pull his head down deeper into the upturned collar of his overcoat. He felt as if his nose and ears were going to freeze off before he reached the school. Once he got there, the place would be utterly frigid until the fire he would start in the stove had burned for a while.

The school was located on South Second Street, close to Mud Creek. The sturdy, whitewashed frame building originally had one large room, but once Leslie Gibson, Abilene's other schoolteacher, arrived, it was divided into two smaller ones. As Simpson approached, he could see frost glittering on the roof of the building.

The schoolmaster habitually wore a rather sour expression, but as he squinted into the cold wind, a puzzled frown appeared on his narrow face. Something was amiss, and after a moment he saw what it was. The front door of the building was ajar; the gap was only an inch or so wide. But to someone as precise as Simpson, it told him something was wrong.

Perhaps Leslie Gibson had arrived first this morning and had already lit a fire in the iron stove. If that were so, the place would certainly be more comfortable. But Leslie would not have left the door open, Simpson decided as his frown deepened. Someone else had to have been in there.

A twinge of apprehension coursed through Simpson, but a surge of anger rapidly replaced it. This was *his* school, and no one had any right to be in there without his knowledge and permission. His stride quickened. Perhaps he could find some evidence that would reveal who the intruder had been. He planned to see that Marshal Travis arrested the culprit immediately.

As he approached the door, Simpson saw that the lock had been broken. The lock had not been very strong, and from the looks of the door frame, someone had simply knocked it loose when they shoved the door open. Simpson curtly thrust the door back and stepped inside, his breath pluming in front of his face in the frigid air.

His gaze darted around the room, but he saw nothing out of the ordinary. Sniffing, he stepped to the doorway in the partition that divided the building. It stood open, and he moved through it to survey Leslie Gibson's classroom.

Again, he saw nothing unusual. Except . . . His eyes flicked back to something in the front corner of the room, beyond the desk Leslie used. He saw a mound of something furry that was a mottled brown color.

Simpson stepped cautiously toward the heap, his nose wrinkling in distaste as he drew closer to it. *Why*

*the devil would anyone, even someone like Leslie, leave
a pile of filthy, molding buffalo hides stacked in the
corner of his classroom?* he wondered.

The object in the corner suddenly rolled over and
let out a massive belch.

Involuntarily, Simpson jumped back and cried out
in fright. He stared wide-eyed as what he had taken to
be a pile of buffalo hides pulled itself to a sitting
position. Bleary eyes set in a bearded, craggy face
blinked uncomprehendingly at him.

As the apparition began to rise from the plank floor,
the schoolmaster kept stepping backward. Panic began to grip his chest. He recognized Nestor Gilworth,
a former buffalo hunter whose staggering, drunken
form had become a common sight in Abilene during
the last few months. Nestor was notorious for the
trouble he caused during his drinking binges, and now
here he was, right in the schoolhouse, a place Simpson
regarded as his own inviolate sanctum. Nestor shuffled toward him, undoubtedly bent on mayhem.
Thurman Simpson screamed.

Nestor's eyes widened. Shaking his head as if to
dislodge something inside his skull, he stared at
Simpson, then bellowed, "Injuns! You ain't goin' to
get my scalp, you heathens!"

His beefy right hand darted inside his coat. With a
whisper of steel against leather, he drew out a bowie
knife. The sunlight coming in through the windows
glittered on the long, heavy blade with its wicked
double edge.

Simpson screamed again, and Nestor, holding the
bowie low and ready to slice upward, lunged. The
terrified schoolmaster desperately threw himself to
the side.

Even when he was drunk, the enormous Nestor was
fast for a man of his size. The blade's lethal point

missed Simpson only by inches. Simpson tried to dart away, but Nestor reached out with his free hand and grabbed the smaller man's coat sleeve. Jerking Simpson toward him, Nestor growled, "I've got you now, you redskinned bastard!" He raised the knife.

Simpson screeched in fear. Slowly Nestor lowered the knife and frowned. Once more, he shook his head. "You ain't no Injun," he said accusingly.

Now that it was apparent to him that he was not going to die, Simpson's anger overtook his fear. "Of course I'm not an Indian, you great hulking idiot!" he blustered. "I'm Thurman Simpson, the schoolmaster! This is my school."

Nestor's frown deepened. "You sure you ain't a Comanch'? No, I reckon you're not. Most of 'em are as scrawny as you, but they don't squall like that when they're fightin'."

"Let me go, you oaf!" Simpson demanded. The tiny voice of reason cautioned him to be more careful—after all, Nestor still had the knife—but Simpson's fury was beyond his control. "How dare you break in here like this!"

Nestor let go of the schoolmaster's coat, and Simpson began to fall. As his feet touched the planks he realized that he had been dangling in the air. Gasping in surprise, he caught his balance and glared up at his huge, unwelcome visitor.

"I was just lookin' for a place to get out of the cold," Nestor muttered. "Nigh froze to death las' night, till I thought to come in here."

"But you have no right to be here!" Simpson insisted. "This is school property belonging to the town, not the back room of some saloon where an inebriated reprobate like yourself can collapse in a drunken stupor!"

The baffled look in Nestor's watery eyes said that

the big man did not understand a word he was saying, so Simpson sighed and gave up. Nevertheless, he cautioned himself to be careful. Nestor still had the knife and an ancient Colt that was known as a Dragoon holstered underneath the coat. Simpson saw now an old Sharps buffalo rifle leaning against one corner of the room. He did not want to make Nestor too angry; he did not even want to imagine what Nestor's alcohol-soaked brain would tell him to do if he was opposed too much.

Nestor Gilworth had been living in Abilene for less than a year, although he had wandered in and out of town several times before coming to stay. That had been in the days, four and five years earlier, when remnants of the huge buffalo herds still roamed the Kansas plains. Once millions of the shaggy beasts had made the prairie their home. A man could stand all day, watching a single herd pass, and not see all the animals in that group. Since he had come to Abilene, Simpson had heard those claims and thought them exaggerated. He had never seen a buffalo, let alone endless multitudes of them.

However many of them there had been at one time, the coming of the railroad had ended their dominance. The buffalo were slaughtered, hundreds and sometimes thousands in a day, for a variety of reasons.

Some men, like Nestor Gilworth, had hunted them to provide food for the soldiers and the even larger army of railroad workers who had come to lay iron rails across the frontier. Other men, able to look at the larger picture, could tell that wiping out the buffalo herds would eventually mean the defeat of the Indians who opposed the westward expansion of the white men, so vital was the creature to the Indian way of life. Yet another group of men killed them simply for the brutal, bloody sport. In the end the buffalo that survived migrated to the south. Some of the hunters followed them; others, like Nestor Gilworth, remained behind to remember the old days and drown those memories in alcohol.

Most of the former hunters and skinners were simply general nuisances, and usually Nestor fit into that category. But on other occasions he could be genuinely dangerous.

Thurman Simpson was thinking about that as he went on, "You get out of here now, Gilworth! You've caused enough trouble in my school, and I want you gone before the children arrive."

Nestor turned toward the door. "All right, I'm goin'," he said. He replaced the bowie knife in its sheath.

"And don't think I won't report this little incident to Marshal Travis," Simpson said, putting his hands on his hips. "I fully intend to lodge a formal complaint against you. You're going to have to pay for that door lock you broke or serve some time in jail to pay for your crime."

Nestor wheeled around. "Jail?" he rumbled. "I ain't goin' to jail."

"You most certainly are unless you can pay for the damage you've caused. Which I seriously doubt, considering the way I've seen you drink up what little money you earn doing those odd jobs around town." Simpson sniffed contemptuously.

Nestor's voice was like the thunder of one of those buffalo herds of the past as he abruptly threw himself toward Simpson and shouted, "I ain't goin' to jail!"

Simpson yelped in pain as Nestor's hands came down on his shoulders. He felt himself lifted again, and before he could even start to struggle, Nestor had thrown him toward one of the tall, narrow windows that lined the schoolroom.

Nestor's aim was not very good. That was the only thing that saved Simpson from smashing through the glass. He slammed into the wall between two of the windows, the impact cutting off the bubbling yell that came from his throat. He slid down the wall, slumped to the floor, and huddled there, whimpering.

Nestor started toward him again, his bearded face twisted with rage.

Suddenly heavy steps pounded in the other classroom, and Leslie Gibson burst through the doorway. Leslie was big and bearded, too, but that was where the resemblance between Nestor and him ended. The teacher was several inches taller, and he moved with a catlike quickness that was a legacy of the life he had led before he entered teaching. Leslie Gibson had been a heavyweight prizefighter in the East, as unlikely as that seemed to anyone who knew the gentle, soft-spoken man now.

Seeing immediately that Simpson was under attack, Leslie hurried over and stood between Nestor and the other teacher. To Simpson, lying on the floor, it was as if he were watching two ancient behemoths facing off against one another. Leslie said quickly, "Hold on, Nestor! I don't want any trouble!"

"I ain't goin' to jail!" Nestor repeated. He swung a clenched fist in a blow that would have taken Leslie's head off his shoulders if it had connected.

Smoothly Leslie moved aside. The punch whistled past his ear. He stepped up and tried to grab Nestor's arms.

Nestor's arms closed around the burly schoolteacher in a bone-crushing bear hug. Leslie let out a groan.

Leslie brought his cupped hands up and slammed

them against Nestor's ears. The buffalo hunter's long shaggy hair and filthy black felt hat absorbed some of the force of the blows, but he grunted and relaxed his grip. Moving with blinding speed, Leslie smashed the heels of his hands up under Nestor's bearded chin and propelled himself backward out of the deadly embrace.

Off balance, Leslie staggered a step or two before catching himself. By that time, Nestor was coming after him again, roaring in anger. Instead of trying to wrestle with him, Leslie dodged aside, planted his feet, and crashed a fist against the side of Nestor's jaw. The punch did not seem to faze Nestor, who turned toward the teacher again.

This time Nestor lunged and snatched up one of the student's desks. He lifted it above his head as if it were a stick of kindling and whipped it toward Leslie.

Leslie threw up an arm to protect his face as he tried to get out of the way of the desk. It only grazed his sleeve, then crashed against the wall and shattered into splinters. Nestor grabbed another desk and started toward Leslie.

Throughout the fracas Thurman Simpson had been huddling on the floor. Now he pushed himself to his hands and knees and scuttled toward the doorway. He hoped he could get outside before the two battling giants brought the building down around their heads. As he reached the doorway to the other classroom, he almost crashed into the legs of several students who had just entered the schoolhouse.

Simpson looked up at the eager faces of the children. Clearly they were trying to find out who was raising such an uproar inside the building. Simpson was not surprised to see that Michael Hirsch was in the lead. The redhead was grinning as he looked down at Simpson. The schoolmaster exclaimed, "Out of the way! Get out before they kill us all!"

Michael Hirsch could not believe his eyes. Mr. Simpson, his sallow face panic-stricken, was crawling on the floor like a dog. The fussy little man who was the bane of Michael's existence was a mess, his hat gone and his hair tousled. And beyond him in the other classroom a battle was raging.

Michael darted past the frightened teacher and ran into the other classroom in time to see Leslie Gibson ducking to avoid the desk Nestor was swinging at him. Leslie stayed close to Nestor, but he was not grappling with the big man in the buffalo coat. Instead, he drove punch after punch into Nestor's midsection, using his speed to land as many blows as possible. Then Nestor's arm swept around, smashed him, and knocked him off his feet.

"Holy cow!" shouted Michael. "I'd better get the marshal before Nestor kills Mr. Gibson!"

By this time Thurman Simpson had scrambled to his feet and started shooing the students out of the building. He gestured urgently at Michael and called, "Hirsch! Come on!"

Michael bounded out of the schoolhouse after Simpson and the other children, but instead of racing to the windows to watch the fight as his friends did, Michael turned and headed toward downtown Abilene. Luke Travis's office was nearly five blocks away, and Michael knew he would have to hurry if he was going to bring back help in time to save Leslie Gibson. As he ran, he could hear the crashing sounds of the ongoing battle inside the schoolhouse.

Deputy Cody Fisher did not know which felt better, the hot coffee sliding down his throat and warming his belly, or the warmth of the cup as he wrapped nearly frozen fingers around it and tried to thaw them. It was about even, he decided. He wondered if he should resign his post and drift back down to Mexico. The one time he had been there, it had been a lot warmer than it was on this morning in Kansas.

Travis had not come in yet, but it was still early. Since Cody slept in the back room, it was his responsibility to get up early enough to stir the embers in the stove to life and start the coffee heating before the marshal arrived. Travis would probably be there shortly.

"Marshal! Marshal!"

Cody's head snapped up as he heard the frantic cries from outside, accompanied by the sound of running footsteps. He quickly put the coffee cup down on the desk and wheeled toward the doorway, his hand hovering over the butt of his Colt. A small figure, bundled up in a heavy coat, muffler, and cap, burst through the door. Cody relaxed slightly as he recognized Michael Hirsch's face, which was redder than normal because of the cold.

"Take it easy, Michael," Cody advised the boy as he came out from behind the desk. "Marshal Travis isn't here yet. What's the trouble?"

Michael had obviously been running. He gasped for breath; tiny clouds of steam hung in front of his face. "It's Nestor—" he finally managed to pant.

Cody stiffened. He had had his share of run-ins with Nestor Gilworth, had arrested him several times in fact. "What's Nestor done now?" he asked sharply.

"He's down . . . at the school . . . trying to kill Mr. Gibson!" Michael wheezed.

Cody grabbed his coat off the back of a chair, slipped it on, then broke into a trot before he reached the door. Later he would take the time to find out what the devil Nestor Gilworth was doing at the schoolhouse; now he had to stop him. If the brawny hunter was on one of his rampages, he just might kill someone.

"Come on!" he shouted at Michael over his shoulder. "But stay out of the way once we get there!"

Cody's horse was in a nice warm stable down the street, but it would take too long to fetch it and saddle it up. He had no choice but to run to the school. His heavy boots slowed him down somewhat, but he still managed to get there in a hurry. He heard the sounds of the battle while he was still a block away.

As he raced into the schoolyard two struggling figures came crashing through one of the windows, shattering the glass and sending shards flying in all directions. The children who had been watching the fight screamed and scurried toward the leafless trees for cover. Leslie Gibson and Nestor Gilworth landed on the cold, hard ground and began to roll over and over. Nestor was trying to get a grip on Leslie's throat, and the teacher was fending him off as best he could.

Cody came to a stop and debated his course of action. He glanced at Thurman Simpson, who was standing next to one of the trees in the schoolyard, carefully keeping its trunk between him and the combatants. Simpson would be no help, Cody decided, and that came as no surprise at all.

He slipped his Colt out of its holster, then dropped the revolver back into leather. The quarters were too close for shooting. Even with his accuracy, there was too great a risk that he would hit Leslie.

It looked as if the only thing he could do was to get right into the thick of the fight himself.

Leslie managed to plant a foot in Nestor's stomach and shoved the buffalo hunter from on top of him. Nestor landed heavily, but he recovered quickly and rolled to his feet before Leslie had a chance to get up. He was starting toward the teacher when Cody grabbed his shoulder and turned him around.

Cody put all his strength into the right cross that he threw. His fist caught Nestor on the left side of the jaw but seemed to have little or no effect. The big man just shrugged it off and backhanded Cody. Cody flew backward, feeling as though a tree had just smashed across his face.

But the delay had given Leslie Gibson enough time to get back onto his feet, and he was set when Nestor turned toward him again. Leslie kicked him in the groin as hard as he could.

Doubling over in agony, Nestor staggered back a few steps. Cody had regained his feet, and he pulled his gun as he leapt forward. He lashed out and sent the barrel of the Colt thudding into the back of Nestor's head. Cody had seen Luke Travis drop the big man with a similar blow a few months ago, and combined with the damage Leslie had inflicted, it did the trick again. Nestor swayed for a moment, then collapsed on the hard, frozen ground.

Cody and Leslie stared at one another over the shaggy figure. Leslie finally managed to pant, "How . . . how long will he be out?"

"If we're lucky . . . long enough for us . . . to get him to jail," Cody gasped. Taking a deep breath, he holstered his gun. "Grab a leg."

"You're joking."

The deputy shook his head. "Not unless you want him waking up on the outside of a cell."

"I don't think so," Leslie replied quickly. He bent over and grasped one of Nestor's booted ankles.

The two men felt as if they were hauling a side of beef, but more men pitched in when they reached

Texas Street. Nestor was still out cold by the time they reached the jail. Luke Travis, who had arrived at the office, must have heard the hubbub that accompanied the little caravan as it made its way down the street, because he emerged with a Winchester in his hands. He scowled as he saw the prisoner.

"Nestor again, eh?" he said. "We've got to do something about him, Cody."

Cody grunted with effort as he and Leslie and the other men dragged Nestor through the office and on into the cellblock. He did not reply until a cell door had clanged shut behind the massive troublemaker in the buffalo coat. Then he said, "I don't think we ought to let him out again, Marshal. He just tried to kill Leslie."

Travis glanced at the teacher. "Is that true, Leslie?"

"It certainly seemed like it," Leslie admitted. "And I don't know what he did to Thurman Simpson before I arrived at school."

"He tried to murder me!" Simpson said shrilly from the office doorway. "I came down here to press charges against that . . . that monster, Marshal. I want him locked up and the key thrown away!"

"I don't agree too often with Thurman, Marshal," Cody commented as they all stepped back into the office and closed the cellblock door. "But this time he just might be right about Nestor."

"I think everybody needs to settle down and tell me what happened," Travis said. "You first, Mr. Simpson."

Quickly Simpson explained about surprising Nestor inside the schoolhouse. "He tried to kill me with a knife," the schoolmaster shrieked bitterly. "He thought I was some sort of Indian! Drunken hallucinations, I'd say."

"That's right, Thurman," Cody said dryly. "Nobody in his right mind would mistake you for a savage."

Simpson sniffed archly. "Then when I told him he was going to have to pay for the damages or go to jail, he went absolutely insane! I swear he tried to kill me, Marshal."

Leslie Gibson picked up the story then, followed by Cody's recitation of his part in the fracas. When they were finished, Travis leaned back in his chair and sighed. "I guess Nestor's gone too far this time," he said. "I don't think he means to hurt anybody, but he's just not in his right mind when he's been drinking."

"He belongs in jail," Simpson insisted. "Or in some sort of institution."

"Nestor Gilworth used to be a good man," Travis pointed out. "Before he hunted buffalo, he scouted for the Army and fought Indians. Men like him helped make this part of the country safe for you and me, Mr. Simpson."

"Perhaps that's true, Marshal," Simpson said coldly. "But those days are gone, and now the man is nothing but a menace. I insist he be put away where he can't harm anyone."

Travis looked at the schoolmaster's angry, determined face and sighed. "I guess we'll have to see what we can do about that," he replied.

Chapter Four

At dawn that Monday morning, Edward, Martha, and Wesley Stillman were some twelve miles west of Abilene. They made good progress right after they had left the town a day and a half earlier, but the norther had caught them, just as it had everyone else in the area, and forced them to stop. During the long night, the wind had rocked the wagon, its icy fingers intruding around the canvas top and between the wagon's planks. The family was chilled to the bone even though they huddled together for warmth beneath a thick pile of blankets. None of them slept much.

As the sun rose, Stillman prodded his son. "Get out there and build a fire," he snarled. "Make sure you do it right, like I showed you."

"But Papa, it's cold!" Wesley protested.

"I know it's cold, dammit! That's why we need a fire. Now get moving, you lazy whelp!"

He sent a slap alongside Wesley's head that stung the boy's ear. Wesley was so cold that he was afraid for an instant that the blow would break the ear right off. Of course it did not, but it hurt cruelly as he crawled out from under the blankets and reluctantly left behind their meager warmth.

Swallowing his hurt, Wesley stumbled toward the back of the wagon. He had slept in all of his clothes, including his overcoat, boots, and cap; nevertheless he still felt cold as he opened the canvas flap and leapt out of the wagon. He landed on the hard, frozen ground, staggered slightly, and realized that his feet were a bit numb. He went to the side of the wagon and reached into the canvas sling that hung under it for the chunks of firewood that were kept there.

One of his jobs on this journey had been to pick up pieces of wood whenever he encountered them and store them in the canvas sling. There were few trees out here on the prairie, and firewood was scarce. Buffalo chips were abundant and made a suitable fuel for fires, but they were sometimes difficult to get burning and did not produce as much heat as wood.

Wesley arranged several pieces of firewood on the ground, trying to find a spot that was shielded by the wagon and out of the wind. Crouching next to the little heap, he pushed his numb fingers into his pocket and fumbled to bring out the matches he kept there. He carefully scratched one into life. The wind plucked at the flame and tried to blow it out, but the boy cupped his hand around it and kept it glowing as he lowered it to the wood shavings that he was using for kindling.

After a moment, the fire took hold, the flames small but bright in the gloom of dawn. Bright and warm . . . Wesley sighed and stretched out his gloved hands toward the warmth.

He looked around. His father had at least picked a decent spot to camp for the night. They were in a small valley, a shallow depression that had probably protected them from the full force of the wind. There was no water nearby, but they had passed close to the Smoky Hill River the day before and had refilled their water barrels and canteens. His father was a thoroughly unpleasant man, but Wesley had to give him credit for getting them this far safely.

When Edward Stillman had first announced his intention to take his family to California, Wesley had thought it was the most foolish thing he had ever heard. They were city folk, and the very idea of making their way across the country in a wagon was ludicrous.

Martha Stillman had suggested traveling by train, but her husband had flatly rejected the idea. He planned to open a mercantile in California with what was left of his stock from the failed business in New Haven, and they could not afford to ship the merchandise west by rail. Instead the stock had been packed into the wagon until there was barely room for the three of them to stretch out and sleep at night. They kept the personal belongings they brought with them to a bare minimum.

Wesley knew his father had been deeply hurt when his store had gone under. Edward Stillman had never been a warm, loving man, but the failure of his business had made him even angrier and more remote. It was impossible to please him now, although Wesley still tried—at least some of the time. But he was reaching the point where he no longer cared what his father thought of him.

His mother climbed down from the wagon as he knelt by the fire. Wesley looked up at her and asked gently, "What can I do to help you, Mama?"

"Why don't you gather some more buffalo chips?" she suggested. "We need to save as much firewood as we can."

Wesley nodded, stood up, and went about the task, ranging several yards from the wagon to pick up the droppings. It was not a pleasant job, even though they were dried out and easy to handle, and Wesley tried not to think about what he was doing.

By the time he returned to the fire, his father had emerged from the wagon, a broad figure in his heavy coat. Stillman stood close to the flames, warming himself, while his wife began preparing breakfast.

Wesley dumped the armload of chips close to the fire, ready to be fed into it, and wished for at least the hundredth time that they were back in the kitchen of their home in Connecticut. He began to imagine the hot stove, spreading its warmth throughout the room, and a lump rose in his throat.

That house—the house where Wesley had been born and grew up—belonged to someone else now. It had been sold to finance this journey. Taking a deep breath, Wesley forced those thoughts out of his head. It would not help to dwell on what had been. But he missed his home; he could not deny that.

Stillman had to chip ice out of one of the water barrels with a knife so that his wife could make coffee. The wind was no longer howling as it had all night long, but the air was bitterly cold. The small campfire did little to dispel the chill. Wesley fed the mules, the steam from his breath blending with the puffs that came from their nostrils. Finally, breakfast was ready, and Wesley returned to the fire eagerly.

After the meal of bacon, pan bread, and coffee, Stillman and Wesley hitched up the team. When they were finished, Martha Stillman walked over to them and said tentatively, "Edward, I've been thinking."

Stillman snorted but refrained from making the sort of contemptuous comment that usually followed such a statement from his wife. He said nothing, waiting for her to go on.

"I think we should turn around and go back to Abilene," she finally said. "That marshal was right about how the weather can change and quickly turn bad out here. I think we should stop for the winter now."

"Don't be ridiculous," Stillman snapped. "This is just a little cold spell. It's still several weeks until the solstice! It's not even really winter yet."

"That doesn't mean it's not cold, Papa," Wesley put in.

"You stay out of this," Stillman said harshly. "You're a child, and this is an adult decision."

Martha began, "I'm just afraid—"

"That's right, you're afraid," her husband cut her off. "You've always been fainthearted, Martha, unwilling to take a chance, to seize an opportunity. Well, Edward Stillman is not like that, by God! We're pushing on! I still say we can make Santa Fe before we have to stop."

Wesley exchanged a look with his mother. Both of them knew there was no point in arguing with him. Once he had made his mind up, nothing would make him vary from the course he had selected.

"Stubborn old son of a bitch," Wesley muttered under his breath as he turned away.

Stillman grabbed his shoulder roughly. "What did you say?" he demanded.

Wesley faced him, his features set in insolent lines. "I said I'm glad we got the team hitched," he replied.

"All right. Now let's get ready to roll. We're going to make a lot of miles today."

As soon as they had cleaned up the campsite and

put the fire out, the Stillmans climbed back onto the wagon. Wesley settled down in the rear while his father took the reins. More than once, Wesley had asked to handle the team, but he had always gotten a curt refusal. *Just as well,* he thought now. *It's warmer inside the wagon.*

Despite the cold, the going was fairly easy at first. The family put several miles behind them during the morning, and nothing more was said about turning back to Abilene. Wesley told himself that was all right, too. After seeing the cities of the East, he had not been impressed with the Kansas cattle town. Like everything else about the frontier, it had been flat and brown and ugly. But he had enjoyed the fight with that orphan boy.

By noon the clear morning sky had been obliterated by low gray clouds that came sliding in from the north and west. The sun disappeared behind them, and the wind began to pick up again, although it was still not as strong as it had been the night before. Once the sun was gone, the meager warmth it had provided was missed.

The rolling terrain was rougher than it looked, and the wagon began to make less speed as the afternoon went on. Rocking back and forth slightly to the motion of the vehicle, Wesley lost track of time. There was nothing to look at, nothing to think about, nothing to do except sit and hope that his fingers and toes did not freeze off.

Suddenly Stillman called, "Whoa there!"

Wesley looked up, his reverie broken by the wagon jerking to a halt. He peered through the gap between his parents' shoulders and saw that they had stopped at the top of a rise overlooking a small, shallow valley. At the bottom of the slope was a broad, ice-covered creek.

"We have to turn around, Edward," Martha Stillman said. "We certainly can't ford that creek in this weather. If the mules get wet, they'll freeze to death."

"Nobody's getting wet, and nobody's going to freeze to death," Stillman replied. "Can't you see that there's ice on that stream? We'll simply drive over it. Crossing it now will be easier than if we were trying to do it in the middle of summer."

Wesley frowned dubiously. "Are you sure that ice is thick enough to drive on, Papa? It doesn't look like it to me."

Stillman turned and glared angrily at his son. "And since when are you an expert on such things, Wesley? If you're worried about the ice, why don't you go down there and test it yourself?"

"All right," Wesley said hotly. "I'll do that."

"No, Wesley," his mother cried and caught his arm as he started to push past them. "I don't want you doing anything dangerous."

"Somebody's got to check the ice, Mama," he told her. "I'll be all right. I promise I'll be very careful, and if it seems too weak, I'll come right back."

"Let the boy go, Martha," Stillman said. "He's right for a change."

Martha Stillman sighed, but she released Wesley's arm. "All right. But be careful."

Wesley leapt down from the wagon and walked quickly toward the bank, while his father urged the mules into motion and drove the vehicle slowly behind him. Wesley saw as he drew nearer the stream that several trees lined its banks. They were leafless— their naked branches silhouetted against the gray sky only added to the bleakness of the scene. The ice covering the water was the same color as the cloud-choked heavens.

Pausing on the creek bank, Wesley studied the frozen stream. It had been cold enough the day before that a little ice might have formed on the edges of the creek, but it could not have frozen over until the previous night. That meant the ice had had less than twelve hours to harden. The temperature was still well below freezing, he estimated, so the ice should have been getting thicker all the time, but there was no way of knowing how strong it was without checking it. He grimaced, then slid down the bank.

Stretching one foot out and tapping it on the frozen surface, he found that the ice certainly felt thick. Then he looked up and down the stream and located a spot where the banks on either side were gentle enough to accommodate the wagon. He headed toward it, hugging the shore and tapping the ice with his foot from time to time.

When he reached the place where the wagon would have to cross, he looked back up the hill and waved at his father, signaling him to veer the team in this direction. Then Wesley turned and faced the stream again. He took a deep breath and stepped onto the ice.

Slowly, carefully, he walked gingerly out onto the frozen creek, pausing at each step, testing the surface. As he neared the center, he thought he heard gentle cracking noises, but the wind was whistling so loudly that he could not be sure. He slid one foot forward, then the other. The ice continued to support him.

At last when he was safely on the other side, he drew a deep breath in relief. He had made it. However, all his instincts warned him that the ice would never support the mule team and the heavy wagon.

He turned and looked back across the stream. His father had drawn the wagon to a stop at the very edge of the creek. Before Wesley could utter a sound,

Edward Stillman flicked the reins and started the mules onto the ice.

Shocked, Wesley waved his arms in the air and yelled, "No! Go back, Papa! The ice isn't thick enough!"

Stillman ignored him and kept the wagon moving.

Barely able to believe his eyes, Wesley watched as his father pressed on. Stillman had not even waited for Wesley to come back across the stream and report on the thickness of the ice.

Wesley frantically motioned for him to stop. "No, Papa!" he called again. "Go back!" He ran out onto the treacherous crust, his feet slipping and sliding and threatening to spill him.

Edward Stillman's features were set in a grim, determined expression. Sitting beside him, his wife clutched his arm, her face pale and frightened.

As the boy and the wagon approached the center of the stream from the opposing banks, Wesley tried yelling once more. "Dammit, go back, Papa!" he shouted, still waving his arms.

Stillman was close enough to understand the words now. "You made it, boy!" he shouted in reply. "So will we!"

"But the ice—"

Sharp cracking noises cut off Wesley's warning. The sounds were much louder than the faint crunching Wesley had barely heard on his trip across the stream. An instant later the front wheels of the wagon dropped through the ice, pitching the front of the vehicle forward and down. His mother screamed. The icy crust on the creek began to shatter in wide, radiating circles.

Water swirled around Wesley's boots. Abruptly something shuddered beneath his feet, and he felt himself losing his balance and falling. When he landed, the ice gave way, and he plunged into the frigid creek. He floundered, half in and half out of the water. He looked up wildly and was horrified to see the ice beneath the wagon collapse.

The mules thrashed frantically; the heavy vehicle was pulling them into the stream. Their hooves flailed in a futile attempt to find a purchase. Wesley heard his father shouting curses as the wagon tipped crazily and started to turn over. He caught a glimpse of his mother falling from the wagon seat and landing in the water with a great splash. "Mama!" he screamed.

Then the dark, icy stream closed over his head. It was deeper than he had thought, and a strong current was running just beneath the surface that threatened to pull him away. In a panicked frenzy, Wesley fought his way back to the surface.

He got there in time to see the wagon disappearing beneath the flow. Neither of his parents was anywhere to be seen.

Wesley knew that all three of them were going to die. A huge area of ice had broken out in the center of the stream, and the wagon had slipped completely beneath the surface. The heavy clothes that his parents were wearing would drag them deeper into the stream's swift current, just as his own boots and overcoat were pulling him down.

But not all of the ice near him had cracked and collapsed. As he thrashed around, trying to stay afloat, he spotted an area about ten feet away that was still frozen. Somehow, he managed to swim toward it, although it seemed as though he swallowed half the creek on his way. Finally his gloved hands slapped the frost-glazed surface. His fingers clutched desperately for a hold and miraculously found one. Then as he hung on for dear life he struggled to lift his leg and put a knee on the surface. Gulping a deep breath, he threw the last of his strength into the effort.

He came up out of the creek, great streams of water trailing from his clothing, and sprawled on the frozen crust. More cracking sounds rang in his ears, and the ice shuddered beneath him. Wesley spread his arms and legs out, praying that the fragile surface would not give way.

A large jagged crack appeared in the frozen layer between him and the bank of the creek. He watched it in horror-stricken fascination, too petrified with fear and cold to move. The chunk of ice on which he lay did not break, but he was afraid that if he shifted even an inch, it would.

Wesley lay there and listened for any sound that might tell him his parents were still alive. He had hated his father's voice, always snappish and complaining, but now he would have given anything to hear it calling out assurances to him that everything would be all right. He would even have welcomed cries for help, because that would have meant that his mother and father still had a chance to survive.

Deadly quiet was all he could hear, that and the occasional lonely sighing of the wind.

Tears rolled down Wesley's cheeks and froze almost immediately. He was alive, but he was not much better off than his parents. He was drenched to the skin, stuck on this chunk of ice in the middle of the stream, unable to move. He was going to die, but it would just take longer for him to freeze to death instead of drowning.

A great sob wracked him, shaking him to the very core of his being. The great adventure his father had promised, the journey to the golden land of California, was over.

Edward Stillman had sought his fortune and found only death for himself and his family.

The two middle-aged cowpokes named Dutch and Robey had seen plenty of blue northers in their lives, but this was one of the worst. They agreed on that as they plodded on horseback toward Abilene.

"If'n you'd laid in the supplies like you was supposed to, we wouldn't have to go into town in weather like this," Dutch complained to his companion.

"How was I supposed to know it'd turn this cold this early?" Robey protested. "I figgered we had plenty o' time to stock the line shack."

"Well, you damn well figgered wrong, didn't you?"

"And you ain't never made a mistake yourself, you old coot?"

Dutch held up a gloved hand. "Hush up. Look yonder, down by the crick."

The two ranch hands stared through the washed-out light of the cloudy afternoon. The creek was frozen over, which was no surprise considering how cold it had been the night before, but there was something out of the ordinary there. A dark shape lay on the ice near the bank.

"By God, Dutch, that's somebody!" Robey exclaimed. "Come on!" The cowboy spurred his horse and urged it to a gallop.

Dutch followed right behind him, and within minutes they were close enough to see that the person sprawled on the ice was a youngster. They drew rein when they reached the bank, and Dutch frowned as he said, "That ice ain't thick enough to go out and get him. How the hell you reckon he got out there in the first place?"

"That don't matter now," Robey said as he took a

coil of rope from his saddle. He shook out a loop and went on, "I got to see if'n I can snag his foot."

With the skill born of years of daily practice, the cowhand cast his loop once, twice, and then three times, dropping it in the right position on the final try. Robey pulled carefully, tugging one side of the loop past the toe of the boy's shoe so that the loop itself could close on his ankle. That done, Robey took a dally around his saddlehorn and started to back his horse up slowly. "Get a fire goin'!" he called to Dutch. "We'll have to thaw him out if he's still alive!"

Within a quarter of an hour, the two cowboys had hauled the youngster off the ice, stripped him of his soaked clothes, wrapped him in blankets, and laid him close to the fire Dutch had built. The boy was breathing, but he had been almost blue when they found him, and he had not yet opened his eyes.

"What'll we do with him, Robey?" Dutch asked anxiously as he knelt next to the motionless youngster.

"Wait a while and see whether he lives or dies," Robey answered practically. "Either way, once we can tell what he's going to do, we'll take him on into Abilene."

They waited then, just as Robey said, crouched around the only spot of warmth within miles on the frozen prairie.

Chapter Five

———◆———

THE COLD WEATHER PLAYED NO FAVORITES AS IT SWEPT across the bleak prairie out of the north. The Sioux warriors led by Claw had more warning than the white men in the area. Civilization had not dulled their senses. But when the frigid air struck, it hit them as hard as it did anyone else. A small raiding party like this one carried no teepees—their bulk would have slowed them down—but they did have an ample supply of buffalo robes and pieces of hide that could be rigged to block the wind. For an Indian it was not too uncomfortable.

For Lucinda Broderick, however, it was just one more hellish chapter in a nightmare that seemed to have no end. It had been less than a week since Claw and his braves had attacked the ranch, killed everyone, and taken her captive. Lucinda knew how much time had elapsed when she was rational enough to think clearly. But most of the time she felt as though she had been a prisoner of the Sioux forever.

As Claw had promised, he had taken her to his blankets. That first night, less than two hours after she had seen most of her family slaughtered, he had raped her. She still had enough spirit to fight back that time, but he seemed to enjoy her struggles, grinning fiercely as he ripped her clothes from her and pounded his body into hers. When he was through, he left her, bruised and sobbing and trying to pull the shreds of her dress around her nakedness.

Her clothes had been ruined. Later she had been given buckskins to wear and a buffalo robe to wrap around herself. Claw warned her not to resist so much the next time. "If I have to tear these garments off you, you will stay naked under the robe after that, Yellowhair," he threatened. "You would not like that."

She had not been able to meet his eyes, but somehow she summoned the courage to say sharply, "My name is Lucinda."

Claw hooked his fingers around her chin and cruelly tipped her head back, forcing her to look at him. "No more," he told her. "You are Yellowhair. You are what the white man calls a slut. And when I am done with you, my men shall have you. So it would be wise for you to continue to please me. Do you understand, Yellowhair?" His grip tightened on her jaw. "Do you understand?"

She had done the only thing she could. God forgive her, she nodded and said that yes, she understood. And that she would please him whenever and however he wanted.

For the first few days she had been in shock, had ridden numbly in front of Claw and paid little attention to where the band was going. Gradually her senses cleared a bit, and she began to realize that Claw did not have a specific destination in mind. He seemed to be looking for more ranches to raid, and he found one during that first week, while Lucinda was with them.

Leaving her guarded by an older brave in a make-shift camp, Claw had galloped away with the rest of the war party to strike at an isolated cattle spread. From a mile away, Lucinda could see the smoke rising into the sky and faintly heard the crackle of gunfire. She imagined despite the great distance that she could hear the screams of the victims as well.

Claw had been particularly excited when he came to her that night. She did not resist, but still he hurt her with his savagery. *This is the life I have to look forward to,* she had thought.

She began to steal glances at the knives the braves carried. If she could only get her hands on one of them . . . It would take only seconds to slit her own throat. But Claw made sure that that opportunity did not arise. A few days later the norther hit, and Lucinda was unable to think about anything except trying to keep warm.

Now, as she huddled in one of the crude hide shelters in the bottom of a wash, she pulled the buffalo robe tighter around her and tried to scoot closer to the tiny fire that burned nearby.

Nestled in the wash, which provided some protection from the wind, were a dozen small makeshift huts. The hides, stretched taut over stakes driven into the ground, kept out some more of the cold. The other braves shared all but one of the shelters. Claw, as the leader of this band of raiders, had a dwelling to himself. Lucinda stayed in his hut, venturing out only when she had to. It was dim and quiet inside. Only a small fire provided light and a little warmth. Smoke drifted out through a small hole in the top of the structure, just the way it did in the teepees in the Sioux villages.

Lucinda was aware that Claw had pushed aside the flap of hide that had been left unfastened to serve as an entrance. But she did not look up at him; instead, she kept staring at the flames.

"See what I have, Yellowhair," he said.

She glanced up and saw that he was sitting on the other side of the fire and was holding the chest he had stolen from the ranch house before setting it on fire. She nodded dully and replied, "I see."

"This is yours, is it not?"

"My husband's," Lucinda said slowly, the word sounding strange to her. The idea that she still had a husband somewhere was almost beyond comprehension.

Claw's mouth curved in an arrogant grin. "I have stolen everything else of your husband's," he said. "Now it is time to see what I have stolen here."

Somewhere in the back of her mind, Lucinda was surprised that Claw had not broken into the chest before. Then she remembered they had spent most of their time on horseback, and she supposed he had not thought it important enough to waste his energy on. Now that they were stuck waiting out the cold weather, he must have grown curious.

He had brought a fist-sized rock with him, and he battered the lock with it for several minutes. Lucinda flinched at each blow. Finally, when he had damaged the lock sufficently, he finished the job by prying it off with his knife. The latch popped loose. Claw eagerly raised the lid.

He stared down into the chest for a moment, then threw back his head and laughed. Lucinda knew quite well what he had found, but she was not sure why he thought it was so amusing.

Claw reached into the chest, raised a handful of greenbacks into the air, and let them flutter slowly back into the wooden container. He was still laughing.

Then he closed the lid and fastened the latch, which caught despite the damage he had done to it with the rock. "Your husband has nothing left that matters to him now," he said. "I have his treasure chest and his woman, and I shall make good use of both."

Lucinda lifted her eyes again. Before she even thought about what she was saying, she spat, "Owen will come after me. He'll come after me, and then he'll kill you."

Claw laughed again. "Let him come." He thrust the chest aside with his bad hand and stood up. Stepping around the fire, he towered over Lucinda. "He will find his woman . . . much changed."

Lucinda's face was set in an emotionless mask now. She opened the buffalo robe and waited.

Not everyone had sought shelter when the cold weather hit. Some fifteen miles northeast of the wash where Claw and his warriors were waiting for conditions to improve, Owen Broderick and his brothers Max and Al plodded through the gloom on horseback, their pack animals trailing behind them.

Owen Broderick's normally florid face was even redder than usual from the bitter cold. He was in the lead. Max and Al followed close behind, each of them huddled in his coat, his hat pulled down snugly.

Max dug his heels into his horse's flanks and urged it up beside Owen's mount. "We'd better find someplace to hole up for the night, Owen," Max said. "Night'll be on us before we know it, and I'd bet it's going to be even colder than last night."

"We'll push on a little while longer," Owen replied. His voice was flat and hard; his tone made it clear he would not put up with any argument.

Max sighed, looked back at Al, and shrugged. There was nothing either one of them could do.

Owen had been a man possessed ever since they had returned to the ranch and found death and destruction. They had located the tracks of the unshod mounts of the Indian raiding party that had committed the atrocities and started following them.

But after several miles the trail had petered out. Owen decided to keep going in the same direction that the tracks were leading, and the three of them had done that for the last several days. Sooner or later, Owen claimed, they would run across something else that would get them back on the trail of the savages.

They had encountered very few people in this sparsely settled section of the state. Twice they had crossed paths with cowhands who were usually eager to talk but could offer no clues as to the whereabouts of the Indians. There were not many travelers at this time of year; most immigrants on their way west had already stopped someplace to wait out the winter.

Owen had been very quiet, saying little except to tell his brothers that they were not stopping yet. He drove them hard, spending eighteen hours a day in the saddle. Max and Al had felt the loss of their families and home very keenly, and both men had cried the first couple of nights on the trail. There was just too much pain for them to contain. But Owen had been dry-eyed, his face cold, hard, determined.

If they did not get out of the weather and stop pretty

soon, however, Owen's thirst for vengeance was going to be the death of them all. Exchanging knowing looks, Max and Al agreed on that without saying a word.

A small dot of light suddenly appeared ahead of them in the murky twilight. Al spotted it first and pointed it out to Max. "Something up there," he called.

Owen had seen the light, too. He turned his head slightly and grunted, "That's Winslow's place."

"I didn't think we were that far south," Max said.

"We are."

All of them knew about Ike Winslow's isolated roadhouse and trading post. It was in the middle of nowhere, seemingly a prime target for Indian raids, but the warriors left the place strictly alone. Some said Winslow paid them off in whiskey and guns, but that was only an unproven rumor. The roadhouse was also a stopping point for all sorts of outlaws, hired guns, and hardcases, and the frequent presence of tough, lawless men might have had something to do with the reluctance of the Indians to bother the place.

Again Max drew up even with his older brother. "If that's Winslow's, it'd be a good place to put up for the night, don't you think?"

"Good as any, I suppose," Owen answered. "I wanted to put a few more miles behind us, but pretty soon it's going to be too dark to see anything."

Max and Al both sighed in relief. "Man, it'll be good to back up to a nice warm fire," Al said. "I could sure as hell use a drink, too."

"And we can stock up on supplies," Max added. That had been a problem. They had been almost out of provisions when they reached their ranch. Since then, they had been on short rations, making do with what they had left and cadging a few things from some of the cowboys they had run across.

"We'll stay the night," Owen said, "but we're pulling out first thing in the morning, understand?"

"Sure, Owen," Al replied. "Whatever you say." Given Owen's mood, neither Max nor Al wanted to cross him. Their older brother was even more dangerous when he was silently brooding than when he blustered and carried on.

The light up ahead grew slowly but steadily brighter until it finally resolved itself into a warm yellow glow coming from a window. The roadhouse was a large, rambling building, one wing devoted to the trading post, the other functioning as a saloon. As the brothers approached they saw several horses tied up at the hitchrack in front of the place. The animals looked miserable in the cold.

As Owen glanced at the horses, he felt something stirring inside him. Winslow had a stable in the back of his roadhouse. That was where the horses should have been, not left out here in the bitter weather.

Owen drew rein and swung out of the saddle. Handing his lines to Max, he said, "You and Al put our horses in that stable back there. I'm going on inside."

"Sure, Owen."

A porch ran along the front of the building. Part of the railing had fallen down and had never been repaired. As Owen stepped up onto it, he could feel the warped planks give beneath his feet. Winslow was not noted for keeping a fancy place, but then he did not have to be out here. The men who frequented the roadhouse cared only that it was warm and had whiskey available.

Owen went to the door, opened it, and stepped inside. Quickly he pulled the panel shut and paused just inside the entrance to scan the big room. He had heard stories about some of the shootouts that had taken place at Winslow's, so he rested his right hand on the butt of his pistol, just in case he had walked into some sort of trouble.

But the roadhouse appeared peaceful at the moment. Five men were lined up at the bar, no doubt the owners of the horses outside. Winslow himself stood behind the hardwood, pouring drinks for his customers. The proprietor was a huge man, sloppily fat, with a gleaming bald skull and a sweeping black mustache. Tucked into his belt was an ancient Colt revolver, a Texas Paterson model. It was an unwieldy weapon with a nine-inch-long barrel, but Winslow, it was said, could bring it into play with surprising speed when trouble threatened.

A few rickety tables were scattered around the room, but no one was sitting at them. The only other person in the roadhouse was a round-faced Indian woman who sat cross-legged and wrapped in blankets in a corner. Beside her was an iron stove that gave off welcome heat.

The men at the bar had looked around when Owen entered the room. All but one of them turned back to their drinks when they saw that he was not wearing a lawman's badge and did not seem to be looking for trouble. The man still watching him stood slightly apart from the others. His dark, watchful eyes played slowly over Owen's hulking form. He was lean, almost gaunt, and his clothes were draped on him like those of a scarecrow. Under his battered hat, his stringy brown hair hung to his shoulders. A mustache drooped on both sides of his mouth beneath his prominent cheekbones. Holstered in the shell belt strapped around his hips was a Colt, and a rifle was leaning against the bar beside him. The other men at the bar were as heavily armed as he.

"Howdy," Winslow called, his voice booming in the low-ceilinged room. He had stopped tending the bar and was looking pointedly at Owen. "What can I do for you?"

Owen started toward him, pulling off his gloves as he strolled across the room. "Whiskey, first of all," he said. "Set up three of them."

Winslow raised an eyebrow. "Are you that thirsty, mister, or are you expecting company?"

"My brothers are putting our horses in your stable," Owen replied. "I hope that's all right."

"That's what it's there for," Winslow said as he placed three glasses on the bar and started splashing whiskey into them.

Owen glanced over at the other men, who were standing a few feet to his right. The one who had been watching him was the closest. Owen nodded to him and said, "Evening, friend."

"Evenin'," the man answered. "Plenty cold out there tonight, ain't it?"

"Yes, it is. Are those your horses tied up just outside?"

"Sure are. Why do you ask?"

"You'd better get them in out of the cold. Even a dumb brute deserves better treatment than that."

One of the other men heard Owen's comment and, straightening, pushed away from the bar. He turned an angry face toward the newcomer and began, "What the hell business is it of—"

The lean man lazily raised a hand and cut him off. "Forget it, Ben," he said airily. A slow smile spread across his features. "I'm sure this feller didn't mean no harm. He was just lookin' out for our best interests. Wouldn't do if we let our hosses freeze to death, now would it?"

"No, I reckon not, Tate," the man called Ben muttered.

"Then maybe you'd best go put 'em up for the night. I sure as hell ain't goin' back out in that cold."

For a moment Ben looked as if he might argue, but then he shrugged and tapped one of the other men on the shoulder. "Come on, Lee Roy. If I got to go back out there and put up the horses, you can come with me and help."

The two men went toward the door. Before they reached it, it swung open, and Max and Al came in, breathing hard and slapping their arms against their bodies to try to drive out the cold. Al spotted the stove and started straight for it. The two hardcases stepped past them and out into the night.

Hardcases are exactly what they are, Owen decided. The whole pack of them had the hungry look of outlaws, especially the one called Tate who seemed to be their leader. *Two-bit outlaws on the dodge,* Owen thought, *but they could be dangerous.*

He picked up his drink and tossed it down. Tate leaned an elbow on the bar and asked, "Buy you another, friend?"

Owen shrugged. "Sure." He knew he would wind up buying drinks for all of the other men, but he had the loot from the bank holdup in his saddlebags; money was not going to be a problem for a while. And once he caught up with the Indians and recovered the chest they had stolen, money would never be a problem again.

Abruptly a red haze of anger filmed his vision, and he felt a surge of rage that was so great he wanted to smash every chair, table, and person in the room to bits. Owen shut his eyes, and with a great effort he pushed those feelings away as he had been doing for days now. After his initial, angry outburst at the Indians, he had kept his emotions under control. The robberies that he and his brothers had pulled off had always been carefully planned and carried out with calm precision. That was why they had been successful. The vengeance they were now seeking would be handled the same way, Owen had decided. When the money was his again, when Lucinda was recovered— or avenged, if the savages had killed her in the meantime—and when the score had been settled for his sons and for the families of his brothers . . . then Owen Broderick would allow himself the luxury of fury and grief. Not before.

Tate gestured at Winslow, and the burly bartender refilled Owen's glass. Max and Al came over to the bar and picked up their own drinks, and Owen asked, "Any trouble putting the horses up?"

Max shook his head, sipped the whiskey, and licked his lips before he answered. "I think they'll be fine. Better than being outside, anyway."

Owen lifted his glass again and nodded to Tate. "Thanks, mister."

"You're welcome." The lean man thrust out his hand. "Name's Tate Driscoll."

Owen tossed off the whiskey, feeling its warmth coursing down his throat and on into his belly. Then he put the glass on the bar and shook hands with Tate Driscoll. "I'm Owen Broderick," he said. "These are my brothers Max and Al."

"Glad to meet you, boys," Driscoll said. A thoughtful frown appeared on his face. "Broderick . . . Name seems a mite familiar. You fellers wouldn't be from over Missouri way, would you?"

"We've been there," Owen replied noncommittally.

Driscoll grinned shrewdly. "The boys I'm thinkin' of sort of helped themselves to the contents of a few bank vaults here and there. Mighty smooth operators, they seem like. I recollect there're three of 'em, too."

"All right," Owen snapped. "There's no point in playing games. You know who we are, Driscoll. That mean anything to you?"

Driscoll held up his hands, palms out. "Take it easy, Owen. You don't mind if I call you Owen, do you? Naw, I always admired you and your brothers. Always seemed to me like you was mighty good at what you do."

"Thanks," Owen grunted. He relaxed somewhat. Driscoll's casual stance told him the man was not about to start a fight.

"You might've heard of me and my boys, too," Driscoll went on. "Ben Dunn and Lee Roy Johnson just went out to tend to the hosses, and this here is Asa Mitchell and Stub Pearson." He inclined his head toward the other two men at the bar. "What brings you to these parts, Owen?"

The brothers' ownership of their ranch had been a secret, but Owen saw no point in continuing to keep it that way now. "We're after some murdering redskins," he said. "They raided our spread north of here."

Driscoll frowned again. "Indians, you say? Hey, Winslow, you didn't say nothin' about no Indian trouble 'round here."

"They haven't bothered me any," Winslow replied with a shrug of his wide shoulders. "I don't know what they've been up to other places."

"It was Indians, all right," Max said in a choked voice. "Nobody else would have done what they did to our families."

Driscoll shook his head. "Damn. That's rough, boys. I'm mighty sorry to hear about it. You're trackin' the heathens, you say?"

"Trying to," Owen replied. "They've got my wife with them."

Driscoll caught his breath, his eyes glowering angrily. "A white woman? They stole a white woman?"

"That's right."

The hardcase put his hand on the walnut butt of his pistol. "This may be kind of sudden-like, but how about me and the boys ridin' with you fellers?"

Owen looked at him warily. "What for?"

"White men have to stick together out here," Driscoll declared. He glanced over his shoulder at Mitchell and Pearson. "How about it, boys? You want a shot at them murderin' redskins?"

"Whatever you say, Tate," one man replied, while the other nodded.

"How about it?" Driscoll asked, swinging back around to face Owen. "Eight guns makes for a lot better odds than three."

That's true, Owen thought. He looked at Max and Al and saw that they were waiting for him to make the decision. Neither of them, however, looked overly eager to team up with Driscoll and his gang.

"All right," he decided, nodding abruptly. "We'll be pulling out early in the morning, Driscoll. If you and your friends want to come with us, we'll be glad to have you."

Driscoll grinned. "And we'll be damn glad to ride with you. I speak for all the fellers when I say that. 'Fore we're done, we'll kill us a bunch of redskins, won't we?"

"Maybe." Owen turned to Winslow and went on,

"Bring the bottle and leave it. We might as well celebrate our new partnership."

He took the bottle that Winslow shoved down the bar and refilled Driscoll's glass and his own. Driscoll picked up his glass and clinked it against Owen's, then said, "Here's to killin' Injuns."

"To killing Indians," Owen agreed.

Chapter Six

"WHAT DO YOU MEAN, DROP THE CHARGES?" THURMAN Simpson cried incredulously.

Luke Travis was sitting at his desk looking at the schoolmaster's pinched, angry face. "I just don't want to see Nestor Gilworth sent to prison," he explained mildly, refusing to be goaded by the irate Simpson. "And that's what's going to happen if you insist on pressing assault charges against him. Drunkenness and disturbing the peace are fairly minor offenses. We can keep him in the town jail for those. But if he's convicted of assault, the judge will have to sentence him to serve time in the state prison."

"Isn't that exactly where he deserves to be?" Simpson snapped testily.

Travis shook his head. "I don't think so. Nestor drinks too much because he misses the old days when he was a scout and a buffalo hunter. But he means no real harm in what he does."

"No real harm?" Simpson echoed, his voice rising in disbelief. "I was almost too sore from the beating he gave me to get out of bed this morning, Marshal! Not to mention the damage he did to the schoolhouse. It's going to take time and money to put that right."

"I know," Travis replied. "But I'm asking you as a personal favor to me, Mr. Simpson, to drop the assault charge." The marshal knew he was pressuring the schoolmaster, knew that as a well-respected lawman there were very few townsfolk who would go against his wishes. Travis saw from the shifting pinched expressions on Simpson's face that the schoolteacher was yielding to that pressure, even though he did not like it.

"What about disturbing the peace?" Simpson's mouth twisted sourly as if he were uttering something distasteful.

"As I said, Nestor can serve his time here for that. Is that arrangement agreeable to you, Mr. Simpson?"

The schoolmaster sighed and replied grudgingly, "All right, I suppose so." His mouth tightened into an angry line again. "But I insist that that big lout be forced to pay for the damage he inflicted on my schoolhouse."

Travis refrained from pointing out that the schoolhouse was the town's property and not Simpson's. "I don't know how Nestor's going to do that," he said, "but maybe we can work something out. I'll go have a talk with the judge."

"You do that," Simpson hissed. "But just make sure Gilworth serves some time. I don't want to see him loose on the streets any time soon."

"I'll see what I can do," Travis said evenly. He stood up and offered his hand to Simpson. "Thanks for seeing things my way."

Rising from his chair, Simpson shook hands with the lawman, although with little grace, then left the office. Travis watched him go, a humorless smile playing around his lips. Then he pulled on his coat and walked up the street to the courthouse. He spent half an hour in Judge Leander Belton's chambers discussing Nestor Gilworth's situation. Judge Belton had come to Abilene just after the murder of Judge Lawrence Fisher, Judah's and Cody's father. An experienced jurist nearing retirement from the bench, he had taken this assignment on an interim basis. The marshal had known the judge for many years, ever since Travis had been the marshal of Wichita, in fact, and Belton was more than willing to follow his suggestions in this case.

Travis returned to the jail a little later and went into the cellblock. He found Nestor lying on the bunk, his face turned toward the wall, but the absence of snoring told Travis that the big man was awake. "Listen up, Nestor," he said. He leaned against the wall and struck a deceptively lazy pose. "I've just been talking to the judge."

"Goin' to send me off to prison, ain't you?" Nestor asked without rolling over. His gruff voice seemed to have lost some of its strength.

"What do you think we ought to do?" Travis replied. "You busted up the schoolhouse, not to mention what you did to Thurman Simpson and Leslie Gibson."

Nestor turned over and swung his massive legs off the side of the bunk. He sat up slowly, hung his shaggy head, and ran his callused fingers through his tangled mop of graying hair. "Aw, hell, I'd just been drinkin' too much the night before," he muttered. "Reckon I was still drunk. I lost my head when that little peckerwood said he was goin' to have me sent to jail."

"Yep, but that's where you wound up anyway," Travis pointed out.

Nestor shrugged. "Never did think too straight when I was drinkin'." He looked up at Travis, his bloodshot eyes filled with remorse. "But I promise I'll give it up, Marshal. I've done had my last drink. From now on, ol' Nestor's goin' to stay on the straight and narrow!"

Travis grimaced and shook his head. "You say the same thing every time we haul you into jail, Nestor. I guess you mean it—right now. But it won't last, and we both know it. If I let you out, you'll be back in here within a week for doing the same thing."

"No, sir," Nestor insisted. "I ain't goin' near that schoolhouse again. Allus said book learnin' was dangerous."

Travis tried to look stern; he fought to keep the grin that threatened to give him away slip onto his face. "That's not exactly what I meant. You tend to get pretty rowdy when you've been drinking, Nestor, and you know it. Now, I've gone to the courthouse and had a talk with the judge. We've decided that you're going to have to serve three days for disturbing the peace."

Nestor let out a groan. "Three whole days in this cell?" he cried. "Shoot, Marshal, I'll curl up and die!"

"No, you won't, because you won't be locked up all that time. The courthouse needs some work, and that's what you'll be doing."

"Work?" Nestor sounded suspicious, as if he feared a trap of some sort.

"There are some holes in the ceiling that need to be patched. Bullet holes, actually," Travis said dryly. "Cody got a little carried away during a ruckus a few weeks ago when that temperance lady was in town. The place could use a new coat of paint, too. If you're willing to do that, you'll only have to spend the nights inside this cell."

Nestor considered it for a moment. "I reckon I could handle that, Marshal. I ain't much of a carpenter, but I'll sure as hell give 'er a shot."

"Fine. That takes care of the next few days. There's still a problem, though."

Nestor sighed and said, "I figger I know what you're talkin' about. It's that there schoolteacher, ain't it?" The shaggy buffalo hunter scowled in disgust.

The marshal nodded and once more fought back the grin. He did not want Nestor to know how closely he agreed with his assessment of Simpson. "I was able to persuade Simpson to drop the assault charges against you and settle for disturbing the peace," Travis said. "But he insists that you pay for the damage you did at the school."

"But I ain't got no money, Marshal! I spent it all on whiskey the night it got so cold. Man's got to stay warm somehow, don't he?"

"Sure, but there's nothing else I can do about this problem, Nestor. Simpson's got a right to demand payment."

"So I'm goin' to rot in here after all," the buffalo hunter said heavily.

"Until we can think of something else, I'm afraid so. But we've got three days, while you're working at the courthouse. Maybe we'll come up with something in that time."

Nestor nodded, but he did not look convinced.

Travis shook his head sympathetically and went into the office, leaving Nestor staring gloomily down at the stone floor of the cell. The last thing Travis wanted was Nestor Gilworth as a permanent prisoner, but as long as Thurman Simpson remained stubborn, it looked as though that was the way it would be. And knowing the schoolmaster as he did, Travis suspected that Simpson could stay stubborn for a *long* time.

Later that morning Cody Fisher took a surprisingly meek Nestor over to the courthouse and got him started working on the ceiling. Nestor had promised Travis that he would cause no trouble while he was out of the cell, but the marshal cautioned Cody to keep a close eye on him anyway. The big man was sober at the moment, but even a sober Nestor could be dangerous.

Travis remained at the office and settled down to do some of the paperwork that always seemed to pile up on his desk. He sat back and put down his pencil as the door opened, grateful for the interruption, whatever it turned out to be. A smile stretched across his face as Sister Laurel hurried into the building and closed the door quickly behind her.

Sister Laurel was wearing a coat over her habit and boots instead of the sensible shoes she usually wore. Even nuns had to make concessions to cold weather, Travis supposed. "Hello, Sister," he said. "What can I do for you?"

"Hello, Luke." Sister Laurel smiled, her blue eyes sparkling warmly. "I've come to speak to you about Nestor Gilworth."

The grin on Travis's face was instantly replaced by an expression of shocked surprise. "What the devil— Sorry, Sister. What in the world has he gone and done now? I thought he'd stay out of trouble for a while, what with Cody keeping an eye on him."

"Oh, he's not in trouble, Marshal. I happened to be running an errand inside the courthouse and noticed Mr. Gilworth working there. Cody told me about the arrangement you've worked out with Judge Belton. I was very interested in it."

"Yes, ma'am." Travis nodded and waited for her to go on. What interest could Sister Laurel possibly have in an old reprobate like Nestor?

"An idea occurred to me as I was talking to Cody," Sister Laurel continued. "I'd like you to parole Mr. Gilworth into my custody, Luke."

Travis frowned. "You want to be responsible for Nestor?" he asked. "Pardon me, Sister, but *why?*"

"Judah and I have been discussing the possibility of hiring a handyman to help out at the orphanage," the nun said. "As you know, the building is quite large, and there is a good deal of work involved in keeping it up, along with the church itself, of course. Judah's duties as pastor keep him pretty busy, and I have to spend most of my time with the children. We could use some assistance."

"And when you saw Nestor working at the court-house, you thought he might be willing to take the job," Travis said, nodding in understanding. "I don't know, Sister . . ."

"We could furnish him with a small room in the orphanage so that he would have a decent place to stay," Sister Laurel went on, "and we could also pay him a small salary."

Travis's interest in her proposal quickened. "Nestor does need some money, all right," he mused.

Sister Laurel nodded. "Cody told me about Mr. Simpson's insistence that Mr. Gilworth pay for the damage he did at the school. All of Mr. Gilworth's salary could go for that purpose until the debt is taken care of. Wouldn't that satisfy Mr. Simpson?"

"It ought to," Travis said. "But I'm not sure it would work out. You know how Nestor likes his whiskey."

Sister Laurel sniffed and shook her head, her wimple trembling with the gesture. "Oh, Judah and I can put a stop to that, Luke, I assure you. With Mr. Gilworth right under our noses all the time, we can break him of his habit."

Travis leaned back in his chair and ran a thumb along his jaw in thought. What Sister Laurel was proposing made sense, all right, but Travis's instincts cautioned him to be careful. The nun was talking about a situation that was ripe for trouble. If there was anybody who could raise Cain wherever he was, Nestor Gilworth was the man.

Besides, Travis thought, he happened to know something that Sister Laurel did not. It had not been long since Reverend Judah Fisher had conquered his own drinking problem—for the second time. Having a booze-hound like Nestor around might not be a good idea, just in case Judah was tempted to backslide once more.

Sister Laurel seemed convinced that the arrangement would work, however, and for the life of him, Travis could not see a better way out of Nestor's dilemma. The marshal nodded and said, "All right. It'll still take him a couple of days to finish his work at the courthouse, but once that's done, Nestor is all yours."

"You don't think Mr. Simpson will object?"

"I'll see to it he doesn't," Travis promised. "No, the way I see it, the toughest one to convince is going to be Nestor himself."

"I'm sure you can handle that, Luke." The nun's eyes twinkled merrily.

A grin played around the corners of Travis's mouth. He had to admit he was looking forward to seeing Nestor's reaction when he told the big man he was going to live in an orphanage.

* * *

"I'm goin' to stay *where?*" Nestor demanded, staring at Travis in shock.

"At the orphanage out at the Methodist Church," Travis repeated. "Sister Laurel and Reverend Fisher have been kind enough to offer you a job as their handyman."

Nestor's breath hissed between his clenched teeth. He looked as if he wanted to spit in distaste. In frustration he reached up and pulled his battered hat down tighter on his shaggy head.

"If you can think of a better way to earn that money you've got to pay to Thurman Simpson, I'm open to suggestions, Nestor," Travis went on. "Otherwise you'll just have to stay in jail."

"Jail, huh?" Nestor frowned, squinting one eye almost closed as he did so. A small splash of white paint decorated his grease-stained shirt.

Cody had brought him back to the jail to eat his lunch, and Travis had taken the opportunity to tell him about Sister Laurel's offer. Travis was not surprised that Nestor did not particularly like the idea. He was accustomed to the rough company of army posts and buffalo hunting camps, not orphans and preachers and nuns.

But even a brain that had been fogged with alcohol for most of the last few years could see that there was probably only one way out of the messy situation Nestor found himself in. Right now, the chance to earn enough money to pay off the damages to the school was more important than anything else.

"Reckon I don't have a hell of a lot of choice," he grumbled. "When do I start?"

"Whenever you're finished patching those holes in the ceiling," Travis told him.

"He's through with that already," Cody put in. The

deputy had been listening to Travis's exchange with Nestor, and his handsome, mobile face had registered as much surprise as Nestor's had when he heard about Sister Laurel's suggestion. Cody went on, "Nestor turned out to be real handy on that chore, Marshal. He's already painted over the patches and has started on the rest of the ceiling."

"No need to paint the whole room now," Travis replied. "I talked to Judge Belton again, and he agreed to commute your sentence for disturbing the peace."

"What'n the Sam Hill does that mean?" Nestor wanted to know.

"It means you don't have to paint the whole courthouse after all," Travis said. "Just finish the ceiling, and then we'll turn you over to Sister Laurel."

"I still ain't sure I like the sound of that. I seen that little nun around town, Marshal. She seems like a pretty strict boss."

"Stricter than the ones you've got around here," Travis admitted. "She'll keep you in line, all right. That might be the best thing for you, Nestor."

The big man looked dubious. "Reckon I'll believe that when I see it," he mumbled.

"I suppose we'll find out." Travis jerked a thumb toward the cellblock and went on, "Your lunch is in the cell on a tray, Nestor. Go on in there and eat so you can get back to work. The sooner you finish painting the courthouse ceiling, the sooner you can go to the orphanage."

Nestor—looking as if he could definitely wait to report to the orphanage, would like to postpone it as long as possible, in fact—shuffled grumpily into the cellblock.

After the three men had eaten, Nestor and Cody returned to the courthouse. Travis remained in the office, planning to ride out to the orphanage later that afternoon and let Sister Laurel know that Nestor would be available for the handyman job sooner than they had expected.

Travis left the office a little later to take a turn around town. He was not surprised to see that there were very few people out and about on the streets. The cold weather still gripped the area, and even though the clouds had cleared and the sun was shining brightly, there was little warmth in its glow.

The marshal was strolling on the north side of Texas Street when he noticed two men riding into town from the west. He ran his gaze quickly over them, ready to dismiss them as no threat—simple cowpokes on some errand for their boss. Then his keen eyes spotted the smaller figure slumped in the saddle in front of one of the riders. Travis stepped down off the boardwalk and started toward them, his pace increasing as he drew nearer.

The two middle-aged riders were hands from one of the ranches west of town, Travis saw. He recognized them from previous visits they had made to Abilene. And unless he was seriously mistaken, the boy with them was Wesley Stillman.

Travis ran up to them as they reined in. They had Wesley with them, all right, his blond head sagging onto his chest. The cowboy who was not riding double said, "Howdy, Marshal. We're lookin' for the doc."

Jerking his head toward the small white house set back several yards from the boardwalk, Travis said, "Dr. Bloom's office is right over there. Where did you find this boy? What happened to him?"

The cowhands walked their horses toward the doctor's office, while Travis strode beside them. The man riding with Wesley, supporting him with an arm around his waist, said, "We pulled him off the ice on one of the cricks west of here, Marshal. Near froze to death, he was. We thawed him out as best we could, then brung him on into town."

When they reached the boardwalk, Travis reached up, took Wesley down from the horse, and carried him up the short walk to Aileen Bloom's office. One of the cowboys hurried ahead of him to open the door.

In the small, neat room just inside, Travis saw there were several patients waiting for Aileen Bloom. Most of them appeared to be suffering with the grippe, he judged from the coughing and wheezing he heard. Suddenly Aileen, apparently responding to the sounds of yet another patient entering the office, stepped out of one of the examining rooms that lined the hallway beyond the small room. At the sight of Luke Travis, standing next to two cowboys and holding a limp youngster in his arms, her gentle, brown eyes narrowed, and her smooth forehead creased into a frown.

"My goodness, Luke, what's wrong?" she asked as she came toward him.

"Exposure, for one thing," Travis replied quietly so as not to disturb the other patients. "I'm not sure what else."

Aileen nodded briskly. Even in her plain, functional office dress, covered with a white coat, and her dark brown hair pinned severely in a bun at the nape of her neck, she was very attractive. "Bring him in here," she said, leading the three men to one of the examining rooms. "I'll be back in a moment."

Travis placed Wesley on the table in the tidy little room, while Aileen hurried down the hall to finish with her patient. As Travis put the boy down, Wesley's eyelids fluttered and then opened. He stared dully up at the marshal for a moment, then sighed, closed his eyes again, and let his head fall to the side. A moment later he was wracked by a sudden cough.

"He'd been in the crick," one of the cowhands told

Travis. "Soaked to the skin, he was. And in that wind, he'd'a been froze stiff 'fore long if we hadn't come by."

The other man said, "This here's Dutch, Marshal. My name's Robey. We ride for the Box T."

Travis nodded. "Glad to meet you, boys. I've seen you around town. Did this youngster tell you what had happened to him? He was traveling with his parents in a wagon."

The cowboy called Robey grimaced. "He was awake enough last night to tell us about it, Marshal. His pa tried to drive across the crick on the ice. 'Course, it weren't near thick enough to hold up a wagon." He gulped. "I reckon both of 'em must've drowned, 'cause there sure as hell wasn't no sign of them anywhere around."

Travis shook his head. He had known that Edward Stillman was a stubborn, arrogant man, but to try such a foolish stunt that was bound to wind up killing somebody . . . Well, it was just blind luck that Wesley had survived.

At that moment Aileen came into the room. She quietly asked the men to leave, then quickly turned to the boy, and began to examine him. Travis, Robey, and Dutch stepped out into the hall. The two cowhands told him the rest of what they knew about what had happened—which was practically nothing. Travis supposed that when the weather improved he would have to take some men out to where the accident had occurred and try to find the wreckage and the bodies. The Stillmans deserved a decent burial.

Their good deed completed, the two men told Travis that, should he need to find them, they were heading over to the Alamo for a drink. Then they would stock up on supplies and start back to the line shack where they would spend the winter. If the marshal wanted to find where the Stillmans' wagon went into the creek, they would help.

Travis thanked Dutch and Robey for bringing Wesley into town and walked them to the office door. After saying so long to them, he went back to wait outside the examining room.

When Aileen emerged a half hour later, she smiled at Travis and said, "The boy is in surprisingly good shape, Luke. Those two cowboys must have done just the right thing and warmed him up gradually, otherwise he'd be in danger of losing his fingers and toes to frostbite."

"He's going to be all right, then?"

"He should be," Aileen assured him. "He has a cold, but that's to be expected. After all, he was exposed to that bitter cold for quite some time. But he's young and strong, so he should recover quite nicely."

"Is he alert enough to talk?"

"I think so. I gave him some brandy, strictly for medicinal purposes, of course."

Travis grinned. "Sure won't hurt," he chuckled and reached for the doorknob. With a smile Aileen moved down the hall to the waiting room. Travis heard her call to a patient as he opened the door and stepped into the room. Inside he saw Wesley Stillman sitting up on the examining table, his shoulders hunched. The boy was coughing. When the spasm eased and Travis was certain he could answer, he said, "Hello, Wesley. Remember me?"

The boy looked up sullenly. "Sure. You're the marshal. You told my father to be careful." He laughed, a harsh, humorless sound that was cut off by another wracking fit of coughing. When he caught his breath he went on bitterly, "I guess you can see how that turned out."

Travis looked sadly at the youngster slumped on the table. "Those two men who helped you told me what happened. I'm sorry about your folks, Wesley."

"It was his fault," Wesley said. "He was so damned stubborn . . ." His eyes began to glisten with tears, and he turned away.

Travis shook his head. He was glad Wesley was going to be all right, but now he was faced with the problem of what to do with the youngster.

"We'll find a place for you to stay until you're feeling better, son," Travis said. "Then we can see about getting you back home."

Wesley avoided looking at the marshal. "I don't have a home anymore," he muttered.

"What about relatives? Surely you've got some folks back East, where you came from."

"No." The reply was curt, bitter. "My parents were the only family I had, Marshal. There's nobody back there."

Travis frowned. If this boy had no family to return to, that complicated the situation. No relatives, no place to go, nothing left except the clothes on his back. Somebody would just have to take Wesley in and give him a place to live.

Luckily, there were two people in Abilene who specialized in doing that very thing. Travis said, "You just stay here and take it easy for a while, Wesley. I'll be back later."

Wesley made no reply, did not look up, or say good-bye. Travis shook his head again, then left the doctor's office after exchanging a few words with Aileen Bloom. She agreed to watch Wesley until he returned.

Five minutes later, Travis was mounted up and riding toward the Calvary Methodist Church. If there was anybody in Abilene who would know what to do about this, it was Sister Laurel and Reverend Judah Fisher.

Half an hour later, Judah and Sister Laurel returned to Aileen's office with Luke Travis. They rode in the church's buggy with Judah at the reins; Travis was on horseback beside them. Both the nun and the minister wore concerned looks—the expressions had been there ever since Travis had told them about Wesley Stillman's plight.

Aileen met them in the hallway just outside the door of the examining room where Wesley waited. "He's still very withdrawn, Luke," she murmured. "But that's to be expected, given what he's gone through."

"The poor lad," Sister Laurel said. "I'm just glad we were here to help."

Travis hoped she still felt the same way after she had dealt with Wesley. He was not the most likable boy Travis had ever met.

The marshal opened the door and led the small group into the room. Wesley was still sitting on the table, Travis saw, wearing the same sullen look on his face. "I've brought somebody to lend you a hand, Wesley," he said.

The blond youth glanced up briefly, then looked again as he recognized Sister Laurel and Judah. His mouth tightened, and he exclaimed, "Wait a minute! I remember you people. You're from that orphanage!"

"That's right, Wesley," Judah said. He stepped forward and extended his hand to the boy. "I'm Judah Fisher, and this is Sister Laurel. We've come to offer you a place to stay."

Wesley pointedly ignored the minister's hand, and Judah finally lowered it. The boy's face was flushed with anger. "I won't go to live in any stinking orphanage, if that's what you mean," he snarled. "My parents were headed for California, and that's where I'm going!" He nodded his head to emphasize his decision and folded his arms defiantly.

Travis frowned. Wesley's determination to continue the westward journey was a new development. He must have come up with the idea while he was sitting here and brooding. "Look, Wesley," he said reasonably, "you can't start out for California by yourself. You're too young to make a trip like that."

"I'm fourteen," Wesley shot back.

"And if you'd lived out here on the frontier all your life and knew its ways and how to handle yourself, some folks would consider you a full-grown man," Travis replied. "But you just got here, son."

Anger flared in Wesley's eyes. "Don't call me son! My father is dead."

Travis turned and exchanged looks with the others. All of them knew that grief and shock were taking their toll on Wesley. Sister Laurel moved forward and tried getting through to the hurt, angry youngster.

"No one is going to try to replace your parents, Wesley," she said in a forthright, yet soothing voice. "And if you want to go to California someday, no one is going to stop you. All we want to do is give you a decent place to live until you're old enough to do what you want."

"What I want is to get out of this stupid town—" Another coughing spell shook Wesley as soon as the harsh words were out of his mouth. Sister Laurel, her eyes filled with compassionate concern, moved to stand beside him and rested a hand on his shoulder. At her touch he looked up sharply and suspiciously and appeared ready to pull away from her. But he stayed where he was, hunched over on the table until the coughing stopped.

"I'll give you some medication to ease your cough, Wesley," Aileen said firmly. "But to recover fully you must rest in a nice warm place."

"Like that orphanage," Wesley snapped. "I know what you're getting at."

"That's right," Travis said firmly. He was growing impatient with the truculent lad. "Legally, you're a ward of the court, Wesley, and if you don't have any relatives back East, you'll stay that way. You can make it easier on all of us—yourself included—if you agree to go to the orphanage."

"The marshal is right, Wesley," Judah said.

"Please," Sister Laurel added softly. "All we want to do is help you."

Wesley looked at each of the adults encircling him and took a deep breath. A feral, haunted expression that reminded Travis of a trapped animal briefly crossed his face, but then he nodded. "I guess I don't have much choice," he muttered slowly. "I've got to have some place to stay. It might as well be the orphanage."

Judah clapped him on the shoulder. "You won't regret that decision, Wesley. I'm sure you'll find plenty of friends there."

"Yeah, maybe." Wesley did not sound convinced.

Travis caught Sister Laurel's eye and whispered that he would like to speak with her in private. As Judah and Wesley went out to the buggy, Sister Laurel waited for the marshal in the hallway. "Yes, Luke," she said, "what is it?"

"I just wanted you to know that Nestor agreed to your suggestion. Judge Belton decided that under the circumstances he won't have to spend the whole three days working at the courthouse. I can bring him to the orphanage any time you like."

Sister Laurel smiled. "That's excellent, Luke!" She

peered at him thoughtfully, then said, "Since Wesley has no bags, there would be room for Nestor in the buggy now. Would it be all right for him to come with us?"

"I don't see why not," Travis replied with a shrug. "He ought to have finished painting the ceiling."

With Sister Laurel at his side, Travis strolled down the street to the courthouse. Judah and Wesley rode beside them in the buggy. Their timing was fortuitous, because they reached the building just as Nestor and Cody were emerging.

The grim expression on Nestor's face told Travis that the buffalo hunter had spotted the marshal and the nun coming toward him. Nestor swallowed nervously and looked more like a prisoner headed for the gallows than a potential handyman.

"I think you two folks know each other," Travis said dryly. He tried not to grin as he watched the big buffalo hunter and the nun size each other up.

"Hello, Mr. Gilworth," Sister Laurel said. "I'm glad you're going to be working with us. I'm sure it will be a satisfactory arrangement for all concerned."

"Uh . . . yes'm," Nestor mumbled in reply. He twisted his hat in his hands.

"You can go with Sister Laurel and Judah now," Travis told him. "Do you have anything you'd like sent out to the orphanage?"

"All I got in the world 'sides what's on my back is my bowie and my Colt and my Sharps," Nestor said. "Don't reckon I'll be needin' them where I'm goin'."

"Indeed you won't, Mr. Gilworth," Sister Laurel agreed.

"Why don't you just give 'em to the Reverend for me, Marshal? I'd like to have 'em handy."

Travis looked at Judah and saw him nod in agreement. "I'll bring them up to the parsonage later."

"Well, come along, Mr. Gilworth," Sister Laurel said briskly. "I believe there's room for you in the back seat of the buggy with Wesley. This is Wesley Stillman, by the way. He's going to be staying with us at the orphanage."

Nestor glanced into the back seat and nodded. "Howdy, boy," he said shortly.

Wesley made no reply. He just wrinkled his nose in distaste as Nestor awkwardly climbed in, his bulk making the buggy sag momentarily.

Cody helped Sister Laurel into the front seat. The nun settled down, then turned and said over her shoulder, "I already know what your first task shall be once we arrive, Mr. Gilworth. I want you to wash that . . . that coat you're wearing and take a bath."

"Yes'm," Nestor muttered sheepishly.

Judah looked at Travis and Cody and grinned. Then clearing his throat, he flicked the reins and got the buggy moving. The vehicle rolled down Texas Street, Wesley and Nestor staring gloomily out of opposite sides.

"What do you think's going to happen, Marshal?" Cody asked, grinning as he watched the buggy depart.

Travis shook his head. "I'm not sure," he said, "but with those two out there, I'll be surprised if there aren't some fireworks sooner or later."

Chapter Seven

MICHAEL HIRSCH ENJOYED SCHOOL—AT LEAST WHEN Mr. Simpson was not being too unreasonable—but the redheaded boy was still always glad to see classes draw to an end for the day. Once he had hurried back to the orphanage and tended to whatever chores Sister Laurel had for him, he was free to play with his friends, explore the area around Abilene, and generally have the kind of fine time that only a youngster is capable of.

Of course, when the weather was as cold as it was today, that cut down on the things that Michael and his chums could do. But there were still plenty of games they could play around the orphanage.

He was in a good mood as he and several of his friends walked into the foyer of the large building that had once been the Methodist parsonage. Judah Fisher still had a room there, but most of the space was now devoted to the children. Michael carried the primer that the students used in school under his arm. Mr. Simpson had told them to read one of the stories in it before class the next day.

Michael did not mind the assignment; he had always liked to read, although his tastes ran more toward the dime novels that he sometimes smuggled into the orphanage than the primer assignments Mr. Simpson came up with. Sister Laurel was somewhat tolerant of his fascination with Deadwood Dick and Old Sleuth and all the other heroes who had such thrilling adventures, but she did not want the yellow-backed pamphlets corrupting the younger children. Michael planned to read the story in the primer right away, so that it would not interfere with his plans for the rest of the day.

As he and the others passed the parlor doorway, Sister Laurel called out to him. "Michael, would you mind coming in here for a moment?"

Michael turned and glanced into the room. He stiffened when he saw the boy sitting on the sofa, crowded into the corner as far away from Sister Laurel as he could possibly get.

He remembered the blond youngster's arrogant face quite well, remembered the taunts that had come out of the boy's sneering mouth. And he recalled how good it had felt to smash a fist into that mouth.

Over his shoulder Michael said to his friends, "I'll catch up to you." Then he went into the parlor. Judah Fisher was sitting in an armchair opposite the sofa. Both he and Sister Laurel had serious expressions on their faces. Michael knew that meant something important had happened. Probably something bad, he thought. It had to be bad, or else why would the kid called Wesley be back here? Michael went on, "What is it, Sister?"

"Michael, this is Wesley Stillman," the nun said. Her solemn voice and demeanor sent a slight tremor through Michael. "I'm sure that you remember him from the other day."

"I remember," Michael replied coldly.

"The sister and I received some bad news this afternoon, Michael," Judah said quietly. "Wesley's parents were killed in an accident."

Michael caught his breath and looked at Wesley again. The blond boy did not meet his gaze. Instead Wesley stared at the braided rug on the polished wooden floor, his features surly. Michael cleared his throat and said, "I'm sorry. I didn't know."

"You couldn't have known," Sister Laurel said gently. "Wesley was brought back to town today by some men who found him. I won't go into the details of the tragedy. Suffice it to say, Wesley is coming to live with us, Michael, and Reverend Fisher and I agree that it wouldn't do for him to start off on the wrong foot. We don't want any ill feelings between you two boys."

"That's why we want the two of you to shake hands and put any trouble you have had in the past behind you." Judah leaned forward in his chair and looked intently at Michael. "How does that sound to you?"

Michael hesitated for a moment, then shrugged. "Sure. I don't want any trouble." He stepped over to the sofa and extended his hand to Wesley Stillman. "How about it, Wes? Why don't we bury the hatchet?"

Without looking up, the other boy said, "My name is Wesley, not Wes. And I suppose that's one of your colorful frontier expressions."

"It's just a way of saying that I don't want any more trouble, all right?" Michael replied tightly. He kept his hand out.

Finally Wesley reached up and took it. He shook it limply, then dropped it. "All right. I don't want any trouble, either."

"Fine." Michael forced a grin. "Maybe we can even be friends."

"Yeah, maybe. But I don't expect to be here for long. I'm going to California."

"We'll discuss that at another time, Wesley," Sister Laurel said firmly, "at some point in the future. For now, though, this will be your home, and we're very glad to have you with us."

Wesley nodded and muttered, "Thanks."

Judah stood up and put a hand on Michael's shoulder. "You seem to know your way around Abilene better than any of the other children, Michael. Why don't you help Wesley learn to get around, too? And Wesley, you'll have to get started in school."

For the first time Wesley showed some animation, but he did not look particularly happy. "I'll have to go to school?" he asked. "My father said I'd had enough education. He said you could learn more from traveling than you can from any school."

"He may have been right," Judah said lightly, "but you're not going to be traveling for a while, so we think it would be best if you went to school. Michael can show you the way in the morning and help you get settled in. How about that, Michael?"

"I guess so," Michael replied with a shrug.

Judah moved over to Wesley and said, "Why don't you come with me, and I'll show you your room. I think you'll like staying there."

Wesley certainly did not look as convinced of that as Judah did, but he got to his feet and followed the minister out of the parlor. He glanced back as they reached the foyer, and for an instant, Michael felt a shiver go through him. Wesley looked as if he would just as soon kill Michael as look at him. Neither Sister Laurel nor Judah could see the expression, but Michael did not miss it. Obviously Wesley had been shamming when he agreed to try to get along.

Michael, his mind buzzing angrily at that realization, heard Wesley follow Judah up the narrow staircase to the second floor. He took a deep breath to push the fruitless anger aside as their footsteps receded down the long corridor.

"Thank you, Michael," Sister Laurel said gently. Michael looked at her and saw that her wise blue eyes were studying him compassionately. "I realize you and Wesley don't get along particularly well, but he's going to need a friend now that he's lost his family."

"What happened to them?" Michael asked.

"Their wagon fell into a creek west of here," she replied softly. "Wesley's mother and father both drowned."

Michael shook his head. Unlike some children, he had seen enough violent death in his short life, and it was vividly real to him. He said sincerely, "I'm sorry. I didn't like Wesley when I met him, but I wouldn't want that to happen to anybody's parents."

"Even to someone as unpleasant as Wesley can be." Sister Laurel smiled slightly. "I understand, Michael, and I appreciate your making an effort to make him feel at home here. I'm sure he'll fit in if we just give him enough time."

Michael was not so sure of that, but he nodded anyway. He knew Sister Laurel expected it. Nevertheless, he had a feeling that Wesley Stillman was never going to fit in, no matter how hard the rest of them tried.

Michael would take only so much of the other

boy's obnoxious behavior. Unless Wesley had really changed—which Michael doubted—the day was going to come when there would be trouble.

All the children who lived in the orphanage had assigned tasks to perform after supper. That evening while the other children were cleaning up, Wesley was excused from the chores because it was his first day at the orphanage. Also, the cold he had caught had weakened him. With Sister Laurel's permission, Wesley went upstairs to his room.

Some of the other boys grumbled at this unusual lapse in Sister Laurel's strict rules. But Michael came to the newcomer's defense. "Take it easy on Wesley," he told his friends. "He lost his parents, and he's in a new place. I wouldn't feel very good, either."

"What's wrong with you?" one of the boys asked in surprise. "I thought you hated the guy. I saw the way you two mixed it up a few days ago."

Michael shrugged. "That was then. Things have changed."

Have they really? Michael wondered. Wesley had been as surly as ever during the meal, eating in silence and ignoring the few attempts the other children made to befriend him. Maybe it would have been better all around, Michael thought, if Judah and Sister Laurel had let Wesley go on to California just the way he wanted.

After the dishes had been washed and put away and the kitchen had been cleaned, Michael and his friends were free to do as they wished, providing that they had already done their homework. While several of the boys gathered in the parlor to play a game, Michael decided to try once more to befriend Wesley Stillman.

He climbed the stairs to the second floor of the large building and went down the hall to the room that had been given to Wesley. Most of the boys shared quarters, but this room had only the one occupant. Michael rapped on the door and heard a muttered, "Yeah? Who is it?"

"Michael Hirsch," he replied.

"What do you want, Hirsch?" Wesley asked, not sounding particularly happy to be disturbed.

"Some of the fellas are getting ready to play a game downstairs. I thought you might like to join in."

"Nah." Wesley coughed. "Now leave me alone."

Michael frowned. He heard Wesley cough again, then he sniffed as a faint, strange odor drifted to his nose. It smelled like something burning. On the other side of the door, a particularly violent fit of coughing seized Wesley.

"Are you all right?" Michael asked anxiously. Wesley did not answer; instead, he continued to cough.

Hesitating briefly, Michael then made up his mind. He grasped the doorknob, turning it with his fingers, and swung the door open. The smell of smoke was stronger now.

Wesley was facing away from the door, but he turned around quickly as he heard the door scraping open. "Dammit, get out of here!" he gasped when he saw who had entered.

Michael noticed the cigarette in Wesley's hand. Somehow the blond boy had gotten the makings, maybe cadged them off one of the cowboys who had brought him back to Abilene, and retreated to his room to roll a cigarette. He had cracked open the window a few inches, letting in cold air but also letting most of the smoke escape.

"I don't think you should be smoking," Michael

said firmly. "Sister Laurel and Reverend Fisher wouldn't like it, and anyway, you're sick. That's just going to make it worse."

"Mind your own damned business," Wesley snarled. He pulled on the cigarette and then coughed again, bending over almost double for a moment. He straightened and wiped the back of his hand across his mouth, then said, "I told you to get out. Are you going, or do I have to make you?"

"I'm going." Michael narrowed his eyes and nodded. Clearly he had wasted his time trying to be friendly to Wesley.

As Michael turned toward the door, Wesley took a quick step forward and grasped Michael's shoulder, jerking him to a halt. "And don't get any ideas about telling the nun or that stupid preacher about me smoking," he warned. "You'll be sorry if you do."

Michael looked coldly at the hand that was holding him, then raised his eyes to Wesley's. "Don't worry," he snapped. "I don't care what you do to yourself. Just don't burn the building down."

Wesley gave him a shove. "Get out of here."

Michael left, glad to close the door behind him and be away from Wesley Stillman. The Eastern youngster was just about the most unpleasant individual Michael had ever encountered. It would be good to get back downstairs to his friends.

As he turned away from the door, Michael thought he heard an odd sound inside the room, something that sounded almost like a choked sob. He paused, then shook his head and went down the hall. Michael did not want to know anything about whatever was going on in Wesley's room now.

Things did not improve the next day. At breakfast, as Michael was walking out of the kitchen into the dining room carrying a plate heaped with ham, eggs, and flapjacks, he passed the table where Wesley was sitting by himself. Michael glanced at the blond boy, then turned away and continued on to another table.

Wesley never stopped eating as he thrust a foot backward between Michael's ankles.

It was a quick move, almost too fast to be seen, and Michael was caught unprepared. He stumbled, tried desperately to catch his balance, but failed. He fell forward, food flying off his plate, and sprawled on the floor. Laughter erupted from the other children in the room.

Wesley glanced over his shoulder as Michael started to pick himself up from the mess that surrounded him. "Pretty clumsy in the mornings, aren't you, Hirsch?" Wesley sneered. "Or are you that way all the time?"

Michael's hands closed into fists. "You tripped me, you sonuva—"

He stopped himself just in time and looked up quickly to see if Sister Laurel or Judah had heard what he was about to say. Neither of them seemed to have noticed his near-slip, but they had seen him fall and were coming toward him. "Are you all right, Michael?" Judah asked anxiously. "What happened?"

His face flushed with anger, Michael opened his mouth to accuse Wesley of tripping him. But he realized that it was unlikely anyone had seen Wesley's action, considering where the newcomer was seated. Michael could not prove a thing.

"Must've tripped over my own two feet," he muttered. "I'm sorry, Reverend. I'll clean up this mess."

"It's all right. No great harm done." Smiling evenly, Judah went back to his seat. Sister Laurel nodded and followed the reverend.

As Michael bent to pick up the fallen plate and the

food, he heard low-pitched laughter coming from Wesley. His face burned with humiliation; he was certain it had to be almost as red as his hair. But he fought back the rage that was coursing through him.

Holding the plate, Michael rose and turned to go toward the kitchen. As he did, he caught a glimpse of a large, bulky figure standing in the hallway just outside the dining room entrance. For a second his eyes met those of Nestor Gilworth, the orphanage's new handyman. Michael knew about Nestor and his drunken binges, as did all the other children. He was also aware of the man's past as a scout, Indian fighter, and buffalo hunter, and his feelings toward Nestor were a mixture of keen interest and fear.

Now, a tiny shiver went through Michael as he saw the intent look on the big man's face. Nestor turned away and disappeared down the hall, leaving Michael to wonder what that was all about. *Why,* he asked himself, *is Nestor watching what goes on in the dining room?* He glanced back, saw Wesley still grinning arrogantly at him, and realized that from where he had been standing Nestor might have seen the whole thing—including Wesley's tripping him.

No point in saying anything, Michael decided. This incident, as embarrassing as it had been, was over.

But Michael was wrong. Over the next few days, as his health improved, Wesley went out of his way to make life difficult for Michael. It seemed every time Michael turned around, Wesley was there with some new taunt. A couple of the younger boys seemed to have fallen in with him, and they were always beside him to laugh at the derisive comments he flung at Michael. Michael tried to keep a tight rein on his temper; he would have gladly tackled Wesley again, along with his two toadies, but he had promised Sister

Laurel and Judah that there would be no more trouble.

Some of the other children were not so restrained. Several fistfights broke out as the other boys grew tired of Wesley's jibes about the orphanage, Abilene, and the West in general. Sister Laurel or Judah was usually close at hand to break up the battles, and no one was seriously hurt beyond a bloody nose or an occasional bruise.

Michael had done as Sister Laurel requested and shown Wesley where the school was located. Wesley attended classes just as he was supposed to, but he did not volunteer to participate, and he answered curtly when Thurman Simpson or Leslie Gibson called on him. At lunch and recess he kept to himself, his only companions the two younger lads who seemed to follow him worshipfully for some reason Michael could not fathom.

But throughout all this, Michael might have been able to keep a lid on his anger . . . had it not been for what Wesley said about his sister, Agnes.

Agnes had come to Abilene with Sister Laurel's group of orphans, but she was older than all of the others, more a young woman than a child. She helped out around the orphanage with the younger children and worked at the Sunrise Café on Texas Street as a waitress. Michael, looking at her objectively, supposed she was pretty. Agnes had thick, lustrous red hair, fair skin, attractive features, and a lithe, well-curved body. But to Michael she was just his sister.

Wesley had reacted quite differently to her, right from the first night he had stayed at the orphanage. More than once Michael had seen him staring at Agnes with a disturbing expression in his eyes. On Friday evening, after Wesley had been at the orphanage for three days, he came sauntering up to Michael after supper. "Listen, Hirsch, I want to ask you something about your sister."

"Agnes?" Michael frowned. They were alone in the dining room, the younger children having gone up to bed, the older ones in the parlor or in their rooms. "Sure. What do you want to know?"

"How much does she charge?"

Michael caught his breath. "What do you mean by that?"

"I just thought I might start saving up my money," Wesley replied with an elaborately casual shrug. "I never saw a redheaded girl yet who wasn't a whore, so I thought I'd try her out."

Michael stared at him for a moment, numb with shock and rage. He could see the amusement in Wesley's eyes. Then something seemed to snap inside Michael. Uttering an inarticulate yell, he threw himself at Wesley, fists flailing.

That must have been exactly the reaction Wesley desired, because the bigger youth was ready. He blocked Michael's punches and hooked a blow into Michael's belly. He was about to follow it with a hard cross to the jaw, when someone grabbed him from behind.

Michael gasped for breath and kept pushing forward, but a big hand pressed against his chest, stopping him as surely as if it had been a brick wall. He looked up and saw that Nestor Gilworth had slipped between Wesley and him. The other boy was dangling from one of Nestor's massive paws, his feet inches above the floor. The front of Wesley's shirt was bunched in the big man's fingers.

"Now hold on, you little rapscallions!" Nestor rumbled. "I've watched you two hoo-rawin' each other all week, an' I'm plumb sick of it!"

"I haven't done anything to him!" Michael protested. "I've just tried to stay out of his way. But you should've heard what he said about—"

"I heard him, boy," Nestor growled. He pushed Michael back. "You go on. I'll have a talk with this feller."

"You put me down, you big ox!" Wesley snarled. "I'm going to call Sister Laurel—"

"No you ain't," Nestor cut in. "Not if'n you know what's good for you, you ain't. Now hush up. Michael, you do like I tell you. I'll handle this."

Michael frowned dubiously. Several times during the week he had caught Nestor quietly watching Wesley but had not said a thing about it to anyone. Evidently the big man was taking some sort of interest in the boy from back East, and it did not appear to be a friendly one at the moment. Michael knew how Nestor tended to try to shoot people who angered him or at least throw them through windows. If something happened to Wesley—

"I ain't goin' to hurt him, if'n that's what you're worried about," Nestor rumbled. "Now git!"

There was no arguing with Nestor Gilworth. You either did what he told you or got ready to fight. Michael knew that quite well, so he did the only thing he could. He hurried out of the dining room.

If he heard any yelling, though, or if Wesley did not come out unharmed in a few minutes, he would have no choice but to go find Judah.

Not that the reverend would be any match for Nestor Gilworth, Michael thought bleakly.

Nestor Gilworth let go of Wesley and allowed the boy to drop to the floor. As Wesley caught himself, he demanded angrily, "What right do you have to butt into somebody else's business, old man?"

"I work here now," Nestor said. "Reckon part of my job is to help look out for you younkers."

"The hell it is," Wesley sneered. "You're just the handyman."

"Mebbe so, but I hate to see a young feller make a damn-blasted fool of hisself."

"What are you talking about?"

Nestor jerked a thumb toward the door that Michael Hirsch had gone through. "Don't you know Michael just wants to be pards with you? How come you're allus pushin' and proddin' at him and the other fellers? You want folks to hate you?"

Wesley laughed harshly. "I don't care," he declared. "Why should I care what these orphans think of me?"

"Well, you're one of 'em now."

"No, I'm not," Wesley insisted with a determined shake of his head. "I'm not like them at all."

"You're a youngster who lost his folks. And I reckon that makes you about as scared and sad as a feller can get."

"That's a lie!" Wesley blazed. "I'm not scared of anything."

"Then you're a fool."

Wesley started to spin on his heel. "I don't have to listen to this."

Nestor's hand came down on his shoulder. "I got to clean out the barn tomorrow. You're goin' to help me."

"The hell I will!"

Nestor's fingers tightened. "You will if'n you know what's good for you, boy." He laughed, the harshness of it matching Wesley's earlier laughter. "Tomorrow mornin' at seven. That's when I'll be startin'. You be there, or I'll come lookin' for you."

"You're crazy!" Wesley gasped. "You're just a drunken old man!"

"Don't count on it," Nestor grated. He released Wesley again, then turned and walked out of the dining room.

When he was out of Wesley's sight, Nestor stopped and drew a deep breath. The craving was on him strong. He wanted a drink, wanted the fiery taste of whiskey to burn away the outside world and leave him in a pleasant, unthinking haze.

But those days were behind him. He had made promises to Luke Travis, Sister Laurel, and Judah Fisher. Nestor intended to keep those promises if he possibly could.

It had been a long week, working hard in the orphanage all day and then staring at the ceiling of his small room all night as he fought the thirst that threatened to engulf him. Sister Laurel had been right about one thing—the place needed work. He had been very busy during the days, cleaning and repairing and painting. Pretty soon the place would be in order again. To his surprise Nestor had found himself enjoying the work. It was not like the old days, when he had been the best buffalo hunter the Great Plains had ever seen, but there was satisfaction in a job well-done, he discovered, no matter what it was. He even liked having the youngsters scurrying around. They brought back memories of his own childhood, memories that he had thought lost in years of hardship and boozing.

Now, after the emotional confrontation with Wesley Stillman, the thirst had come back to Nestor stronger than ever. He shook his head, looking for all the world like a shaggy buffalo trying to drive off some bothersome flies, then trudged toward his room. He had sensed from the moment he first saw him that Wesley and he had something in common. The pain of losing something important, Nestor supposed. That was what it was. And he sensed as well that the boy had some goodness in him—if somebody could just dig deeply enough to find it.

Nestor snorted as that thought crossed his mind. "Damn," he muttered to himself, "now I'm thinkin' like a blasted preacher." He shook his head again, licked his lips, and tried not to think about how good a drink would taste.

Chapter Eight

NESTOR WAS IN THE BARN NEXT TO THE PARSONAGE AT seven the next morning, just as he had told Wesley Stillman he would be. Judah Fisher's saddle mount, the mare that drew Sister Laurel's buggy, four spare horses, and three milk cows were kept in the big wooden building. Cleaning it out would not be a particularly difficult chore, but neither was it a pleasant one. Nestor fully expected Wesley to ignore his warning and not show up.

He was wrong. A few minutes after seven, the hinges of the barn door squealed slightly, and the door swung open. Wesley came in, his head and shoulders drooping.

Nestor was shoveling out one of the stalls. He stopped what he was doing and stepped toward Wesley, picking up another shovel on the way. He held it out toward the boy and grunted, "Mornin'. You can start on that stall right there. Muck it out good and put some fresh straw down."

Wesley did not take the shovel. Instead he raised his eyes and glared at Nestor. "Why should I?" he demanded. "You don't have any right to make me do your work for you."

Nestor shrugged big shoulders. "Reckon you're right. I can't make you do nothin'. Just figgered you'd want to do your part around here, pull your own weight. Like when me an' Jim Bridger and some other fellers was scoutin' the Bozeman Trail a few years ago. Ever'body had a job to do, and we done what we was supposed to. That's how we made it through there 'thout losin' our hair."

"Sure," Wesley snorted sarcastically. "Even I've heard of Jim Bridger. Do you expect me to believe that a drunken old man like you rode with him?"

"It's the God's truth," Nestor declared. He thrust the shovel at Wesley again. "Here, take this, and I'll tell you about the time me an' Kit Carson was pinned down by Injuns when we was openin' up the Santa Fe Trail."

Wesley laughed in disbelief, but this time he reached out to take the shovel. "Now it's Kit Carson," he scoffed. "Who else did you know, old-timer?"

"Oh, I reckon I knew most of the fellers on the frontier back in the wild times," Nestor said, raking his fingers through his tangled beard and grinning. "Bridger and Beckwourth and Carson, Joe Meek and the Sublette brothers. . . . Hunted buffs with Bill Cody, Tuck McCall, Billy Dixon, and that Masterson feller. Scouted for Custer along with Cap'n Bob Pryor. You name it, I reckon I've done it."

As he talked, Nestor went back to work, starting to shovel out the stall he had assigned to Wesley. The boy was still frowning dubiously at him as he said, "If you've done all those things, how in hell did you wind up here in Abilene"—Wesley's lip curled in contempt —"mucking out stalls?"

"Man's got to do somethin'," Nestor answered simply. "All the buffalo left and headed down south to the Texas panhandle. I figgered I was gettin' too old to go gallivantin' all over creation after 'em. That was the biggest mistake I ever made. I should've gone down to the panhandle with Dixon and Masterson. There's still some fine huntin' down there, and I heard tell they even got into a Injun fight at a place called Adobe Walls." Nestor grinned ruefully and shook his head. "Reckon I miss out on all the good times. Here, push this on out for me, will you?"

Using the shovel Nestor had given him, Wesley shoved the pile of soiled straw out of the barn without seeming to think about what he was doing. When he came back, he said, "I always thought all that stuff about the West was just made up for the dime novels and the papers. Are you trying to tell me that it really happens?"

"Not so much anymore," Nestor admitted. "Some places out here are gettin' downright civilized. But it was plumb untamed just a few years back. Them newspapers never told the half of it, boy. If'n they did, most folks would've been too scared to ever come out here." He laughed. "Maybe it would've been better that way, come to think of it."

Wesley did not reply. Nestor moved over to the stall he had been cleaning before the boy came in and resumed mucking it out. A minute later, Wesley followed him and began working beside him. The big man glanced down at the boy out of the corner of his eye and tried not to grin.

"What was that you were saying about Kit Carson and the Santa Fe Trail?" Wesley asked, breaking the silence at last.

"Interested in that, are you?"

"My father said we were going to make the Santa Fe Trail before winter." Wesley's mouth twisted bitterly. "We didn't make it."

"Heard about that," Nestor replied, keeping his voice matter-of-fact. "I'm a heap sorry 'bout your folks, Wesley. I know how hard it is to lose 'em sudden-like."

"Oh, you do?" Wesley snapped. "What do you know about it?"

"Injuns got my ma and pa when I was only a younker, too. Must've been about eight or nine, I reckon. I don't rightly know when I was born, you see. This was back in Illinois, a long time ago 'fore it was all settled like it is now."

"What did you do?" Wesley asked. "You weren't old enough to take care of yourself, were you?"

"Weren't nobody else to do it," Nestor said simply. "If'n I hadn't took care of myself, I wouldn't be here today." Noticing the self-pitying look on Wesley's face, he decided to steer the conversation away from the touchy subject and around to another topic. "And I wouldn't't've been there to save ol' Kit Carson's hide when around a thousand of them murderin' redskins had him trapped."

"A thousand Indians?" Disbelief rang in Wesley's voice. "What could one man do against a thousand Indians?"

"Well, not much, I reckon, under normal circumstances. But you see, these heathens was chasin' Kit through a canyon there in the Colorado country. I heard the shootin' and come a-runnin', and I got to the rim of the canyon in time to see Kit's horse step in a hole and go down." Nestor leaned on his shovel and grinned at Wesley. "Well, sir, Kit jumped right up, of course, and run over behind some rocks. He forted up there and commenced to pickin' off them Injuns with his rifle as they charged him. It was only a matter of time until they overrun him, though, so I did the only thing I could to help him. I aimed that big ol' Hawken rifle of mine at the other wall of the canyon and let 'er rip."

Wesley frowned. "What good did that do?" he wanted to know.

"Well, you see, that canyon was narrow enough that when my ball hit the far side, it bounced right back to the near side and creased an Injun on the way. Then it ricocheted back again and knocked another one off his hoss. Back and forth that ball went 'tween the walls of that canyon for a good ten minutes, and on ever' bounce it grazed an Injun on the head just enough to knock him silly and make him go flyin'. When it finally lost all of its steam and plunked down on the ground, ever' damn-blasted one of them Injuns was a-layin' there on the floor of the canyon, out colder'n coons! Kit come out from behind them rocks and looked up at the rim and hollered, 'Howdy there, Nestor! It must be you, 'cause you're the onliest man I know who could make such a shot!' Well, I hollered back to him and allowed as to how it was me, all right, and Kit climbed up out'n that canyon right quick, so's we could get away 'fore all them Injuns woke up again. I reckon they was right peeved when they did, what with the headaches they must've had and no white men around to massacre."

Wesley had been staring incredulously at Nestor during the big man's tale. Now he said, "That's crazy! How could one bullet ricochet that many times?"

"Them ol' Hawkens packed one hell of a kick, boy," Nestor replied solemnly.

Wesley laughed. "Sure, Nestor. I'm sure it happened just the way you told it."

The sarcasm in the boy's tone made Nestor frown. "You doubtin' my word, son? Then, hell, I reckon you wouldn't believe what happened the time I was trapped in the middle of a buffalo stampede with Bill Cody. Ain't even no point in tellin' you 'bout it." He turned back to his work.

A moment of silence passed, then Wesley said, "Nestor? What happened? Tell me the story."

Nestor paused and lifted a big hand, rubbing it across his mouth so that Wesley would not see the quick grin that was springing to his lips. "Really want to hear about it, do you?"

"Please."

The word sounded strange coming from Wesley's lips, but his tone, Nestor judged, was sincere.

"Well, I 'spose it wouldn't do no harm. You see, me and Bill—Buffalo Bill, some folks are startin' to call him now 'cause he shot so many of the critters, but not as many as ol' Nestor—we was chasin' this buffalo herd, and danged if we didn't ride so fast that we got in front of 'em without even knowin' it. So there we was, smack dab in the way of about a million or so of them mangy beasts, and they had fire in their eyes, boy, fire in their eyes. . . ."

By midday Nestor and Wesley had cleaned out the barn. All morning Nestor kept spinning yarns, but he and Wesley continued to work as he told the tall tales, and the time went by very quickly. Wesley still did not believe most of the things Nestor had to say, but that did not matter. The important thing was that they were getting the job done together.

After lunch the hulking man and slender boy returned to the barn, and the amiable relationship continued while they tackled the chores Nestor had to do that afternoon. Nestor had to mend some harness, and the strange pair settled down on some hay bales to do the work. As he showed Wesley how to repair the torn leather, he wove even more tall tales. At one point Nestor happened to look up, and he saw Sister Laurel standing quietly in the doorway. Wesley did not notice the nun; he was wrapped up in Nestor's story of how he had helped Wild Bill Hickok clean up Dodge City. As Nestor continued the story, he noticed a slight smile twitch on the nun's lips. He could tell that she knew as well as he that most of the tales he was telling were pure whoppers. But more significantly, Wesley was cooperating for a change, and he was even being pleasant about it. Sister Laurel gave Nestor a nod of thanks and disappeared silently.

Owen Broderick barely felt the bitter cold. He knew somewhere in the back of his mind that his brothers Max and Al were miserable, had heard them grouse once or twice about how uncomfortable they were. Owen would not listen to any talk about turning back—not with his wife and his money in the hands of the Indians. He had silenced them with an angry look and went on with his own burning thoughts.

Since leaving Winslow's roadhouse with Tate Driscoll and his men, the Brodericks had been ranging south, searching for any sign of the Indians who had raided their ranch. Cold days had turned into frigid nights and then back into bleak, gray days again. It was hard to remember just how long they had been out here looking for the savages.

But so far they had had no luck in finding the trail of the murderous band—until today.

Now the Brodericks and Tate Driscoll lay on their bellies just below the crest of a slight rise and lifted their heads only high enough to see over the top of the incline. On the other side of the slope in the little valley, about seventy-five yards away, a group of a dozen Indians walked their horses slowly across their line of vision. Their heads and bodies were bent against the cold wind.

"Is that them, Owen?" Driscoll asked in a voice that was little more than a whisper.

Owen grimaced slightly and squinted. "How the hell would I know?" he grumbled. "I wasn't there when they hit, none of us were."

"Lucinda's not down there, Owen," Max put in. "And I don't recognize any of those horses as some of the ones the Indians stole, either. I don't think this is the right bunch."

Al spoke up. "We can't be sure of that. This ain't all of them, that's certain, but these braves could be part of the same raiding party."

"Keep your head down when you talk, dammit," Driscoll hissed. "That way the steam from your breath don't show as much."

Al's lean face tensed. "You can't talk to me that way, mister," he said angrily. "You don't give the orders around here."

"Al." Owen's voice was quiet, controlled, but it held enough menace to make his youngest brother immediately fall silent. After a moment Owen went on, "There's no way of being sure from this distance, but we can't just let them ride away."

Driscoll grinned. "Now you're talkin'." He turned and signaled to Dunn, Johnson, Mitchell, and Pearson, who were waiting at the foot of the slope with the horses. The four hardcases mounted up as Driscoll and the Brodericks hurried down to join them.

As they mounted up, Max asked, "What are we going to do, Owen?"

"The only thing we can do," Owen replied, his voice flinty. "We're going to hit that bunch of redskins—hard. But I want at least one of them left alive. Does everybody understand that?"

"Sure, Owen," Driscoll said lazily. "We savvy that, don't we, boys?"

The others nodded. So did Max and Al, but they looked considerably more uncomfortable at the prospect of fighting than did Driscoll's companions.

Owen swung his horse around. "Come on," he ordered curtly.

They did not hurry to attack the band. Owen saw no need for it. The Indians had been moving as if the cold had beaten them down and drained their energy. He led the seven men along on their side of the slope, aware that it gradually leveled out a couple of hundred yards ahead. When they had covered about half that distance, Owen slid his Winchester out of its saddle boot and jacked a shell into the chamber. The others followed his example. Owen kept riding, reins in his left hand, the rifle gripped tightly in his right and pointing up.

His head was turned to the right, his eyes tracking the gradually decreasing slope. When he judged that the Indians would be coming in sight in a matter of moments, he banged his heels against the flanks of his horse and yelled, "Now!"

The white men swept up the rise, topping it quickly. They spread out in a line as they charged down the other side. Rifles cracked sharply in the frosty air.

The Indians were bunched together, their huddle an easy target for their attackers. The slugs tore into them, spilling several of the braves from their horses. Some of the Indians tried to respond to the deadly charge, but they were too slow. More shots crashed. A couple of the Indians started to wheel their horses and flee.

Owen worked the lever of his rifle and fired almost mechanically. Beside him Max and Al did the same. Shooting at something from the back of a galloping horse and hitting it was tricky, but the attackers overcame whatever disadvantage they had by pumping a huge amount of lead through the air.

The small band of Indians never had a chance. By the time the white men came pounding up, all of them lay on the hard, frozen ground, except for the two who were trying to get away. Several Indians were crying out in pain from their wounds. Owen, Max, and Al reined in and dropped from their saddles, keeping their guns trained on the survivors as they checked to make sure the ones not moving were actually dead. Driscoll and his men stopped, too. Driscoll stood up in his stirrups, his Winchester at his shoulder, and took a moment to sight it in. The rifle blasted, and one of the fleeing Indians threw up his arms and spun off his horse. Driscoll shifted his aim and fired again, sending the last escaping Indian plunging limply to the ground. Ben Dunn whooped exultantly, and Stub Pearson slapped Driscoll on the back as he shouted, "Hell of a shot, Tate! Hell of a shot!"

Owen noticed that Max and Al had gone pale under the ruddiness the bitter wind had burned on their faces. They were looking at each other over the sprawled body of an Indian, and he could tell both of them were about to be sick.

Driscoll dismounted and walked among the bodies, carrying his Winchester in one hand and slipping his Colt out of its holster with the other. He paused as he passed an injured brave who was moaning and thrashing. Expressionless, Driscoll triggered the pistol and slammed a shot into the Indian's head.

"I said I wanted one of them alive!" Owen called angrily from a few yards away.

Driscoll shrugged. "That buck couldn't have helped you any, Owen. He couldn't talk no more. Half his jaw was shot off."

Owen grimaced. He supposed Driscoll was right, but he still did not like the way the hardcase had finished off the wounded brave. He began to grow frantic. So far he had not found one Indian in any shape to offer some useful information.

Hope came back to him as he spotted one of the warriors suddenly reaching for a fallen gun. Owen lunged forward, his booted foot coming down on the man's wrist with a crunch of bone. The Indian screamed in pain. Owen had heard all the stories about how stoic the savages were, but clearly they were lies. Maybe the Indians were not quite human, he thought, but they felt pain just the way anybody else did.

Owen kept his boot on the Indian's arm and used his other foot to push the man's opposite shoulder down. Holding him pinned, Owen placed the muzzle of the Winchester within a foot of his face.

"You speak English?" Owen grated.

A torrent of curses came from the wounded brave, which proved nothing. Owen scanned the man's body and noticed that he was wounded in the leg, a deep bullet crease across his left thigh. But that seemed to be all that was wrong with him, other than the broken wrist Owen had just given him. Even in this cold, beads of sweat stood out on the Indian's face.

Driscoll came up beside Owen. Over the profanity the Indian was spewing, Driscoll grunted, "Got a mouth on him, don't he?" Driscoll swung his Colt until it was pointed at the Indian's groin, then he eared back the hammer.

Seeing that, the young brave fell silent. He *was* young, Owen realized now. Most of the Indians were, he noted as he looked around. Max and Al were covering a couple of braves who did not appear to be severely injured. All the others were dead, and Driscoll's men were rifling among the bodies, searching for anything of value.

Driscoll grinned. "Figured that would shut him up," he said. "Now, boy, do you understand English or not?"

"I . . . I speak the white man's tongue," the brave gasped, managing to sound defiant despite the pain he was in.

"Did you attack a ranch about forty miles north of here, a little over a week ago?" Owen asked. "There were several white women and children there, and a white woman was taken captive."

"I . . . know nothing . . . of this," the Indian answered haltingly.

"He's lyin'," Driscoll declared. "All Injuns lie. It's second nature to 'em."

"No! I speak the truth," the young man insisted. "We are Kaw . . . We want no trouble with . . . with the white man."

Max and Al had been listening intently as their brother and Driscoll questioned the brave. Now Max said, "I think he's telling the truth, Owen. Look at the markings on their buckskins. I think I recognize them. These are Kaw, all right, not one of the hostile tribes."

Owen looked over his shoulder at his brother. "You sure about that, Max?"

"Well . . . I think so." Wearing a puzzled frown,

136

Max went over to one of the Indian ponies that had not run off during the gunplay and began to rummage through the hides and blankets on its back.

Driscoll spat. "Hell, Owen, I ain't sayin' nothin' against your brother, but an Injun's an Injun as far as I'm concerned. I'll just bet these are the murderin' heathens who hit your place."

"No!" the brave declared again. "I . . . I swear that we are not."

Owen placed the barrel of his rifle against the Indian's forehead. "If you're telling the truth," he said, "maybe you've seen some other war party out here in the last few days. What about that?"

The young man nodded as best he could with the Winchester pressed against his head. "Two days ago, we see tracks east of here. . . . Look like many braves, maybe thirty."

"Two days east of here, you say?"

"Yes. Maybe these are the warriors you seek."

"It's bound to be, Owen," Al said. "I'm sure of it."

"You can't be sure about anything some damned Injun says," Driscoll protested. "I never seen one yet who told the truth when he didn't have to."

"Maybe this one figures he has to," Owen replied quietly. Abruptly, he pulled the rifle away from the Indian's forehead and stepped back. The brave immediately rolled onto his side and clutched his broken wrist to his body.

"I don't see anything from our ranch among their gear, Owen," Max said, his face grim. "We've made an awful mistake."

"Maybe," Owen admitted. "But maybe we can pick up the trail again now." He looked intently at Driscoll. "What do you think?"

The hardcase shrugged. "Shoot, we just came along

for the ride and to lend you a hand, Owen. You're in charge. You want to head east and look for them tracks, that's fine with us."

Owen nodded and said, "All right, that's what we'll do. Come on, Max, Al. Driscoll, how about a couple of your men rounding up some of those ponies for these wounded men, so they can still get where they were going?"

"I'll take care of it myself, Owen," Driscoll promised.

The Brodericks headed back to their horses. Max and Al still looked sickened by the needless violence, and even Owen's icy reserve had been shaken. They mounted up and turned their horses toward the east. Driscoll's men lagged behind with their leader. The Indian ponies had scattered quite a bit during the shooting, and it might take a while to catch enough of them for the survivors to ride on to their destination.

Owen and his brothers had gone only a couple of hundred yards when a flurry of shots rang out behind them.

Reining in, Owen bit off a curse as he swiveled in his saddle. He saw that Driscoll and the others were mounted up and riding toward them. He waited along with Max and Al until the five hardcases caught up with them.

Driscoll was grinning. Owen stared at him and asked, "What happened?"

"Well, those redskins decided to make a try for their guns," Driscoll replied. "We didn't have no choice but to shoot 'em."

"Why would they do that?" Max asked sharply. "We were going to let them go."

"Reckon they didn't understand that," Driscoll drawled, the grin never leaving his face. "Injuns ain't too bright, you know. Still, it works out for the best.

This way there ain't none of them heathens left alive to spread the word that we're lookin' for the others."

Owen nodded. "Yes," he said slowly. "I suppose you're right."

"I know I am." Driscoll's horse danced nervously. "Well, are we ridin' or not?"

"We're riding." Owen's voice was heavy, but he urged his mount into motion. He saw the looks that Max and Al gave him and knew that they were wishing he had never gotten them mixed up with someone like Tate Driscoll, but it was too late to worry about that now.

He had to keep thinking about Lucinda . . . and the money.

Chapter Nine

I SHOULD BE INSANE BY NOW, LUCINDA BRODERICK thought. She shivered and hunched closer to the meager warmth of the small fire. Any normal woman who had seen her family murdered and who had been raped repeatedly would have lost her mind by this time. But she supposed that her plan to kill Claw someday was the only thing that was helping her cling to her sanity.

Lucinda thought about what she had lived through during these last seemingly endless days. She was surprised when she realized her strength was growing. The long days on horseback did not exhaust her now nearly as much as they had at first. Whenever the band made camp, Claw always ordered her to fetch firewood and to cook for the warriors. Lucinda found she could easily handle those chores. This was not a life of leisure by any means; it was even more arduous than life on the ranch had been. But she was managing. She was even able to hide her revulsion when Claw came to her blankets every night.

Those thoughts occupied Lucinda as she huddled in one of the little buffalo-hide shelters. Sitting across the fire from her was a middle-aged brave called Sore Toe. The ailment that had given him his name was painful enough to keep him out of most of the fighting whenever Claw led a raid, but he was tolerated because he was a medicine man of sorts. He claimed he could read the omens and portents in the stars and the weather, as well as those in ancient buffalo droppings. Lucinda had seen the way the shaman worked and regarded him as a complete charlatan, but Claw seemed to have faith in Sore Toe's pronouncements. Sore Toe also came in handy at times like this, when a prisoner had to be guarded while the other braves were away on a war party.

For the past few days several of the warriors had been grumbling and complaining. Winter was closing its icy grip around them, and they needed to find some place to establish a camp and wait out the coming months. They could have gone down to the reservation in Indian Territory, been welcomed by the naive bureaucrats who ran the place, stayed there until spring, then broken out again. But Claw did not wish to be under the white man's thumb for even that long. Sore Toe had supported his stand, claiming that the spirits had promised Claw one more great victory over the whites before the first snow fell.

Then Claw noticed that their provisions had dwindled to an extremely low level. He had no choice but to find a spot and make a temporary camp. Once it was established in yet another dry wash, he left Lucinda with Sore Toe guarding her, then led the rest of the band in search of an isolated ranch to loot.

Undoubtedly, Lucinda thought, Claw would locate

just such a spread. He seemed to have a sixth sense that always enabled him to find victims for his blood-thirsty raids.

Claw and the others had been gone since midday. Now it was night, and Lucinda could tell that the long hours of waiting had made Sore Toe sleepy.

When the sound of the galloping ponies had died earlier that afternoon, Sore Toe had gazed at her with undisguised lust, his eyes roaming lewdly over the thrust of her breasts and the curve of her hips. Lucinda could not help but cringe. She knew Claw had promised that, when he grew tired of her, she would be given to the others. Lucinda could see Sore Toe was clearly anxious for that day to come. But Claw had not turned her away thus far. And she believed that if any of his men attempted to molest her, Claw would punish them cruelly. At least she clung to that hope and prayed all afternoon that it would prevent the medicine man from touching her.

Gradually Sore Toe's eyelids began to droop until they closed entirely. His head sagged onto his chest, and he began to breathe deeply. Lucinda's eyes widened at the sight, and her body grew taut with anticipation. If he sank into a sound slumber, there would be nothing to stop her from slipping out of this crude tent and making her escape. Sore Toe's horse and a couple of spare mounts were tied up at the bank of the wash. It would be a simple matter to steal one and chase the others off. She would have to renounce her vow to kill Claw, but she would gladly trade that for her freedom. All she had to do was be certain this blasted Indian was asleep. She watched him intently, scarcely breathing, not wanting to do anything to disturb him.

A low-pitched, ragged snore issued from the man

across the fire. Lucinda's pulse began to race even faster. Moving ever so slowly in the cramped shelter, she unfolded her legs, raised herself onto her hands and knees, and began to crawl silently around the fire. The tent's entrance was beyond him, and she would have to be very careful as she slipped past him.

She was not breathing at all as she inched up to the medicine man. The blood was pounding in her head, seemingly loud enough to wake him by itself. But Sore Toe did not stir, and the snoring continued.

Lucinda reached out and pushed back the flap of hide that covered the entrance. The opening faced away from the wind, so she knew that no chilly breezes would blow into the tent to wake up Sore Toe. Twisting her body, she worked her way around him, and then suddenly her head emerged from the shelter into the cold night air. The wash was almost as dark as a tomb; the thick clouds that had hovered over the area for days completely obscured the moon and the stars.

Lucinda carefully crawled the rest of the way out of the crude hut. She kept moving until she was a good ten feet away from it. Then she stopped long enough to draw a deep breath. As the frigid air filled her lungs, she felt her head clear; the stuffy feeling, which had come from sitting inside the smoky hide shelter for all those hours, evaporated.

She heard Sore Toe snore faintly once more and felt a surge of excitement. She had made it. She would escape; she knew it. Where she would go once she left, how she would make her way back to civilization, she had no idea. But she would worry about that later. All she wanted now was her freedom.

One of the horses whickered as she stood up and hurried toward them. They were little more than bulky, darker shadows in the gloom. She spoke to the startled creatures softly, trying to make her voice as soothing as possible, while she worked to untie all the animals. The bitter night wind whistled down the wash and plucked at her buckskins, worming its icy fingers between the seams of the crudely sewn clothing. Lucinda tried to ignore it and concentrate on freeing the horses.

Finally, she was ready to swing up onto the back of one of the animals. She twined her fingers in its mane and tensed her muscles.

A hand came out of the darkness and closed on her upper arm. It jerked her around and away from the horse. Lucinda's nerves, already stretched taut, snapped. A scream of terror erupted from her lips.

Someone pushed aside the opening of the shelter, and a pool of firelight spilled out into the darkened wash. In the dim yellow glow Lucinda saw Claw standing in front of her, lines of anger etched on his cruel face.

Before he could say anything, Lucinda's free hand flew up to strike at him. Her fingers jabbed at his eyes, making him pull back slightly. With strength born of desperation, she wrenched her arm out of his grip, then whirled around and started to run.

She had no idea where she was going, could not even see a yard in front of her. But she kept running anyway, not even thinking now, just fleeing like a terrified animal.

The thunder of pursuing hoofbeats suddenly penetrated her fear-stunned brain. She flung herself aside just in time to avoid being trampled. Stumbling, she fell and landed heavily on the hard ground. She looked over her shoulder and saw that Claw had pulled his horse to a stop. He swung lithely off its back and strode toward her, his face grim. Several other braves had ridden up as well, and they carried burning brands that cast a garish, flickering light.

Claw was holding his lance, and she saw fresh scalps hanging from it. One of them had long, flowing blond hair very like her own. Her stomach knotted at the sight, and she lost the scant supper she had eaten earlier.

She heard laughter and slowly became aware that it was coming from Claw. He thought her sick terror was amusing. "So, Yellowhair," he said arrogantly. "You try to slip away. This was not a wise thing to do. Sore Toe is very upset that you did not care for his company."

Lucinda could make no reply other than a low moan.

"I am not happy with Sore Toe," Claw went on, "but I will forgive him. I shall not be so generous with you, Yellowhair. I am warning you now that I will kill you if you try to escape again. I will be sorry that you are no longer warming my blankets, but I will not be made a fool of by a white slut." He turned and ordered imperiously over his shoulder, "Come."

Lucinda fought back the nausea that was still gripping her and pushed herself to her feet. He was only a few feet away, striding toward his horse and ignoring her. Her eyes locked on the knife sheathed on his hip.

She lunged, her hand clutching at the weapon. Her fingers closed around it and ripped it out of its sheath, but before she could plunge it into Claw's body as she so desperately wanted to, he spun around and backhanded her. The blow cracked across her face, knocking her down and making the knife slip out of her hand. Claw laughed again and bent to retrieve the blade.

"And if you try once more to kill me," he said, his voice low and mocking, "I shall see to it that you take a very long time to die, Yellowhair. Remember that."

She would remember, Lucinda vowed, as she hauled her aching body up and started to trudge after him, her head and shoulders bowed. *I will never forget what he has done to me,* she promised herself, *until one of us is dead.*

For the first time since Wesley had come to the orphanage, two days went by without any new trouble erupting. Wesley spent all of Sunday with Nestor, still occasionally scoffing at the big man's yarns but less sure of himself now. *Maybe,* Wesley started to wonder, *just maybe Nestor is telling the truth about some of the things he claims to have done.* Nestor did seem to know everything there was to know about living in the West.

Wesley was in a much better frame of mind when he went to school on Monday morning. He walked by himself; the two younger boys who had been playing up to him the week before had drifted back to their old friends. As Wesley entered the schoolyard, he spotted Michael Hirsch crouching behind a tree.

He had not said anything to Michael since Friday evening, when Nestor had stepped in and stopped their quarrel before it exploded into a fistfight. But the tension between them had eased a bit, and Wesley was thinking about going over to Michael and saying hello. Suddenly, the redheaded boy looked up, caught his eye, and motioned for him to come over to the tree.

Wesley frowned, puzzled by Michael's actions, but he answered the summons and ambled over to the tree to join the smaller youth. The gray morning was quite cold, and Wesley hoped that whatever Michael wanted would not take too long. He was anxious to go into the schoolhouse where it was warm.

"Hi, Wesley," Michael said pleasantly. He seemed to have entirely forgotten the hostility of their last encounter. "I want to ask you something."

"Sure, Hirsch," Wesley replied casually, not wanting to appear to be too friendly until he was sure of Michael's intentions. "What is it?"

"Have you ever heard of Jesse James?"

Wesley snorted. "Of course I have. I'm not an idiot just because I come from the East, you know. Jesse James is a famous bank robber."

"He and his gang hold up trains, too," Michael said. "They stuck up one not far from here a few months ago, and rumor has it they took over five thousand dollars!"

"What's that got to do with anything?"

"A posse went after them real quick that time, and they had to stop and bury their loot, just in case they got caught. They were passing through the edge of Abilene when they stopped."

Wesley shook his head. "I still don't understand."

Michael pointed dramatically at the ground beside the tree. "I think this is the spot where Jesse James buried that money!"

"That's ridiculous!" Wesley cried. "Why would Jesse James bury stolen loot in a schoolyard?"

Michael grimaced and gestured to Wesley to keep quiet. "Don't you see?" he hissed. "Who would ever think to look for it in a place like this? Remember, there was a posse hot on his trail. Ever since I heard about that, I've been looking around the schoolyard thinking that maybe I could find the money. And now I think I have!"

"What?" Wesley exclaimed.

"Sssshhh! Don't attract a lot of attention." Michael glanced around nervously, and Wesley followed his lead. The other children seemed to be ignoring them; they were busy playing, enjoying their last minutes of freedom before Thurman Simpson called them to go into class. Michael went on, "Look here. See how this dirt is looser."

He bent and brushed some leaves aside, revealing a place close to the tree trunk where he had evidently been digging with his hands. Wesley studied it for a moment, then asked, "Why are you telling me all this?"

"I'm tired. I need somebody to help me dig for a while. I'll split the money with you, Wesley."

Narrowing his eyes, Wesley asked cautiously, "You'd split with me? We're not even friends, Hirsch. Why cut me in on something like this?"

Michael's voice rang with sincerity as he replied, "I thought maybe that would make you see that I don't want us to be enemies, Wesley. Call it a gesture of friendship."

Wesley grimaced as he considered Michael's words. Then he said, "We've still got a few minutes before school starts. I don't guess it would hurt to dig a little."

"Great!" Michael grinned. "I'll move over here and get between you and the rest of the kids so they can't see what we're doing."

Wesley knelt next to the tree and started scooping dirt out of the hole with his hands. The digging went fairly easily, a sign that the earth had been recently turned, just as Michael had said. After a few minutes Wesley suddenly stiffened. His fingers had touched something that was not soil. When he recognized that it was the rough texture of canvas, his pulse began to race.

"Hirsch!" he whispered hoarsely. "I've found something! It feels like some kind of bag."

"The money bag that Jesse James took off the train. It's got to be!" Michael sounded just as excited as Wesley. "It's probably got a drawstring top. Can you find it?"

Quickly Wesley scraped away more of the dirt and exposed the top of a bag. There was the drawstring just as Michael had predicted. It was pulled tightly shut. "I've got it!" Wesley announced.

"Great! Now open the bag and reach down inside it to make sure it's the one with the money."

With fingers that fumbled slightly in his excitement, Wesley pulled open the drawstring and bent over to plunge his hand into the bag, expecting to find the crisp feel of greenbacks.

Instead an unmistakable odor abruptly rose from the hole, and Wesley's hand sank into a cold, sticky mass of . . . something.

He screeched in horror, jerked his hand out of the bag, and rocked back, losing his balance and sitting down hard on the ground next to the hole. He stared at his hand, now covered with horse manure. Laughter erupted all around him and washed over him. He tore his gaze away from his hand to look up and see all the other children gathered around him. Evidently they had been summoned by Michael Hirsch to witness his humiliation. From the looks on their faces, they had all been in on the joke.

Michael stopped laughing long enough to say, "That's some buried treasure you found there, Wesley!" His comment sparked a fresh outbreak of hilarity.

Rage exploded inside Wesley. He surged up off the ground and glared. Michael crouched and raised his fists.

But then, suddenly, Wesley felt it was not worth it. His face a hard, bleak mask, he bent and wiped his hand off on a clump of dead grass. He straightened, looked into Michael's eyes, and said in a cold, quiet voice, "You bastard."

Then he turned and walked away, the laughter dying behind him.

Thurman Simpson appeared in the doorway of the schoolhouse as Wesley stalked out of the yard. Wesley heard him cry, "Stillman! What do you think you're doing? Come back here, boy!"

Wesley did not stop or even slow his pace. He clenched his teeth as he felt a tear slide down his cheek and dry quickly in the cold wind.

He was through with Abilene. If the others did not want him here—and obviously they did not—that was just fine with him. He had never wanted to stay in the first place.

California. The thought burned in his mind. That was where his parents had wanted to go.

Now it was up to him to carry on, just the way Nestor Gilworth had when he was orphaned. He would miss the big old buffalo hunter and his tall tales, Wesley realized, but that was not enough to hold him here.

California . . . He would go there or die trying.

Chapter Ten

SISTER LAUREL WAS SITTING IN THE PARLOR OF THE OR-
phanage, reading to several of the younger children,
when Wesley stepped into the front hallway. As he
walked toward the stairs past the parlor doorway, the
nun looked up and frowned. "Wesley," she called. "Is
something wrong?"

Wesley paused in the foyer to look at her. "I don't
feel so good," he said truthfully. He was still so angry
he was trembling, and his stomach felt queasy.

"I'm sorry," Sister Laurel replied, her voice filled
with concern. "Should we summon the doctor?"

Wesley shook his head. "It's just something that
didn't agree with me," he said, thinking that that
statement was certainly no lie. The prank Michael
Hirsch had pulled on him had not agreed with him at
all.

Because all of Wesley's clothes had been lost when

his family's wagon tumbled into the stream, the orphanage had provided new clothes for him, most of them donated by Abilene's merchants. Among the clothing had been several handkerchiefs, and he had tucked one of them in his pocket as he left for school this morning. On the way back from the scene of his humiliation, he had used the handkerchief to wipe the rest of the manure off his hand. Then he tossed the soiled cloth away. But the stench seemed to be sticking to him, even though he knew he might be imagining it.

The smell will go away sooner or later, Wesley kept telling himself. But his rage at Michael Hirsch and the other children would not.

"Well, if you're sure you're all right and don't need to see the doctor, why don't you go up to your room and lie down for a bit?" Sister Laurel suggested. "Perhaps you'll feel like returning to school later."

"Yeah, maybe," Wesley replied dully, although he knew he would never go back to the schoolhouse— ever.

He trudged up the stairs and went to his room. Pushing the door closed behind him, he flung himself across the bed and stared at the wall. Plans whirled inside his head, plans for what he would do once he reached California. He could not continue his father's dream of opening a store, that was for sure. But he had plenty of experience at helping out around one. Maybe he could start that way, working in a store and saving his money until he could set one up on his own.

Or maybe he would just find some gold and start a new gold rush, like the one that had made so many men rich back in '49. Wesley had to grin as that thought occurred to him. That would be something, all right.

He spent the morning lying there and formulating schemes that would make a fortune for him . . . once he had arrived in the Golden State. At midday Judah Fisher knocked on the door. He was carrying a tray containing a bowl of soup and some biscuits. Wesley ate ravenously, forgetting that he had told Sister Laurel that he was sick to his stomach. Judah's brow creased in a puzzled frown, but the minister said nothing. Once Wesley realized how he had slipped, he considered himself lucky. Judah must have believed that he was simply playing hooky and decided not to force the issue.

During the afternoon Wesley continued contemplating the future. He would have liked to even the score with Michael, but there was no time. More than seeking revenge, he wanted to be away from Abilene. The fury he felt after being the victim of Michael's practical joke had been replaced by an iron resolve. Nothing was going to stop him from leaving the orphanage.

Late in the afternoon, after the older children had returned from school, someone knocked tentatively on Wesley's door. He ignored it, and a moment later he heard Michael's voice calling, "Wesley, are you in there? I want to talk to you."

Wesley said nothing.

After a minute of silence, Michael went on, "Look, I'm sorry. I know that was a bad thing I did to you at school this morning. Why don't you come on out?"

Again Wesley made no reply. He had nothing to say to Michael Hirsch.

"All right," Michael finally said in an exasperated, angry voice, "if that's the way you want it, Wesley. But I know you're in there, and I know you heard me. You're just too blasted stubborn to listen to reason."

Reason! Ha! Michael Hirsch is a fine one to talk about that. Wesley sneered at the closed door and at the sound of retreating footsteps beyond it.

About an hour later, as the evening shadows began to darken his room, Sister Laurel entered, carrying his supper. Setting the tray on the dresser and lighting the candle that stood waiting there, she turned and looked at him, her blue eyes assessing. "Are you feeling any better?" she asked.

"I suppose," Wesley grunted noncommittally.

"Do you think you'll be all right by tomorrow? I could still ask the doctor to come to examine you."

Wesley shook his head. He had recovered from the cold he caught when his parents died, and he had no desire to have any doctor poking and prodding him, especially when he knew quite well that there was nothing wrong with him. "I'm sure I'll be fine by tomorrow," he replied, again telling the truth—just not all of it. *By tomorrow I'll be out of Abilene for good,* he mused.

After finishing his supper, he briefly thought about going to sleep, but the excitement growing inside him would not allow it. It was about time he took a step on his own, he believed, instead of letting everyone else make decisions for him. As he had told the marshal, he was fourteen and old enough to decide what was best for himself.

Wesley blew out the candle and let the darkness engulf him. He sat in the shadows, staring out his window at the gloomy night and listening to the wind moan. Suddenly a shiver of doubt went through him. He could see a few lights glittering in downtown Abilene, but the rest of the world was a field of deep, black velvet. There were no stars, no moon, just frigid darkness.

Wesley could hear the other children moving around in their rooms. The creak of floorboards, the murmur of voices, an occasional laugh . . . all the noises reminded him of how alone he was. That was the way he wanted it now, he told himself. He depended on no one, and he liked it that way.

Gradually, as bedtime for the children came and went, the big parsonage fell silent. Wesley waited, listening intently, until he was certain that Sister Laurel and Judah Fisher had also gone to sleep. There was no sound to be heard anywhere in the orphanage. And still he waited some more, just to be sure.

When he was certain that everyone else was asleep, he gathered up the new clothes he had been given and tied them into a bundle. Then he slipped out of the room and tiptoed down the stairs. Wesley guessed it was close to midnight.

All the lamps had been turned off, but even though he had been at the orphanage for only a short time, he knew his way around. It was not difficult to locate one of the side doors, open it silently, and slip out into the night.

The stable was about fifty yards away, the big frame building looming darkly in the gloomy night. Last Saturday, when he had helped Nestor Gilworth clean it out, Wesley had learned the layout of the barn, knew in which stalls the saddle horses were kept. Quietly opening the large front door, he went straight to the tack room. Its door was kept closed but was seldom locked. Tonight Wesley was lucky—the knob turned easily in his hand, and he stepped into the room.

Working by feel, he located a saddle and bridle and carried them to the stall where the spare horses were bedded down. The animals moved around nervously as Wesley opened the stall and went inside. He was afraid, but he told himself sternly that he had no time for such emotions. Awkwardly he swung the heavy saddle on the back of one of the horses, cinched it in place, and slipped the bridle's bit into the animal's mouth. He stashed his bundle of clothes in one of the saddlebags, then led the mount out of the stable.

Wesley glanced up at the orphanage. It was still shrouded in darkness. Evidently no one had heard him. Moving as silently as he could, he walked the horse back to the door he had used when he slipped out and tethered it to a shrub growing next to the building. Then he tiptoed back inside and headed toward the kitchen.

Wesley had learned his way around the kitchen on Saturday night, when Sister Laurel made him clean it up after supper. Within a few moments he had gathered some biscuits, hard cheese, apples, and cooked meat, all of which he stashed in an empty sack he had found in the pantry. On Saturday night he had also noticed some small packets of flour, sugar, salt, and coffee. Now he added those to the bag, then hurried back to the spot where he had left his horse.

Hanging the bag over the saddlehorn, he took a deep breath and swung up onto the animal. He paused for a moment and looked up at the dark bulk of the orphanage. His breath plumed before his face in the cold night air, and the sprawling house seemed to float in the haze. He had stayed here only a short time, and he would take a few good memories with him. But now he had to take this big step. For the first time in his life, he would be on his own.

And damn well about time, he seemed to hear his father's voice saying. Wesley grinned humorlessly. He pulled the horse's head around and urged it into motion, circling around the orphanage and then kicking it into a trot. Bouncing a little in the saddle, he rode west toward the open prairie.

* * *

Michael Hirsch woke up with a start. For a moment he had no idea where he was or what time it was. It was either very late or very early. The world was cloaked in darkness, he saw as he peered out of the window next to his bed.

He had been restless all night, slipping in and out of a fitful slumber. When he did doze off, he found himself in vivid dreams that made no sense but were undeniably frightening. The uneasiness stayed with him as he sat up in bed and swung his legs out from under the covers.

As his feet hit the cold plank floor, he winced and thought about curling up once more under the warm blankets. But he knew he could not sleep until he had put to rest the thing that was bothering him, so he pushed himself up and ignored the tingling sensations in his feet.

As soon as he saw the look on Wesley Stillman's face, Michael knew he had done a bad thing. The joke with the bag of manure, as funny as it had seemed when the idea occurred to him, had been wrong. Wesley had not deserved such humiliation, even though he had insulted Agnes. Agnes herself had been very angry when she heard about Wesley's ribald comments, but she would never have taken her revenge in that way. Michael knew his sister well enough to be certain of that.

Throughout the morning Michael brooded about how wrong he had been. He began to feel so guilty that he could not concentrate on his work. It distracted him so much that he was constantly in trouble with Thurman Simpson. By the time school was dismissed and he returned to the orphanage, he was so upset that he went straight to Wesley's room to apologize.

That had not even come close to working. When

Wesley refused to talk to him or even acknowledge his presence, Michael's anger resurfaced. Wesley was in his room, Michael knew, because Sister Laurel and Judah had told him so. He did not blame Wesley for being angry with him; he deserved it. But the time came when fellows had to hash things out and settle their differences.

Now, as he slipped out into the dark corridor, Michael was convinced that the time had come. He was going to Wesley's room, and he would make the boy listen to his apology even if he had to bust in and sit on him.

Reaching Wesley's door, Michael knocked softly on it and hissed the other boy's name, not wanting to wake up anyone else. There was no response, which did not surprise Michael. Fumbling slightly in the darkness, he found the doorknob and tried it. It turned easily, and the door swung open. The blond boy had not locked it or put something in front of it.

"Wesley," Michael whispered as he stepped into the room. "Wesley, are you in here? Answer me, blast it! I've come to apologize for all the mean things I did to you."

Silence greeted him. Michael listened intently, thinking that he ought to be able to hear Wesley breathing if the other boy was in the room. There was no sound at all.

Michael went to the bed and slid his hand over the covers. Empty. The blankets were smooth, unrumpled. Wesley had not even slept in it tonight. But if he was not here in his room at this hour, then where in blazes was he, Michael wondered?

Suddenly one possible answer occurred to him, and as it flashed across his brain, he caught his breath. Wesley could have run away.

A gust of wind rattling the window made Michael

jump. The sound reminded him of how cold it was outside and how dangerous it could be for someone who was not accustomed to these conditions to try to travel in them. Wesley was still a tenderfoot, no doubt about that. He could not manage on his own.

If he *had* run away, somebody was going to have to go after him and bring him back.

There was only one logical candidate for that job, Michael knew. He had made Wesley's life here too miserable for him to remain, so it was his duty to find him.

But first he had to make sure that Wesley had indeed left. Thinking about what he would do if he were running away, Michael quietly headed for the kitchen. He swung the door closed and found the single candle and matches that Sister Laurel kept in the drawer of the long, scrubbed table. Lighting it, he went into the pantry and quickly discovered that some food was missing.

His suspicions confirmed, Michael snuffed out the candle and, taking the matches with him, slipped back upstairs. He hurriedly dressed in silence so that he would not wake up the other boys who shared his room. He pulled his coat on as he went downstairs.

Tiptoeing into the parlor, he took one of the matches from his coat pocket and used it to light the oil lamp that sat on the desk. Then he found some paper and a pen and, dipping it into the inkwell, rapidly scrawled a note that he addressed to Reverend Judah Fisher. In it he apologized for borrowing one of the saddle horses without permission, then concluded, *This is just something I have to do, Reverend. I have to find Wesley and bring him back before he gets hurt.*

Michael signed the note, weighted it down with the inkwell, then blew out the lamp and headed for the stable. Long familiar with horses and tack, he was able to saddle a mount much more quickly than Wesley had. Within five minutes Michael had left the barn and was riding away from the orphanage. As the bitter wind slapped his cheeks, he turned up the collar of his coat and pulled his hat down tightly. He tried not to think about how cold it was.

He remembered how Wesley had talked about going to California. If he were in Wesley's shoes right now, Michael realized, that would be exactly what he would try to do. Following his instincts, Michael swung his horse away from Abilene. He just hoped Wesley had been able to find west in the dark. If the boy had veered off in some other direction, Michael might have some trouble finding him.

Nevertheless, Michael was confident he would find Wesley. After all, he knew this country a lot better than that newcomer did. He would head west himself, and then in the morning he would be able to pick up Wesley's trail. The two of them would probably be back before noon.

And then he would have to face the trouble he was going to get into because of this, Michael thought. But he would take whatever came; it was his fault that Wesley had run off in the first place. If he had not been such a fool and held a grudge . . .

"Sister Laurel!"

As soon as he heard the anxious tone in Judah's shout, Nestor Gilworth knew something was wrong. The former buffalo hunter opened his eyes and slowly sat up, the bunk creaking slightly as he shifted his weight. The little room he had been given was on the first floor of the orphanage, near the staircase, and he had no trouble hearing Judah's worried voice calling from the parlor.

Yawning, Nestor stood up, stretched, and started for the door. He slept in his clothes, except for his boots and hat, so he was as presentable as he ever got when he stepped out of his room. He saw Sister Laurel hurrying across the foyer into the parlor.

Nestor started to follow her, then suddenly stopped in his tracks as he abruptly realized something startling. For the first time since he had come to the orphanage, he had awakened in the morning without a powerful craving for whiskey. In fact, the thought of taking a drink this early in the day was repellent to him. He shook his head. Once he would have considered this a revolting development; now he was grateful.

When Nestor stepped into the parlor, he saw Sister Laurel looking at a piece of paper. He grunted, "Mornin', folks. What's wrong?"

Judah's lean face was taut with worry. He glanced at Nestor and gestured at the paper in Sister Laurel's hand. "Two of the boys have run away," he replied grimly.

"The hell you say!" Nestor exclaimed. Then, realizing what he had just said, he went on hurriedly, "Sorry, Rev'rend. I guess I ain't used to watchin' my language yet. Which of the little rascals has run off?"

"Wesley Stillman and Michael Hirsch," Sister Laurel said, her brow creased in a frown. She held the paper toward Nestor. "Here, Mr. Gilworth, you can read Michael's note for yourself."

"Uhhh . . . Reckon I can't, Sister. Never had the schoolin'. Sorry."

The nun paled slightly, then shook her head. "Oh. No, Mr. Gilworth, I'm the one who's sorry. I meant no offense. I'm just so . . . so startled by all of this."

Nestor was surprised, too. After those two days they had spent working together he had thought that

Wesley was getting along much better. And the boy seemed to have accepted the idea of remaining at the orphanage. He could not understand why Michael had run away.

"Didn't figger them two would run off together," he commented, "knowin' how they got along."

"They didn't go together," Judah said as he ran his hand through his sandy hair in a worried gesture. Quickly, he explained what Michael's note said. When he had finished, he turned to Sister Laurel and asked, "What are we going to do?"

"We have to tell the marshal so that he can organize a search party," the nun replied. "That's all we can do. Those two boys have no business being out in this bitter weather. If we don't find them quickly, I would hate to think what might happen to them."

Nestor's features settled in grim lines. He knew all too well what could happen to the boys if they were not found. Veteran frontiersmen could survive a winter on the plains without too much trouble, but a couple of young boys were a different matter entirely.

"Hold on a minute," he called to Judah as the minister started toward the door. "Ain't no need to bother the marshal with this. I can track down them little scamps 'fore they get into too much trouble."

Sister Laurel, her eyes wide with astonishment, turned toward him. "You, Mr. Gilworth?"

Nestor thumped a big fist against his chest. "Ain't no better tracker 'tween here an' Oregon, Sister, now that my head ain't muddled by whiskey."

"I don't know . . ." Judah began dubiously.

"I can do it," Nestor declared. "Did them youngsters take some supplies with 'em and go on horseback?"

"They did. Michael says in his note that Wesley

took provisions with him, and I'm certain both boys used horses from the stable."

"That makes 'em hoss thieves," Nestor said. "You bring the marshal in on this, and them boys'll wind up in a heap o' trouble, you mark my words."

"Nonsense," Sister Laurel replied. "Luke Travis is not going to charge two young boys with horse theft."

"He might not want to, ma'am, but he wouldn't have much choice." Nestor looked back and forth between Sister Laurel and Judah and then went on, "Please let me go after 'em, folks. I've gotten right fond of them little fellers. I want to help find 'em."

Sister Laurel stared at him for a long moment, then drew a deep breath and said, "Very well, Mr. Gilworth. We won't notify the marshal at this time."

"What?" Judah exclaimed. "Sister, we can't—"

"Mr. Gilworth wants a chance to help," the nun interrupted him. "I think we should give it to him, Judah—on one condition."

Nestor's bearded face split in a broad grin. "You name it, Sister."

"I'm going with you, Mr. Gilworth."

Nestor and Judah both gaped at her. The minister cried, "You can't be serious!" Nestor slowly shook his head.

"I'm very serious," Sister Laurel assured him. "Mr. Gilworth, how long do you estimate it will take to locate the boys and bring them back?"

Nestor shrugged his massive shoulders. "Shouldn't take too long," he said. "I reckon if we're lucky, we ought to have 'em back here by noon or a little after."

"All right." Sister Laurel turned to Judah. "If Mr. Gilworth and I have not returned with Michael and Wesley by the middle of the afternoon, Judah, then you may go to the marshal and request his assistance."

"You can bet on it," Judah replied. "I'll tell him the whole story. Are you sure about this, Sister?"

"Very sure." Sister Laurel's response was calm and measured.

Judah sighed. "All right, but I don't like it. Why don't I come along with the two of you?"

"You'll be needed to stay here with the children," Sister Laurel pointed out. "Besides, someone has to alert Luke if we aren't back by early afternoon." She turned to Nestor again. "Mr. Gilworth, how soon can you be ready to leave?"

"Give me five minutes, Sister. That good enough for you?"

"I'll be ready," she promised.

"I suppose I should go hitch your horse to the buggy and saddle a mount for you, Nestor," Judah said. "At least I'll be doing something to help." He started toward the parlor door, then turned to look at Nestor. "You know, I'd feel better about all this if you had your weapons, Nestor. Why don't I give them to you . . . just in case?"

Nestor nodded and clapped the preacher on the back with a big hand. "Don't you worry none, Rev'rend," he boomed heartily. "We'll find them boys and be back 'fore you know it. Shoot, how far can a couple of little fellers like that have gone since last night?"

Chapter Eleven

WESLEY STILLMAN WISHED THAT HE HAD NEVER LEFT Abilene. A cold wind blew in his face. It seemed to be coming from a massive bank of heavy gray clouds that were moving steadily toward him. The sun had shone briefly at dawn, but it quickly disappeared, swallowed up by thinner clouds that moved ahead of the blackish wall of an approaching storm.

That the clouds held a storm in their midst, Wesley had no doubt. He could not even glance up anymore without shuddering in fear.

Pride was the only thing that had brought him this far, but he had a sinking feeling that it would not save him once the storm hit. The only sensible thing to do would be to turn his horse around and race the animal for all it was worth toward Abilene.

At first, after stealing away from the orphanage, he had been full of hope. Despite the darkness, he had been able to see the railroad tracks as they glistened in the light that spilled from the saloons on the western edge of Abilene. He knew that the railroad tracks and the wagon road, which ran parallel to it, led west, so he struck out between them, keeping the rails to his left and the road to his right. He could have ridden on the road, but if he had done that, he would have risked encountering someone who would want to know what a boy was doing out alone on the plains. Besides, the gently rolling terrain was easy; there was no reason why he could not cut across country.

The night had been bitterly cold then, but in his excitement he barely felt the chill. However, by early morning, he wished he were somewhere warm. When those thoughts started doubts growing in the back of his mind, he remembered what Michael Hirsch had done to him the day before.

That was all it took. Even being cold and alone was better than staying someplace where he was so despised.

The air had warmed up a bit after the sun rose, but that had not lasted long. Wesley had paused to eat a little breakfast, and as he munched on an apple, he stared to the south, looking for the telegraph poles that he knew ran along the Kansas Pacific railroad tracks. A worried frown appeared on his face when, searching the rolling countryside as hard as he could, he failed to spot them.

The wagon road was nowhere in sight, either. He wondered if he could have crossed it sometime in the darkness without being aware of it. That was possible, he supposed.

But if that was the case, then where was he now, and where was he going?

He began to feel more nervous as he started riding again. For a short while, he was able to put the rising sun at his back and feel sure that he was headed west, but then the clouds moved in and blotted it out. He tried his best to keep moving in the same direction, but his doubts continued to grow. They increased as the wind began to blow more bitterly and the temperature dropped again.

Now he had no idea in which direction he was going. Even if he turned back, it would be pure luck if he wound up heading toward Abilene. But one thing was certain—he could not continue riding directly into the path of the storm. He reined in, forced himself to stare up at the gray clouds, and flinched as something cold and wet brushed against his cheek.

Snow.

More white flakes floated down around him, few and far between at the moment, but they seemed to be increasing in frequency. Wesley could feel panic growing inside him like a living thing. "Come on, horse," he growled. Then swinging his mount's head around, he banged his heels against its sides.

The wind was at his back now, and that helped matters a bit. Then he recalled his father saying that most winter storms moved from northwest to southeast, so if he kept the wind at his back, he would stand a good chance of winding up near Abilene. Sooner or later he would run across the road, and he could follow that right into town.

With each stride his horse took, Wesley's confidence grew. He would feel like a fool when he got back to the orphanage and had to listen to the ribbing he would take for trying to run away, but at least he would be alive and not some frozen corpse out on the prairie.

His pride was important, but it was not worth his life.

Michael remembered that Wesley's father had followed the road west when he drove the family's wagon out of Abilene. Given the disaster that befell the family, Mr. Stillman had evidently not stuck to it. But that was understandable. The road sort of petered out and became an overgrown trace the farther west it went. That was because few people heading in that direction took exactly the same route. Only an experienced hand, Michael had heard, could follow the trail once the railroad dipped south, and it would be all too easy for an inexperienced traveler to wander off into the sparsely settled plains south of the Smoky Hills.

Michael had a bad feeling that that was where Wesley Stillman was.

He had stayed on the wagon road as best he could, figuring that Wesley would go that way. Occasionally, he would rein in and shout out the other boy's name. But there was no answer, not even an echo in the wind. Michael bundled his coat more tightly around him and pushed on.

Not long after dawn he saw tracks on the road. The hoofprints cut across the trail at an angle, coming from the southeast and continuing to the northwest. As he spotted them in the dim light, Michael reined in, then dropped out of his saddle to study them more closely. It was impossible to identify them as belonging to the horse Wesley had taken, but the tracks were fresh. The wind had not yet blown enough dirt over them to obliterate them. It certainly seemed worthwhile to follow them, at least for now.

Who else but Wesley would be crazy enough to be out here in the cold before dawn? Michael reasoned.

As the sun rose it became easier to see the tracks. Even after the clouds blew in and obscured the sun, there was still enough light to see the hoofprints. Michael glanced up at the clouds as he rode. They were thick and gray and heavy with snow. He had only spent one winter in Kansas, but in that time he had seen enough snowstorms approach to recognize one.

Where the devil was Wesley?

Sometime around midmorning, snow began to fall, the first flakes spiraling down in gentle arcs. There was a beauty to them, but Michael was too worried to appreciate it. As the snowfall increased and the wind blew more vigorously, the tracks he was following became harder to spot. He blinked against the blowing snow and held his head down to concentrate on the hoofprints. It was not long before he realized he could no longer see them. He looked up and saw that the world around him was obscured by a swirling white haze.

Wesley Stillman had ridden right into a blizzard. Michael's stomach knotted at the thought. *How could anyone be so stupid?* he wondered. Then he reminded himself that he was thinking about Wesley Stillman, after all.

Michael shook his head. Those sorts of ungenerous thoughts were part of the reason Wesley and he were out here in this mess. Still, the boy from back East should have had the sense to turn around before now. Surely he had seen the storm coming.

Lowering his head, Michael pushed on. He was going to have to turn around soon, he knew, or else he would not be able to make it back to Abilene himself before the storm trapped him. But if he did turn around, he was consigning Wesley to death. He was certain Wesley would not be able to make it by himself.

The wind chafed Michael's face, crept into his clothes, and stole every bit of warmth from him. The snow made it increasingly hard to see. Michael pulled his horse to a halt again. *This is hopeless,* he thought. He had not been able to see any tracks for a while; blind instinct had guided him all that time. There was nothing left for him to do but turn around and try to make it back to civilization and shelter. He hauled on the reins and started to wheel the horse around.

"Hey!"

The faint shout came from behind him, somewhere in the direction he had been traveling. Michael stopped short, swiveled his head, and tried to see through the falling snow. He saw nothing and began to wonder if he was imagining things.

"Wait! Oh, God, please wait!"

The cry was unmistakable now. Michael's heart raced as he made out a figure on horseback pushing through the curtain of white. He thought the voice was familiar, and then, when he got a better look at the horse, he was sure of it.

The rider hunched so miserably in his saddle was Wesley Stillman.

Michael jerked his horse around and kicked it into a trot. He raced toward the other boy, calling, "Wesley! Wesley, it's me, Michael!"

As he rode up to Wesley, Michael could not tell if the other boy had heard him. Wesley was shivering, and his face was contorted in fear. Michael drew up beside him, and Wesley reached out to grasp his arm. Wesley's fingers seemed to claw through the coat sleeve and dig into Michael's flesh.

"Hirsch!" Wesley exclaimed, staring at Michael in surprise. "My God . . . you . . . how . . . ?"

"Never mind," Michael said sharply. "Come on, we've got to get out of this storm."

"I thought I saw somebody . . . never d-dreamed it

would be you. . . . I'm so cold, and it's snowing so hard—"

Michael jerked his arm out of Wesley's grasp and leaned over to grab the reins of the other boy's horse. Wesley's speech was rambling, almost incoherent, and Michael knew that being lost in the storm had taken quite a toll on him.

"Don't worry about it," he said, trying to sound reassuring. "We'll get back to Abilene, and everything will be fine."

He wished he could be sure of that. The way the storm was closing in, it might already be too late. But if he had turned back even a minute or two earlier, he would not have run into Wesley. At least they were together. They had a chance. That was all they could hope for now.

Leading Wesley's horse, Michael started in what he thought was the right direction. It was more difficult than ever to tell now. The snowfall was so thick that he could see only a few feet in front of him. At first Michael tried to use the wind as a guide, keeping it at their backs. But after a few minutes he realized it was swirling and gusting from different directions. He could not tell whether they were on the right course.

For all he knew, they were really headed directly into the teeth of the blizzard. If that was the case, they would both die. It was that simple.

It was impossible to estimate how far they had traveled in the wind-whipped snow, but after they had been riding together for about half an hour, Wesley raised his voice and asked, "Why don't we stop and build a fire?"

Michael laughed grimly. "You can't build a fire in weather like this," he told the blond boy. "Not without some sort of shelter."

"Then we could just stop for a few minutes. I'm so damned tired—"

"No," Michael cried firmly. "We can't stop. We'll freeze to death if we don't keep moving. We've got to get back to Abilene."

"We can't," Wesley wailed. "You know we can't make it all the way to Abilene."

"Then we'll just have to find some shelter. We'll find someplace to hole up, and then we can have a fire."

Even as he spoke the words, Michael realized just how true they were. Unless they stumbled onto someplace where they could get out of the wind, they would not stand a chance of surviving. He squinted against the grayish-white nightmare they were pushing through and tried to make out more details of the terrain.

His hands and feet were just beginning to go numb when his horse stumbled and almost fell. Michael wobbled and almost slid out of the saddle. He clutched the saddlehorn and righted himself, then stared in front of him. His heart began to beat faster when he saw what they had almost ridden into.

Before them lay one of the dry washes that cut across the Kansas plains. It was no more than a dozen feet wide and perhaps eight or ten feet deep, with steep, ragged banks. Michael was jubilant. Inside that gully they would find the shelter they desperately needed. Somehow they had to get down that bank.

Michael looked one way, then the other. He could not see very far and could not tell where the sheer bank had somehow broken and become a gentler slope. He prayed that it had. It was their only hope. But he had to make a choice now.

"This way," he decided and abruptly turned his

172

horse to his right. Over the moaning wind he could hear Wesley's horse following.

They had ridden a couple of hundred yards, Michael's spirits sinking with every step, when he spotted a caved-in area of the bank on their side of the gully. The slope was rough and still steep, but the horses would be able to manage it. Michael pointed it out wordlessly to Wesley, then urged his mount toward it.

The horses picked their way carefully down the slope. It seemed to take forever, but neither animal lost its footing or stumbled. Michael heaved a sigh of relief once they reached the bottom of the wash.

Inside the narrow channel the wind was blowing less forcefully. Snow still swirled around them and coated the floor of the gully, but the cold was not so intense.

"I don't see what good this does us," Wesley complained. "Can we have a fire now?"

"We can if we can find a big overhang," Michael told him. "Let's go." New hope and enthusiasm gripped him.

Within minutes he had located a suitable spot for a camp. An area several feet deep and nearly ten feet long had been gouged out by the elements beneath one of the banks. The overhang was so large that the snow did not fall directly onto the ground beneath it, although the swirling wind had blown a faint white carpet across the earth. Michael dismounted and motioned for Wesley to do the same. They led the horses under the overhang.

The animals did not need any urging to move all the way up to the bank. They huddled there, and Wesley leaned against them, drawing what warmth he could from them.

Michael began to hunt for fuel. He gathered some clumps of dried grass from the edge of the wash, found some small branches, and returned to the overhang. The grass was wet and snowy, but Michael dried it as best he could. Then crouching down, he fluffed it into a loose pile, gently placed some twigs on top of it, and took out one of the matches he had brought from the orphanage. Holding his breath, he scratched it into life.

The match flickered and went out before the grass caught fire. Undaunted, he lit a second one, and that one did the trick. Tiny flames leapt up in the pile of grass and twigs. Michael shielded them with his hands and his body and watched as they grew. Wesley crowded in beside him, trying to get as much of the warmth as he could.

Maybe, Michael thought, *just maybe we'll come out of this alive after all.*

Michael's hands and feet began to tingle, as sensation returned to them. He did not think that they had been numb long enough for frostbite to have set in. He and Wesley knelt by the small fire for long moments, relishing the meager heat. When he felt a little warmer, Michael went to Wesley's horse, got some food from the saddlebag, and returned to the fireside. The boys were in the middle of their meal when they both heard a rhythmic noise clattering over the howling of the wind.

"Listen," Michael hissed. "Hoofbeats."

Wesley's eyes widened. "I hear them!" he said excitedly. "Come on!" He started to surge to his feet.

Michael reached out, caught his arm, and jerked him back down. "Where do you think you're going?" he asked.

"To get help! Somebody's out there, Hirsch. They can help us."

"Maybe, maybe not," Michael said sternly. "Out here on the frontier, it's always a good idea to find out who you're dealing with before you go yelling for help."

"What the hell are you talking about?" Wesley sounded incredulous. "Why wouldn't they help us, whoever they are?"

"Might be Indians," Michael said. "Or outlaws. They might want our horses. Now keep your voice down and help me put out this fire." He started throwing snow on the flames.

For a moment Wesley looked sick as Michael heaped the cold, wet stuff on the fire, and it began to sputter. Then he reluctantly began to help Michael. Within a few seconds the fire was out.

"Now keep quiet," Michael whispered. He stood next to his horse and stroked its neck to keep it calm, motioning for Wesley to do the same.

The hoofbeats grew louder, coming closer all the time. Michael's pulse began to race as he realized that there were several riders and that they were moving toward them right down the wash. Whoever the strangers were, they had sought shelter from the storm in this gully just as he and Wesley had.

Ghostly shapes suddenly appeared, emerging from the blowing snow only yards away from the overhang, where the two silent, frightened boys waited. Michael gulped as he saw the buckskin-clad forms draped with buffalo robes that were coated with snow. Some of the men carried lances, while others held old, long-barreled, single-shot rifles.

A sob escaped from Wesley's throat. The strangers walked directly toward the overhang, leading their horses. Their heads were bowed against the wind, but the man in the lead looked up sharply when he heard the sound.

Michael and Wesley stood there, petrified with fear, staring into the lean, impassive face of an Indian warrior.

Chapter Twelve

NESTOR GILWORTH REINED IN AND LEANED FORWARD IN his saddle, his deep-set eyes narrowing as he studied the horizon. Sister Laurel called to her mare, pulled lightly on the lines, and brought the buggy to a halt beside him. She was wearing a heavy coat over her woolen habit against the cold. The swirling wind tugged at her wimple.

"What is it, Mr. Gilworth?" she asked, turning to look up at him. "Why have we stopped?"

Nestor lifted a big hand and gestured toward the bank of dark, ominous clouds that were advancing toward them. "Got a bad storm movin' in, Sister," he grunted. "A real blue norther from the looks of it. It ain't a good idea to be caught on the open prairie when one of them things hits."

"But we don't have any choice, Mr. Gilworth. We haven't found Michael and Wesley yet, and we certainly can't leave them out here to face such a storm by themselves."

"No, ma'am," Nestor agreed.

He began to rub his bearded jaw thoughtfully. It had been quite some time since he had last seen the sun, and he had no way of knowing what time it was. Judging from the way the shadows were gathering, it might have been early evening, but Nestor knew that was an illusion caused by the thick cloud cover. It had to be early afternoon, he decided, which meant that Judah Fisher was probably notifying Marshal Travis about the missing boys.

Nestor had expected to locate the two runaways long before this. He was quite disturbed that in all this time they had seen no sign of Michael and Wesley, except for the last vestiges of some tracks that might or might not have belonged to the youngsters. Nestor's frustration began to gnaw at him. He had been following cold trails for years; there was no way a couple of wet-behind-the-ears kids should have given him the slip.

"What sort of problems do you expect from this blue norther of yours, Mr. Gilworth?" Sister Laurel asked. Shivering slightly, she hunched her shoulders and pulled the coat around her.

Nestor grinned down at her. "It ain't mine, Sister. I ain't claimin' it. But as for what it'll do . . . well, more'n likely it'll dump a couple of feet of snow across this part of the country, an' the wind'll push up some drifts a heap deeper than that. Probably won't be much colder than it's already been, but it's liable to feel like it, what with all that snow. It'll be dark as midnight a couple hours before what's normal for dusk. Not a fit night to be out, that's for da—for sure."

"Very well." A faint smile tugged at Sister Laurel's lips, and Nestor knew she had noticed how he had almost slipped into profanity. She continued, "I think we should push on immediately. It's important that we find those boys as soon as possible."

"Yes'm." Nestor clucked at his horse and got it moving again.

They kept heading west, talking very little as they rode. From time to time, Nestor glanced over at Sister Laurel and was struck by the strength and determination on her face. Of course it took a strong woman to become a nun in the first place, he reflected. It was a hard, lonely life, and the women who had the calling voluntarily gave up a great many things that might have made their existence easier. But Sister Laurel had retained her sense of humor and zest for living, and Nestor found himself both respecting and genuinely liking her. And as far as preachers went, Judah Fisher was about the best Nestor had ever run across. The big man had been surprised to discover he had actually enjoyed the time he had spent at the orphanage.

That was really why he had been so determined to come out here and find those two boys himself. It was a way to start repaying the debt he felt to Judah and Sister Laurel and all the children who had befriended him.

Less than half an hour after Nestor had stopped and warned Sister Laurel about the approaching storm, the snow began to fall. It was sparse at first, a few gentle flakes fluttering softly to the ground. But all too quickly it became heavier. Nestor blinked as the wind whipped some of the flakes into his eyes. He looked over at Sister Laurel again and saw the growing concern on her face.

"What about it, Sister?" he rumbled. "Do we keep pushin' on?"

The nun hesitated for a moment. Then she lifted her chin and replied, "As I said earlier, we have no choice, Mr. Gilworth. We are responsible for the safety of those boys, and they will surely die out here if we don't find them."

Nestor took a deep breath. He was worried about Michael and Wesley, too, but unless Sister Laurel and he turned around immediately, they would be caught by the full force of the storm. As it was, they might be too late. Even if they headed back right away, they would not have time to reach Abilene. They would have to hole up somewhere and wait out the bad weather.

But despite what his years of experience were telling him, he knew he could not refuse to do as the sister wanted. He owed her too blasted much not to pull his freight now. . . .

Nestor nodded. "We'll keep lookin'," he said.

The snowfall grew heavier, closing in around them until it was hard to see more than a few yards in any direction. Nestor's beard and mustache became wet as the flakes collected there and melted, and he knew that if they kept moving into that cold wind, he would soon be sporting a fine collection of icicles.

Abruptly Sister Laurel's gloved hands pulled back on the lines, stopping the buggy. Nestor reined in and, turning his horse to face her, opened his mouth to speak but caught himself. The nun, her eyes closed, was crossing herself. Deeply moved, he slipped off his hat and watched as her lips moved in silent prayer. He kept quiet, and a moment later she opened her eyes and looked up at him.

"We must turn back, Mr. Gilworth," she announced over the whistling wind. "It pains me to reach that decision, but I've searched my soul and asked for the Lord's guidance. There is no way we can find Michael and Wesley in this storm."

"No way but blind luck, ma'am," Nestor agreed, shoving his hat on his now damp hair.

"We'll start back to Abilene immediately—"

Nestor shook his head. "No, ma'am. No point in that. This storm's movin' in too fast. We can't even hope to outrun it; we ain't got a chance of reachin' town now. What we got to do is find us a hidey-hole, someplace where we can wait for this mess to blow over."

"I suppose you're right." Sister Laurel sighed. "I'm sorry, Mr. Gilworth. I've probably doomed us both."

"We had to look for them youngsters," Nestor pointed out. "That ain't your fault, Sister."

"No, but you would have turned back an hour ago if I hadn't insisted on continuing."

A grin split Nestor's face. "I wouldn't be so sure of that. I can be a mite stubborn, too, ma'am."

Sister Laurel stared up at him, then suddenly returned the smile. "I'm aware of that, Mr. Gilworth," she replied, her blue eyes twinkling. "Now, shall we try to locate that . . . hidey-hole you spoke of?"

Nestor nodded. He reached up and rubbed his bearded jaw, thinking back to the times when he had ridden these plains in search of the great buffalo herds. That had been nearly ten years ago. Kansas had been so different then. The railroad was just starting to make its way across the prairie. The few, widely scattered settlements had been sleepy little farming communities. The booming, brawling cattle towns were still years in the future.

Nestor remembered it all, even better than he ought

to have, considering the amount of whiskey he had consumed since then. And as he searched his memory, something occurred to him that just might save their hides.

Out here on the prairie, trees were few and far between. But he recalled that a good-sized stand of them were somewhere nearby—if he was anywhere close to correct in his sense of where Sister Laurel and he were. Salina was somewhere to the southwest, Abilene far back to the southeast. The Smoky Hills were to the north. He remembered seeing the low line of hills from that grove of trees when he and some other hunters had made camp there one evening.

Nestor pointed in a direction he judged to be northwest. "Let's strike out that way for a spell," he said. "We might get lucky and happen onto a place where we can get out of the weather. Who knows, maybe we'll even run into them two boys."

Sister Laurel nodded. "An excellent suggestion, Mr. Gilworth. Lead on. I shall follow."

Nestor knew what a great risk he was taking and would bet anything that that smart nun knew it, too. But he was heartened by her encouraging reply.

"Yes'm," he cried with a broad grin. "But I think you'd best let me lead that little mare o' yours. She's gotten a mite skittish."

The tracker had noticed that as the storm intensified Sister Laurel's mare had become increasingly nervous, and he was not sure how much longer the nun would be able to control her. The last thing they needed was a frightened mare losing her head and bolting.

Nestor saw Sister Laurel's agreement in the relieved smile she gave him. He urged his mount into motion and walked it forward until it was even with the mare. Leaning over, he grasped her harness firmly and led the buggy through the whirling snowfall.

As the afternoon wore on, the small amount of light that penetrated the clouds and snow grew dimmer. Nestor pushed on stubbornly. He was well aware that, if Sister Laurel and he missed the trees by even a few yards, they would never know it. They would keep moving until they could no longer continue. The end would probably be pretty quick then. Nestor realized grimly that he was not even certain the grove was still there. Some sodbuster could have cut down the trees and used them for firewood years ago.

There was no conversation now. Neither of them had the energy for it. All their strength went into fighting the life-sapping cold.

Suddenly, Nestor reined in. Through the swirling white mist he saw something dark and dense looming up in front of them. He felt the ice crystals that clung to his beard and mustache break as he smiled broadly. The tracking instincts he had honed during his years as a hunter and scout had not failed him. The trees were still there, and he had found them.

Twisting in the saddle, he called back to the nun, "This is it, Sister! Drive the buggy up in here as far as you can!"

Stiffly, Sister Laurel twitched the reins, and the mare pulled the buggy into the stand of trees. Nestor rode in front of it. Instantly he felt a difference—it was warmer. The growth, scrubby though it was, broke the wind. The snowfall seemed not quite as thick.

Nestor stopped his horse and swung down from the saddle. Hurriedly he tied his mount and the mare to one of the slender trees. Then he went over to help

Sister Laurel climb down from the buggy. "Stay close," he told her. "I'm going to fix a place to hole up."

The nun looked around at the trees and said, "But how—"

Nestor reached under his coat and slipped his bowie knife from its sheath. "This ol' pigsticker's saved my skin before, ma'am," he said, displaying it proudly. "Reckon it can do it one more time." He turned, selected one of the trees, and started hacking at its trunk with the massive blade.

For the next few minutes Nestor worked to cut down the tree, the bowie biting deeply into the trunk with each swing of his powerful arm. Once it was down he left its branches intact and quickly moved on to another one. In less than half an hour he had felled about ten small trees. He pulled them into a pile, crossed the trunks, and arranged the bare branches so they supported one another, creating a small hollow underneath. Then, crawling beneath the twiggy nest, he brushed as much snow as he could from the ground and packed it around the interlaced branches, anchoring them. When he had finished, Nestor scrambled out, pushed aside a few limbs, and motioned to Sister Laurel. "It ain't much," he said, "but it's all we got."

Her face was red, her lips almost as blue as her eyes. Looking a little doubtful, she said through chattering teeth, "You mean that we should . . . both of us . . ."

"You bet. Crawl in, Sister. We got to keep each other alive now."

Sister Laurel gave a short laugh. "I suppose . . . survival is . . . more important than propriety." She bent and slid into the crude shelter.

Nestor turned to look at the two horses. Both of them were still tied and were huddling against one another. It would have been better if he had constructed some sort of shelter for the animals, too, but there simply was not enough time. He shrugged, shook as much snow as he could off his buffalo coat, and then joined Sister Laurel under the branches.

It was almost pitch dark now. Nestor could barely see the nun as they huddled together to share what little warmth they had. Suddenly her face seemed to be a pale image floating in the blackness, and for a moment Nestor thought crazily that she looked like a ghost. He had been haunted many times during his drunken binges, but never by anyone like this.

"You know, ma'am," he mumbled, "if'n you wasn't a nun, you'd be a right handsome woman."

"Mr. Gilworth!" Sister Laurel said, but she did not sound angry. "I am indeed a nun, as you know quite well. Besides, it's freezing and snowing, and we're probably both going to die out here."

"Well, I reckon that's true. I'm sorry, Sister. Didn't mean nothin' by it. . . ."

"That's all right, Mr. Gilworth." Sister Laurel's voice was gentle. "I know what you meant."

Time and its passage became meaningless. There was nothing to see, nothing to hear except the constant howling of the wind, nothing to feel except the bitter cold. Somehow Nestor's buffalo coat wound up covering both of them. He fought the powerful urge to drift off to sleep, trying to stay awake as best he could because he knew the dangers of dozing off in a situation like this. Sometime during the seemingly endless nightmare, he heard Sister Laurel chuckling softly. He stirred and rasped, "Ma'am?"

"I just realized that I have something to be thankful for, Mr. Gilworth," she replied dryly. "You *did* wash this coat."

"Yes'm," he agreed and found the strength somewhere deep inside to grin. "And maybe it'll help save us both."

Chapter Thirteen

MICHAEL AND WESLEY STAYED WHERE THEY WERE, TOO frightened to move, as the tall, slender Indian stared down at them. If he was surprised at finding two white youngsters crouched under the bank of the dry wash, he did not show it. His lean face was gaunt; the copper-colored skin stretched across the prominent bones was pockmarked. Exhaustion and sadness were visible in his dark eyes, but Michael also saw determination there.

Michael's tongue darted out to lick his dry lips. In a voice that sounded strange even to himself, he said, "H-hello." He had no idea if the Indian spoke English.

The buckskin-clad warrior stared at the boys for a moment longer, then looked over his shoulder at the other members of his band. Michael glanced past the man, following his gaze, and saw that there were perhaps two dozen Indians in the group. Only a few of them were braves; the others, Michael could see now as they drew closer, were squaws and children.

Michael looked at Wesley and saw that the other boy was ashen and trembling fearfully. "Take it easy," Michael hissed. "I don't think this is a war party. It sure doesn't look like one."

Wesley made no reply, but the Indian who was standing in front of them turned back to them and grunted. "You right, boy," he suddenly said in passable English. "We peaceful Injuns. Not look for trouble." He made a loose fist and tapped it against his chest. "Me Beaver-Tail."

Michael, his confidence growing now that he knew the Indian spoke his language, repeated the gesture. "Michael Hirsch," he declared. "And this is Wesley Stillman. Are you folks lost?"

A faint smile appeared on Beaver-Tail's face. "Not lost," he said. "Look like you are, maybe?"

Michael had to nod. "We sure are. We got caught in this storm when we were trying to get back to Abilene. That's where we're from."

"You alone?"

Michael hesitated before answering. Beaver-Tail seemed friendly enough, but Michael was still not certain he wanted to admit that Wesley and he were alone out here in the middle of nowhere.

As if sensing his thoughts, Beaver-Tail said, "You not worry. We friendly Injuns, I tell you. Sometimes white men not wait to find out, maybe shoot first."

Beaver-Tail was concerned for the safety of his people, Michael realized. The Indians were probably just as afraid of them as they were of the Indians. Taking a chance, he said, "Wesley and I are alone. We could sure use some help."

"Michael!" Wesley hissed. "You said we had to be careful—"

"There's a difference in being careful and never putting any faith in folks," Michael said.

Beaver-Tail's smile widened into a grin. "Maybe we all help each other," he said. Then he slid his knife from its sheath.

Panic surged through Michael. The brave turned his head and barked a command over his shoulder. Several other men came forward, also pulling their knives. Michael and Wesley shrank back against the hard earth of the bank.

Beaver-Tail and his braves moved past them and started digging at the bank with their knives. "We make this place big enough for all of us," the Indian said. "Be good place to wait for storm to be over."

"Yeah," Michael finally managed to say. "A good place."

During the next hour the Indians gouged out the earth beneath the overhang until the shelter was more like a cave. They had to be careful not to dig too deeply, so that the bank would not collapse. But when they were through, it was large enough to allow everyone to crowd into the area out of the storm. The horses had to be left outside, and at Michael's suggestion, Wesley and he tied their mounts with the Indian ponies. As important as the horses were, it was more vital to give the people access to the small fire's warmth.

Beaver-Tail proved to be surprisingly talkative for an Indian. They were Arapaho, he explained, and he was expressing the sentiments of every man in the group when he said that they had grown tired of fighting the expansion of the white man across the plains. It was a fight they could not win, and the real losers were the women and the children, as more and more of them were left without husbands and fathers. So, along with these others, Beaver-Tail had given up and decided to head for the reservation down in Indian Territory. At least the families of the men would be taken care of there.

The only problem was they had started too late. Winter had closed in while they were still over a hundred miles from the reservation.

They were a pretty ragtag bunch, Michael saw, as Beaver-Tail slowly fed twigs into the fire and built it up some more. Their buckskins and robes showed signs of age and hard use. The men were all thin, as were most of the squaws and children. Life had not been kind to them.

Despite that, as the Indians gradually warmed up, they began to laugh and trade comments in their own language. Michael had no idea what they were saying, but from the occasional glances they cast at Wesley and him, he supposed they were laughing at the two white youngsters who were foolish enough to be out on the plains in this weather.

Wesley still looked a little wild-eyed, and Michael hoped he could keep his emotions under control. Michael's instincts told him that they had nothing to fear from Beaver-Tail and his people. Michael found a spot to sit and pulled Wesley down beside him. The ground was cold, but he felt warmer sitting with his back against the bank.

Beaver-Tail sat down cross-legged beside Michael. He regarded the boy gravely and said, "Bad for child to be out in weather like this. You two running away, maybe?"

"I guess you could say that," Michael replied, casting a glance at Wesley. The other boy had drawn his legs up, his head resting on his knees as he huddled in a tight ball to ward off the cold.

"Maybe Injun do the same," Beaver-Tail mused.

"Maybe we run away *to* white man's reservation." He shrugged. "Not much honor in taking what white man wants to give us, but there no honor at all in letting babies starve, I think."

Michael looked around at the other Indians and saw Beaver-Tail's point. Food had probably been scarce on their journey.

Abruptly Michael made a decision. He patted Wesley on the shoulder and stood up. "I'll be back in a minute," he told Beaver-Tail.

He made his way through the people crowded under the overhang and stepped out into the wash. Their horses were tied up only a few feet away, and Michael went directly to Wesley's mount. He unfastened the saddlebags, slung them over his shoulder, and returned to the cavelike depression in the bank.

"Here," he said, handing the saddlebags to the Indian. "It's not much, but it's all we've got. You're welcome to split it up among you."

"Wait a minute, Hirsch!" Wesley exclaimed, looking up. "Those supplies are mine."

Michael's expression was almost as cold as the wind blowing through the wash as he said, "I know as well as you do where you got them, Wesley. These folks need food, and I reckon Sister Laurel and Reverend Fisher would want us to share what we've got, don't you?"

"I suppose so," Wesley muttered. "It doesn't matter. I'm not hungry anyway, and we're never going to make it out of here alive."

"That's where you're wrong," Michael told him firmly. "We are going to make it, and you're going to eat like everybody else. You've got to keep your strength up, and food'll help ward off the cold."

Beaver-Tail opened the pouches and began pulling

out biscuits and salt pork and apples. "White man's food," he said with a grin as he looked up at Michael with gratitude in his eyes. "Not as good as Injun food, but better than nothing."

Michael returned the grin. "That's what I figured."

He saw several of the Indians glance warmly at him as Beaver-Tail distributed the food, and he sensed that the rude shelter was warming up from more than the leaping fire.

Michael pressed a biscuit into Wesley's hand, then began gnawing on one himself. Cold biscuits had to be the hardest substance known to man, he thought, but not bad under the circumstances. He watched the snow falling as he ate. It seemed to have slacked off a little, but it was still coming down steadily. Already there was nearly half a foot of the sticky white stuff on the floor of the wash. Michael was sure that the drifts were much higher than that up on the plains.

Still, he was safe and not quite as cold. As he leaned back against the bank, he realized that he was almost enjoying himself. This was turning out to be quite an adventure. He knew that once he got back to Abilene, he would catch hell from Judah and Sister Laurel, but there was nothing he could do about that now. He was just glad to be alive and in the company of these friendly Indians.

He watched the snow and the dancing flames of the small fire and waited out the storm.

In an old line shack that they had stumbled onto an hour earlier, Owen, Max, and Al Broderick, Tate Driscoll, and Driscoll's four men were thawing out around a fire they had built in what was left of a rusted-out stove.

All of the men had been on the frontier long enough

to recognize the signs of an approaching storm. Driscoll had suggested stopping around noon, but Owen had been as determined as ever to push on. It was hard for any of the brothers to believe that less than two weeks had passed since they returned to their destroyed ranch. They had put plenty of miles behind them in that time, but as far as they knew, they were no closer to the Indians they were seeking than they were when they had started out.

Driscoll's men were passing around a bottle of whiskey. Stub Pearson took a swig from it, then offered it to Al Broderick. Al cast a glance at Owen and saw that his older brother was staring into the fire, not seeming to see anything except whatever dark scenes were playing out inside his head. Al looked at Max, shrugged, and took the bottle. After a healthy swallow, he passed it to Max.

There were no chairs in the shack. All the men except Owen and Tate Driscoll were sitting on the floor around the stove. Owen stood a few feet away. Driscoll hunkered on his haunches and rolled a cigarette.

Suddenly Owen came out of his reverie and announced, "I'm going to go check on the horses." They had left the animals tied in what was left of a tumbled-down corral. It did not offer much shelter, but at least the horses were out of the wind in the lee of the shack.

Driscoll took a drag on his cigarette and straightened. "I'll go with you," he said. "Sounds a mite strange to say it, but the way that fire's heatin' up this room, I could use a little fresh air."

"It's fresh, all right," Owen grunted as he opened the door. The wind whipped into the shack, bringing snowflakes with it. Quickly Driscoll followed Owen.

But just before he shut the door behind him, he glanced meaningfully at Ben Dunn. Dunn gave a minuscule nod.

Max started to hand the bottle of whiskey to Dunn, but the hardcase shook his head. "You and your brother might as well finish it off," he said. "There's plenty more where that came from."

"Thanks," Al said, reaching out to take the bottle from Max again. "That's mighty kind of you, Dunn."

"Hell, ain't nothin' too good for the Broderick brothers," Dunn replied with a grin. "You fellers are sort of heroes of ours, ain't that right, boys?"

The other three agreed loudly. A puzzled frown creased Max's brow as he took the bottle. "Us? Heroes? Why in the world would you say that?"

"Shoot, ever'body who rides the outlaw trail has heard of the Brodericks. Folks say you've gotten over two hundred thousand in loot the past few years and never once come close to gettin' caught."

"That's because Owen's so smart and plans every job so well," Al said proudly. "I don't always agree with him, mind you, but I got to admit he's good at what he does."

"Still, we never got any two hundred thousand," Max put in. "Maybe half that, and a lot of that went into our ranch."

Al reclaimed the bottle and took another swallow of the rapidly dropping contents. It had been a long, hard ride, and this was the first chance Max and he had had to relax since they had started. This storm might turn out to be a blessing in disguise.

"I'll bet we didn't have more'n fifty grand stashed away when them Indians hit us," Al said. "Maybe not that much."

Asa Mitchell let out a low whistle. "Fifty grand's a whole hell of a lot of money, Broderick."

Al shrugged. "Reckon it is, at that. We was planning on giving up the bank-robbing business after our last job. Owen wanted to stick to ranching, and so did Max and I. We figured it was time to start keeping our noses clean, what with our . . . our families—"

His voice broke as the memories came flooding in. Al had to bite back a sob, and Max's face was set in lines as hard as granite as he reached for the bottle.

"We're sure sorry about your kinfolk," Dunn said after a moment of awkward silence. "Reckon that's why us and Tate come along with you boys. But I was just wonderin' . . . What happened to that money you was talkin' about?"

"Why, them damned Indians—" Al started to say.

His brother's hand came down hard on his leg, cutting off his words. "Far as we know," Max said, "it burned up in the house along with everything else. Like my brother started to say, those damned Indians destroyed everything."

"That's a cryin' shame," Dunn said, trying to sound sympathetic. But the quick look he exchanged with his partners showed that he doubted Max's story.

Driscoll had figured all along that there might be some money to be made by riding with the Brodericks, and he had arranged with his men to pump Max and Al about it the first chance they got when Owen was not around. It could be that Max was telling the truth about the cache of stolen money burning up when the Indians torched their ranch house. But Dunn and the others had noticed the sharp way Max stopped his brother from answering the question. There was a chance that the raiding party had taken the loot with them.

Which meant that when they finally caught up with the Indians, fifty thousand dollars might just be up for grabs.

It was an interesting possibility, one that the men would share with Driscoll as soon as they had an opportunity. And once this storm moved on, they would be back on the trail, searching for the Indians who had taken Lucinda Broderick—and maybe a whole lot more.

Less than five miles from the line shack, Lucinda huddled on the floor of yet another dry wash and wondered just how long it would take her to freeze to death. There was no way she could escape it this time, she was sure of that. And this new storm had leeched all her strength.

The Indians had known early in the day that bad weather was approaching. Sore Toe had spent several minutes haranguing Claw and warning him that the band should seek shelter. The only shelters available to a war party were these barren splits in the earth, and when they had come upon one of the washes, Claw had agreed to stop, even though it was only noon.

The crude hide huts had quickly been erected. Fires were started inside them, but the blazes were small ones. Fuel was becoming more and more scarce. Lucinda stayed close to the fire in Claw's hut, but as the blizzard struck and the temperature plummeted, she could feel the cold seeping deeper and deeper into her bones.

Claw and Sore Toe sat on the other side of the fire, talking quietly. Occasionally Claw would glance over at Lucinda and scowl at her shivering frame. Finally he asked contemptuously, "You are cold, woman?"

"Of course I'm c-cold," Lucinda answered.

Claw snorted in disgust. "You have a buffalo robe,

and you sit next to a fire. What more do you want? A real Indian squaw would not even be uncomfortable in this weather."

"I-I'm not a squaw."

"I know this," Claw said harshly. "You are a white slut. But I will make a squaw of you someday. Either that, or give you to my warriors for sport. Which would you prefer, Yellowhair?"

For a long moment, Lucinda said nothing. Then, in a whisper, she answered, "I will be a squaw."

Claw laughed, and Sore Toe joined in. "We will see," Claw said. "We shall certainly see about that, Yellowhair."

Lucinda stared silently into the fire and tried to draw warmth from the hatred that was steadily growing inside her.

The storm had not yet reached Abilene, but Luke Travis could see it moving in fast. When he had noticed the ominous dark clouds on the western horizon, he paused on the boardwalk outside his office to watch them. He had seen plenty of blue northers before, and this one looked as though it was going to be bad. Abilene was in for it.

There were quite a few people on the streets this afternoon. Folks who had been in the area for a while would be able to tell that bad weather was approaching, and they were getting ready for it. The mercantiles would do a good business as people stocked up on food and staples.

"G' afternoon t'ye, Lucas," rumbled a deep voice. The marshal looked over his shoulder and saw the brawny, red-bearded form of Orion McCarthy, the exuberant Scotsman who was the owner of Orion's Tavern and probably Travis's best friend in Abilene.

Orion went on, "Looks like we're goin' t'get a bit o' a blow."

"I'd say so," Travis agreed. "I'm surprised you're not down at the tavern selling a few last drinks before the storm comes in."

"Augie's tendin' bar; he kin handle tha'. I come down t'invite ye an' Doctor Bloom t'have supper wi' me an' Jocelyn tonight."

Travis grinned. To hear Orion tell it, there was nothing at all romantic between him and Jocelyn Paige, a gambling lady who had come to Abilene recently. They were just friends, according to the burly tavern keeper. Travis suspected it might turn into more than friendship in time.

Of course, people probably thought the same thing about Aileen Bloom and him, he mused.

"If the storm's not too bad, I'm sure Aileen would enjoy that," Travis replied. "I know I would."

"'Tis done, then. I—" Orion broke off suddenly and gripped Travis's arm. With a nod, he gestured down Texas Street. "Judah's comin', Lucas, an' he looks a mite upset about somethin'."

Travis followed Orion's gaze and saw Judah Fisher riding toward them at a quick trot. The minister was hatless and wore his usual dark suit with no overcoat. Travis was puzzled at the sight; the minister had to be cold.

Judah, his face a grim mask, swerved his mount toward them. "Thank the Lord you're here, Luke," he said breathlessly.

"What is it, Judah?" Travis asked as he stepped into the street to grasp the horse's bridle. Judah slid down from the saddle.

"There's a problem," he began. "Two of the boys

198

ran away from the orphanage last night, and they're not back yet."

Travis frowned, glanced at the clouds, then looked at Judah again. "That is bad," he said. "A couple of youngsters sure don't need to be out in weather like this."

Judah shook his head. "That's not all of it, Luke. Sister Laurel and Nestor Gilworth went to look for them, and they haven't come back, either."

"Wha'?" Orion exclaimed. "The sister rode out wi' tha' daft Nestor? Wha' was she thinkin'?"

"Nestor wanted to help," Judah said. "He claimed he was a good tracker, that he could find the boys and bring them back before they got into more trouble. You see, they stole some supplies and a couple of horses from the orphanage."

"Just who are these two runaways?" Travis asked.

"Wesley Stillman . . . and Michael Hirsch."

Travis stiffened. "Michael? The Stillman boy I can understand. He was pretty unhappy about having to stay here. But Michael! Why, he and Michael didn't even get along! They were at each other's throats most of the time, weren't they?"

Quickly Judah explained about the note that Michael had left behind. Travis's expression grew grimmer as the Methodist pastor spoke. When Judah finished, Travis said, "You and Sister Laurel should have come to me right away, Judah."

"I know that," Judah admitted. "But I promised Nestor and her that I wouldn't tell you unless they didn't come back by afternoon. Nestor was so anxious to help, and you know Sister Laurel. She wanted to give him the chance. He had straightened himself up so much since he's been staying with us. . . ."

Travis nodded, his face grim. He knew Sister Laurel, knew that what Judah said was probably true. She would willingly risk her own life if she thought it might help someone.

The marshal turned to Orion. "Go see if you can find Cody, Orion. Tell him what's happened and that I want him to start lining up volunteers for a search party."

"Aye!" Orion nodded. "Will we be leavin' right away?"

Travis looked at the clouds again, and as he lifted his face toward the gray, leaden sky, he felt a snow-flake hit his cheek. He shook his head. "It'd be sheer suicide to ride out now," he said bleakly. "We're going to have to wait until this storm blows over. Might be tomorrow, might be the next day."

Judah grabbed Travis's arm. "But they're still out there somewhere, all four of them!" he cried. "We can't just abandon them!"

"There's nothing we can do right now, Judah," Travis told him, his voice hard. "They'll have to take their chances until the storm blows over. If they come through it all right, we'll find them and get them back here."

"But—"

"Dammit, Judah, I don't like it any better than you do!" Travis snapped, letting his frustration show for a moment. "I've known Sister Laurel and Michael even longer than you have. That hardheaded nun helped save my skin once or twice. But we can't do a thing now." Travis sighed heavily. "From what I've heard, Nestor Gilworth used to be a good man. Maybe with him out there, all of them can make it through somehow."

"Used to be," Judah echoed bitterly. The guilt he was feeling etched deep lines on his thin features.

If he had only broken his promise and alerted Travis to the danger earlier . . . He shook his head. "Do you really think Nestor can save them?" he asked.

"I reckon that's what we'd better all be praying for," Travis said.

Chapter Fourteen

WHEN LUCINDA AWOKE THE NEXT MORNING, SHE WAS surprised that she was still alive. Slowly, she opened her eyes to the brilliant rays of sunlight lancing into the rough shelter, through the gaps where the hides were tied together. Something else struck her as strange, and after a moment she was able to figure out what it was.

The wind was no longer howling and gusting outside. The world was quiet . . . quiet and peaceful.

The blizzard had been fast-moving as well as intense. It had blown over during the night, leaving clear skies and what she was certain had to be sub-zero temperatures.

Lucinda shifted beneath her blankets. Claw had not forced himself on her the night before; it had evidently been too cold even for him. Lifting her head slightly, she saw him lying covered in his own robes on the other side of the hut. His face was turned away from her, but she could tell from his deep, rhythmic breathing that he was asleep.

The fire had died down to a pile of ash. Lucinda felt no warmth emanating from it. A few feet away, Sore Toe sat hunched over. His eyes were open, yet he appeared to be seeing nothing. He was muttering to himself and swaying back and forth.

Lucinda methodically moved each finger and toe and discovered to her surprise that she could still feel all of them. She had avoided frostbite for another night. Quietly, she raised herself, pulling the blankets more tightly around her.

"So, you are awake, woman," Sore Toe said, keeping his voice pitched low so as not to disturb Claw. The shaman continued sullenly, "A good squaw is always awake before the warriors, so that she may build up the fire and prepare a meal."

Lucinda made no reply. After a moment Sore Toe rose awkwardly onto his hands and knees, favoring his afflicted foot, and started crawling toward the entrance.

"Where are you going?" Lucinda asked quickly.

"Claw told me to check on the horses first thing this morning and to take care of them if they are still alive. I will do this before he awakes." Sore Toe sneered. "I follow my chief's commands, not like some stubborn squaw."

Lucinda glanced at Claw again and saw that the conversation did not seem to have roused him. Looking back at Sore Toe, she said, "Can I come with you?"

The shaman frowned. "Why? What do you want, Yellowhair?"

"I need to go outside," Lucinda replied. The lie tumbled easily from her lips. She suddenly felt her cheeks flush and hoped that Sore Toe would see that and believe she was embarrassed. A vague plan had suggested itself to her, and she was operating on instinct. "Besides, I could use some fresh air. Maybe I can help you with the horses."

Sore Toe regarded her skeptically. "I do not know if that would be wise. Claw gave me no orders concerning you."

"A warrior like you should be able to think for himself," Lucinda heard herself saying boldly.

Sore Toe still looked doubtful. He was probably remembering how she had tried to slip away from him before. If Claw and the other warriors had not returned at just the right moment, Lucinda might have escaped. But that had been several days ago, and the white woman had become more meek and subservient since then, her spirit broken by Claw's harsh strength. At least that was what Lucinda wanted all of them to think.

She let the buffalo robe that was around her slip slightly. It fell down on her shoulders and hung open so that Sore Toe could see her full breasts pressing against the tight buckskins underneath. She felt his eyes licking over her, saw him glance nervously at Claw, then recognized the triumph of lust over common sense in his expression. She knew he was still afraid to touch her until Claw gave his permission. But if she went outside with him, he could have her to himself for a few minutes.

"All right," he hissed. "Come on."

He pushed aside the entrance flap and crawled outside. Lucinda followed quickly behind him. She paused as she reached the flap and cast one last glance at Claw. He had not moved; clearly he was sleeping deeply.

As she slipped out of the shelter, she saw Sore Toe scramble to his feet, then he reached out to help her stand. Clasping his arm, she pulled herself up and staggered; her legs after the long hours of inactivity and cold were weak. She panicked; the plan she had vaguely formed would fail. But her strength returned surprisingly quickly, and she stopped wobbling after only a moment.

She looked around and gasped. This was a different world from the one she had left the night before. Snow was everywhere, a thick white carpet that dazzled in the sunlight. The reflections from the white expanse were so brilliant that she had to squint to make out things. And this was inside the dry wash; she could not imagine what it was like out on the prairie itself.

Her breath fogged thickly in front of her. She rubbed her hands together to keep them from getting too cold. Sore Toe started slogging through the snow toward the place where the horses had been tied the night before. Lucinda followed him, the cold air harsh in her throat and lungs as she panted with the exertion of walking through the snow. She looked over her shoulder to make sure that no one else was stirring in the camp. She smiled faintly. She and Sore Toe were the only people in sight.

The horses had been left around a bend in the wash. As Lucinda and Sore Toe turned the corner, she saw with a surge of relief that the animals had survived. Their manes were dusted with snow, but they were all on their feet and several whinnied at them.

Sore Toe paid no attention to Lucinda as he went over to check the horses. She crept up behind him, her hands cupped over her mouth. She was breathing on her fingers to warm them and keep them supple. A part of her brain seemed to have stepped back and was controlling her from outside her body. She was not even thinking about what she was doing, but she was taking action—at last.

She reached out, slipped the shaman's knife out of the sheath on his hip, and said, "Sore Toe." He started to swing around, an alarmed expression on his face, his mouth opening to shout in anger. Lucinda lunged.

She drove the blade into his throat, her aim guided by instinct. The Indian's mouth remained open, but the cry of pain or surprise could not pass beyond the cold steel she had lodged in his windpipe. Drawing on all her strength, Lucinda yanked the knife to the side and sliced his throat open. She did not even wince as a crimson flood spurted onto her hands and arms. Sore Toe sagged and fell. Lucinda hung onto the knife and let the man's own weight rip it free from his flesh.

As she stepped back, she was only vaguely aware of the bright red pattern that the splashing blood had painted on the pristine snow. Sore Toe made a gurgling sound, and one of his hands twitched, then he was quiet and still. His sightless eyes stared up at the bright but cold sun.

Still moving instinctively, Lucinda hurried around him. She went straight to the horse that she had ridden after that first ride behind Claw. It was one of the animals the Sioux had taken from their ranch and was a fairly gentle mare that had not given her any trouble. But now, as she approached her, the horse shied away and regarded her with wide, suspicious eyes. The other animals were nervous, too. Lucinda realized they must be smelling the blood and death on her. She had heard animals had that sort of reaction but had never witnessed it until now. She began to speak softly to them, hoping to prevent them from making too much noise and waking the sleeping camp.

Shoving the knife under the strip of hide that was her crude belt, she jerked loose the line that tied the mare to the other horses. She grasped her mane, still whispering soothing words, and pulled herself up onto her back. The mare danced skittishly beneath her for a moment, then quieted somewhat as she recognized the familiar weight. But the scent of blood still bothered her.

Lucinda drew the knife again. Clasping her knees tightly around her mount's belly, she leaned over and slashed at the lines that held the other horses. As the ponies were freed, they began to prance up the wash away from the camp. Lucinda glanced at the corner that shielded her from the little shelters. There was no one in sight. She had been very lucky so far, but her luck could run out at any second.

She wheeled her mount and started to ride behind the other horses. She swung her arm and hissed at them to keep them moving. She had to drive them off, so that Claw and his men would spend valuable time rounding them up. She desperately needed that time to escape. The next challenge she faced was finding a break in the steep bank that was gently sloped. She had to get out of the wash.

Lucinda began to pray as she kept hazing the horses down the wash, looking for a way out.

It came within fifty yards, just around another of the bends. She recognized the place where they had entered the wash the day before. But the heavy snowfall and swirling wind had clogged the cut with a deep drift. Lucinda almost cried and gave up, but some inner strength refused to yield. The drift would make things more difficult, an inner voice told her, but she still had to try to make it.

She knew she could not drive the other horses through that drift, so she urged them farther down the wash. Then turning her mare toward the slope, she dug her heels into her flanks and urged her on. The horse hesitated and shied away as she reached the drift, but Lucinda forced her to continue, using her hands and feet to drive her and speaking to her in a low, urgent voice.

The horse started up the slope, her legs flailing and kicking up a white cloud. Lucinda felt her slip occasionally, but each time the animal found a new foothold and pushed on. Finally as she leaned over her neck and whispered frantically, the mare reached the top and surged out onto the prairie.

Lucinda blinked as the sun's rays bounced off the snow and stabbed her eyes. She had been right; the glare was even worse up here. But after a moment her vision adjusted, and through narrowed eyes she studied the snow-covered expanse.

Everything was covered with white; she could see no landmarks to guide her. Suddenly she heard an outraged shout. She jerked around on the horse's back and stared toward the place in the wash where the camp was located. Someone had gotten up, discovered Sore Toe's body, and learned that the horses were gone. Within seconds the cold, still air was filled with more angry yelling.

Lucinda banged her heels on the mare's sides and urged her into a gallop. She had to hurry now. It did not matter in which direction she rode, as long as it was away from here.

Hanging on for dear life, Lucinda pressed the mare even harder. The horse fairly flew over the prairie. Lucinda was thankful that the snow muffled its hoofbeats. Normally the thunder of hooves on hard-packed earth was audible for a long way on the plains. Were it not for the snow, Claw and the others would know immediately in which direction she was fleeing.

Now they would have to catch their horses and find her tracks before they would learn where she was headed.

Of course once they found her trail, they could follow it easily. The racing mare was cutting a wide swath through the snow.

Lucinda did not look back. She did not want to know if the Indians were already on her trail. She concentrated instead on getting as much speed as she could out of the horse. Wind whipped her hair, tugged at the robe she was trying to hold around her, sliced into lips that were already split and sore from the cold.

It was a nightmarish ride across a frozen hell, but the prospect of freedom at the end of it kept Lucinda going.

She had no idea how long she had been riding away from Claw's camp when the horse suddenly stumbled. There was a loud crack of bone. The horse screamed, and so did Lucinda as she sailed through the air, thrown clear by the wildly tumbling, injured horse.

Lucinda slammed hard onto the ground, the snow cushioning her fall only a little. The air was driven from her lungs. Blackness swam in front of her eyes in stark contrast to the whiteness that had been all she had seen for so long. She tried to lift her head, and red streaks shot through the ebony.

No hope now, she thought. The horse's leg had to be broken. It was only a matter of time before Claw and his men tracked her down.

She sank back, eyes closed, head pillowed in the snow. There was no point in going on. She might as well lie here and wait for the end. With any luck she would freeze to death before Claw found her.

A faint voice in her head insisted that she had not survived for this long by giving up. Lucinda tried to ignore it, but finally she groaned, opened her eyes, and forced herself to roll over. Her hands and feet were starting to go numb, but she managed to push herself up to a standing position. She looked around and saw the mare lying a few yards away. The animal was still; her head was at a strange angle on her slender neck. Clearly, the mare had broken more than her leg in the fall. Lucinda was thankful she was dead. She had only Sore Toe's knife and would not have been able to put the mare out of her misery with that. It would have been difficult to leave a suffering animal.

She looked at the tracks she had made; her gaze followed them into the distance and out of sight. Scanning the horizon, she saw no one in pursuit, but they would come. She was sure of that.

Lucinda turned and forced one leg to take a step, then the other. She kept moving in the direction she had been going, half walking, half staggering.

I will not die easily, she told herself. *I will not.*

Sunshine had never looked prettier to Michael Hirsch. The clear skies meant that the temperature had dropped even more than it would have if the blizzard had still been blowing. But that did not matter to the impish redhead. He could see, and that was better than the blinding misery of the day before.

Neither of the boys had slept much, and this morning they were both stiff and cold. Beaver-Tail distributed what little food remained of Wesley's supplies. He made sure all the young ones had something to eat. As Michael chewed on a strip of jerky, he noticed that Beaver-Tail himself had not taken any food.

"What do we do now?" Wesley asked. He was standing beside Michael, watching the Indians suspiciously as they munched on their meager breakfast.

"I'd say that depends on Beaver-Tail and the others," Michael answered.

"What do you mean?"

"I think we should stay with them, if they'll let us," Michael said.

"But they're not going to Abilene," Wesley protested. "I thought you wanted to go back to town."

"Do *you* know which way Abilene is?" Michael asked sharply. "We're not even sure where we are. If we go wandering off blindly, we're liable to wind up in even more trouble. I think we should stick with the Indians. We're bound to hit a settlement or a ranch house where we can get some help. We'll get back to Abilene sooner or later."

Wesley looked doubtful, but he did not say anything. Considering the trouble he had already caused both of them, Michael thought that was a wise decision.

Beaver-Tail came over to the boys a few moments later and regarded them gravely. "Where you go now, maybe?" he asked.

"We were just talking about that," Michael told him. "I know it might make things harder for you and your people, Beaver-Tail, but we'd sure appreciate it if we could come with you."

The Indian nodded. "That what I think, too. You help us, give us food. Now we help you. Find white man to take you home."

"Thank you," Michael said sincerely. "We'll do anything we can to help along the way."

"You good boys. You not be any trouble," Beaver-Tail assured him.

Michael turned to Wesley. "Come on. Let's get ready to ride."

All the horses had made it through the night, but they were gripped by a weariness that also seemed to be slowing the small band of Indians. Michael patted his mount on the flank as he cinched up the saddle. He glanced at Wesley to make sure that the other youngster had fastened his saddle properly.

Beaver-Tail and his people were mounting up. Michael and Wesley followed their lead. Beaver-Tail turned slightly and motioned for them to ride beside him. As Michael joined him, he asked why the Indian had wanted them next to him in what would be considered a place of honor. "Maybe see someplace you remember," Beaver-Tail answered.

"I'll keep my eyes open," Michael promised, "but I wouldn't count on anything. With all this snow one place looks pretty much like another."

"Snow hides many things," Beaver-Tail agreed. "But always there are differences in the land."

"Not out here," Wesley spoke up. "I've never seen country that's so much alike as these plains."

"Let me worry about the landmarks," Michael told him, the words sounding more like a reprimand than he intended.

"Sure, Hirsch," Wesley grumbled.

Michael sighed and tried not to shake his head. Wesley sounded just as unfriendly and unpleasant as ever. Now that they were no longer in danger, his true nature was coming back out. Well, Michael supposed, he could put up with Wesley for a while, at least until they were safely back in town. He could even make a few more friendly overtures.

"Look," Michael said as the group started slowly down the wash, "I'm sorry about all the rotten stuff I did to you, Wesley. That's the real reason I came after you. I wanted to apologize."

"Is that so? You sure made me feel like you hated my guts."

"I reckon I did for a while. But shoot, there's no point in staying mad at folks. That just wastes everybody's time."

Wesley made no reply. Time dragged by, and Michael began to think the other boy was not going to say anything. But finally Wesley spoke. "Maybe you're right," he said slowly, and for once Michael thought he heard something besides sullen resentment in Wesley's voice. "You did try to help me, after all. I'd have died out here yesterday if you hadn't come along and then found that overhang."

"Well, I just wanted to help." Michael grinned at Wesley. "And I didn't want to freeze to death, either."

Beaver-Tail, who was riding only a few feet away from them, overheard the conversation. He looked at them and asked, "You two boys not friends?"

Michael shrugged. "We haven't been. I'm not sure about now." He looked over at Wesley. "How about it?"

Wesley hesitated. He started to extend his hand to Michael, stopped, then thrust it out. "What the hell," he muttered. "I guess we can give it a try, Hirsch. But no more jokes like the one you pulled on me!"

Michael took his hand and shook it. Grinning, he said, "No more jokes, I promise."

Beaver-Tail nodded solemnly. "Good for boys to be friends," he declared.

Michael sensed Wesley still had some reservations, but at least they had made a start. If they ever got to Abilene, he might be able to break down that reserve and build a solid friendship.

After they had traveled about a half-mile, Beaver-Tail led the party up out of the wash. On the open plain the glare from the snow was blinding, and Michael had to lift his hand and shade his eyes for a few minutes until he got used to it. He was squinting off to the left when he suddenly reined in and said, "Look!"

Beaver-Tail drew his horse to a halt; his eyes followed Michael's pointing finger. A dark shape stood out vividly against the snow, and it was moving slowly toward them. After watching it for a moment, Michael realized that it was a person staggering along on foot.

"Who the devil is that?" Wesley asked, staring at the stranger. Everyone else in the group was watching it as well.

"I don't know, but we have to help," Michael cried. He heeled his horse into motion and rode quickly toward the stumbling figure.

"Wait, boy!" Beaver-Tail called. He galloped after Michael, overtook him, and caught his horse's bridle. When he had stopped Michael's horse, the Indian slid an ancient single-shot Jennings rifle from a beaded sheath that was slung on his horse's flank. "Better to be careful out here," he warned firmly.

That was exactly what Michael had told Wesley the day before, but in this case the caution seemed unwarranted. "But it's just one person," Michael argued, gesturing at the figure that was now only fifty yards away. The stranger was still plodding along as if he had not noticed the approaching riders.

Beaver-Tail nodded. "Come." He urged his pony to a walk and rode toward the stranger, the rifle held ready. Michael and several braves followed closely behind him.

As they drew nearer, Michael saw that the person was wrapped in a buffalo robe. Beaver-Tail and the others drew rein a few yards in front of the shambling figure. The Indian spoke sharply in his guttural native tongue. The stranger jerked to a stop, looked up at the Indians on horseback, and screamed.

It was a woman, Michael saw with a shock. A white woman with blond hair and wide, terrified blue eyes. Her buffalo robe was splattered with a dark red stain that looked like blood. She shrieked as if she were in mortal torment.

Michael dropped off his horse and ran toward the wailing figure, stumbling a little in the deep snow. "It's all right, ma'am," he called, thinking that hearing English might calm her. "It's all right. I'm white, and they're friendly Indians."

He stopped short as the woman's hand flashed out from under the robe. Clutched tightly in her hand was a knife, its blade glinting in the brilliant light. "Stay back!" she cried wildly, her face contorted with rage. "Stay back, or I'll kill you!"

Michael stood still. Ever so slowly he lifted his hands and held them up with the palms out. Daring to tear his eyes from the hysterical woman for an instant, he saw that his hands were trembling. "Just take it easy, ma'am," he said in what he hoped was a calm voice. "You're all right now. You're among friends. Nobody's going to hurt you."

"Friends?" she moaned. Slowly the wild expression in her eyes changed, and she began to look at Michael as if she were finally seeing him for what he was. She lowered the knife slightly. "You . . . you won't hurt me?"

Michael shook his head. "Nobody will hurt you," he promised gently.

Suddenly the woman's cold-reddened face crumpled. A sob that seemed to come from deep inside her erupted from her lips. The knife slipped from her fingers, and she fell to her knees and cried.

Beaver-Tail had dismounted, and now he moved up quietly to stand beside Michael. "Bad. Something very bad," he murmured.

"Reckon she's been through something awful," Michael whispered. "She looks frozen. Do you think we could build a fire and warm her up some?"

Beaver-Tail glanced around, then nodded. "Bushes over there," he said softly and pointed to a spot behind Michael. "Old buffalo wallow, maybe. We stop for a while."

Michael stepped forward gingerly, his hand extended toward the woman. "Will you come with us?" he asked gently. "My name is Michael."

For a moment she did not respond, but simply huddled on the ground and cried, the sobs shaking her body. Then she looked up, her tearful blue eyes meeting his, and slowly reached out to take his hand.

"I'm Lucinda," she mumbled in a choked voice. "Lucinda Broderick."

Beaver-Tail had pointed out a small depression in the ground that was ringed by a few bare bushes. Several Arapaho dismounted and cleared the snow from a spot shielded by the brush. Michael broke off some branches and, as soon as the Indians had finished, started a small fire. Lucinda Broderick crouched next to the flames, her hands outstretched toward the warmth.

Then Beaver-Tail, his face filled with concern, spoke softly and walked slowly toward her. When she noticed him, her eyes widened in terror, and she shrieked and began to cringe away. Michael rushed to her, placed his hands on her shoulders, and spoke soothingly. It took the boy several minutes, but he managed to calm her. At last the Indian was able to check her hands and feet, and he grimaced at what he saw. Then he began to rub snow on her skin. "Frost-bite, maybe," he commented grimly. "Maybe not."

"Do what you can for her," Michael replied. Lucinda still shivered, and a moan occasionally escaped from her lips, but she let Beaver-Tail work on her feet. Michael stood up and quietly stepped back.

Wesley, who had been watching silently, moved toward Michael and grabbed his sleeve. "Where the hell did she come from?" he whispered.

Michael shook his head. "I don't know. But I think it'd be a good idea for us to find out." He went to Lucinda and knelt beside her. "Miz Broderick, ma'am," he said, "do you think you can tell us what you're doing out here?"

"Running," she replied with a short, humorless laugh. "Running away from the savage who killed my family and made me a slave."

"Indian?" Beaver-Tail asked, his face expression-less.

"A man named Claw."

Beaver-Tail caught his breath. "I have heard of this one," he said, sounding worried. "He is nearby?"

"I don't know. I've been on foot since early morn-ing. I thought he would have found me by now. . . ."

Michael glanced at Beaver-Tail and saw the concern in the Arapaho's dark eyes. "You'd better tell us what happened," he said to Lucinda.

In a halting voice, she recounted what she had lived through during the last two weeks. Michael was horri-fied, and Wesley's face grew pale. But neither boy uttered a sound while she spoke. Throughout her story, Beaver-Tail continued to put snow on her hands and feet. Once or twice Lucinda winced, but she told her tale, leaving out none of the gruesome facts.

When she had finished, Michael looked at Beaver-Tail. The stricken expression on the Arapaho's gaunt face told him that they were concerned about the same thing. They had to do everything possible to prevent Claw and his war party from catching them. They could never defend this group, with its women and children, from that bloodthirsty band of renegades. "I think we'd better get out of here," Michael muttered. "We don't want to run into that Claw fella."

"No. He is a bad man, a killer. We must leave quickly."

Lucinda lifted her head. "You'll take me with you?" she asked in a voice edged with panic.

"Sure," Michael said quickly. "You can ride double with me."

"Or with me," Wesley offered. "You can switch back and forth. Don't you worry, ma'am. We won't let anything else happen to you."

Michael thought he heard more strength and determination in Wesley's voice than he had ever heard before. Feeling concern for someone else's welfare was probably one of the best things that could happen to him.

The Arapaho party quickly extinguished the fire and mounted up. Michael helped Lucinda climb onto his horse, then swung up behind her. He looped an arm around her waist and suddenly felt embarrassed that he was holding a grown woman in this way. Lucinda stared longingly at the ashes of the fire as if she hated to leave them. Michael turned his horse around and nodded meaningfully at Beaver-Tail.

They rode swiftly, heading southeast as far as Michael could tell. Beaver-Tail was probably hoping to run across a settlement, maybe even find the railroad tracks and follow them to a place where they would all be safe from Claw. Michael knew that

Beaver-Tail and his men would fight if they had to, but no one wanted to risk the women and children.

Beaver-Tail turned frequently to scan their back trail, and Michael appointed himself to keep an eye on the flanks. He was the one who spotted movement about an hour later, just as he had been the first to notice Lucinda.

"Somebody coming up on the left!" he called to Beaver-Tail. Lucinda stiffened against him, and he knew that her fear had returned. Instantly, the Arapaho waved a hand to signal the group to halt. The braves who were armed with rifles lifted their weapons, while the other men reached for arrows and nocked them on their bows.

Michael had caught only a fleeting glimpse of someone before whoever it was rode into a depression and disappeared behind a little hill. The three whites and the Indians waited tensely for them to reappear. When they finally did, Michael frowned. Wesley muttered, "What the hell . . . ?"

A buggy was rolling through the snow, and beside it rode a man on horseback. Even though they were over a hundred yards away, Michael could tell that the rider was a big man, made even more massive by the buffalo coat he wore—

Suddenly Wesley banged his heels against his horse and galloped toward the approaching pair. He snatched his hat off his head, waved it, and let out a whoop. Michael shouted, "Wesley, you crazy fool, come back here!"

Wesley turned just long enough to cry, "It's all right! It's *Nestor!*"

Then Michael recognized the big buffalo hunter. Nestor spurred his horse to a gallop to meet the boy from the East. And coming along quickly behind him in the buggy was someone wearing a black outfit.

Michael gulped as he saw the white wimple flutter and tremble with the buggy's movements. They were in for trouble now. There might be a revenge-crazed Indian somewhere behind them, but in front of them was an angry Sister Laurel.

At the moment Michael was not sure which was worse.

Chapter Fifteen

———◆———

OWEN BRODERICK JERKED HIS HORSE TO A STOP AND stared down at the tracks that marred the snow. Beside him, Tate Driscoll reined in as well, while Max, Al, and the others came up behind.

Driscoll took out the makings and began lazily to roll a cigarette as he studied the tracks. "Looks like unshod ponies," he commented. "A couple dozen at least. You know what that means, Owen."

"We've found them," Owen breathed through clenched teeth. He could feel the pulse at his temple throb.

"We can't be sure of that, Owen—" Max began.

"Dammit, Max!" Al exclaimed. "This bunch is the right size, and we're about where that Kaw said we'd find the ones we're looking for. What more do you want?"

"It's just that I remember how we killed all those innocent Indians—"

This time Driscoll interrupted Max. "No such thing as an innocent Injun, mister," he said scornfully.

Max flushed and started to urge his horse toward Driscoll, but Owen put out an arm and stopped him. "Take it easy," he warned. "I know we made a mistake before, but this time we'll make sure. The chances we're right are a lot better now."

"Maybe so, but I still think we ought to be careful."

"Oh, we'll be careful," Driscoll said. "You don't go ridin' up to a bunch of redskins this size without lookin' 'em over first. So don't you worry about that, Max."

"All right," Max agreed grudgingly.

"All I need to do is see Lucinda," Owen said. "It won't take any more than that. If she's with them, we'll know we've got the right ones . . . and then we'll kill every one of the bastards."

Driscoll grinned. "That's the kind of talk I like to hear." He waved an arm and kicked his horse into a trot, following the broad trail in the snow. "Come on, boys. Let's go find us some heathens to shoot!"

The reunion between Nestor, Michael, and Wesley was a happy one. The blond boy was thrilled to see Nestor. "I know everything's going to be all right now," he cried. "You can get us back to Abilene, can't you, Nestor?"

"Sure as shootin'," the big man replied. "Now that that ol' blizzard's blown over, it ain't goin' to be hard to figger out where we are."

"How did you manage to make it through the night?" Michael wanted to know. "Did you find someplace to get in out of the storm?"

Nestor glanced at Sister Laurel and said, "I reckon

you could say so, boy. We stayed warm enough. Almost right cozy, I'd say."

"The important thing is that Mr. Gilworth and I found the two of you," Sister Laurel said firmly. "You had us both very worried."

"We were pretty worried for a while ourselves," Michael admitted. "Then Beaver-Tail and his people came along and gave us a hand."

Nestor turned to the leader of the Indian band who had been sitting quietly on horseback, observing the reunion. The burly tracker uttered a rapid stream of Arapaho, and Beaver-Tail nodded. "I speak English," he told Nestor. "And I am glad we could help boys. They do good thing for us, too. Share food with Injuns."

Lucinda Broderick moved from the back of Michael's horse and sat in the buggy next to Sister Laurel. She recounted her ordeal again, but this time she abbreviated the story. The nun found more blankets for the former captive to wrap herself in, and Lucinda stopped trembling and began to look warmer. "Shouldn't we go?" she asked nervously. "Claw is still out here somewhere."

"The lady's right," Nestor rumbled. "I've heard of that Claw feller. He's a bad 'un, all right. We best head for Abilene as quick as we can."

Michael turned to Beaver-Tail and asked, "Why don't you come with us? I'm sure the folks in Abilene would be glad to help you."

The Indian shook his head and smiled. "No, we go on to reservation now that boys have friends to take them home. You not need our help anymore."

Michael felt something catch in his throat as he looked at the slender brave. Despite the bad fortune that had befallen him and his people, there was an inner strength and dignity in Beaver-Tail. And more than that, there was compassion as well. The encounter had been a short one, but Michael knew he would never forget the Arapaho.

"Thank you," Michael said. "Good luck to you and your people, Beaver-Tail."

The Indian nodded solemnly. Wesley Stillman urged his horse up closer and said, "Yeah. Thanks for helping us."

Beaver-Tail inclined his head. "You are welcome. Farewell, boys."

Beaver-Tail turned his horse to face his people and lifted his arm to signal to the group that they were ready to be on their way again.

Michael was sitting on his horse ten feet away, and tears began to fill his eyes as he watched the Arapaho prepare to lead his people away.

Suddenly a bullet thudded into Beaver-Tail's chest. An ugly bloodstain blossomed on the Indian's buckskins, and Beaver-Tail rocked back from the impact of the shot.

The crack of a rifle blended with Michael's anguished shout of "Nooo!" as Beaver-Tail tumbled to the snowy ground, dead.

Nestor spun in the saddle. Fifty yards away a band of men were galloping toward them from behind a small ridge. They were whooping and firing rifles.

The big buffalo hunter reacted instinctively. He reached for the butt of his Sharps and pulled the heavy buffalo gun from its saddle boot. His horse moved skittishly underneath him as more gunfire rang out.

"Get down!" he shouted at Sister Laurel and Lucinda. He turned to Michael and Wesley and went on, "Get behind the buggy and stay there!"

The buggy was scant cover for the two women and the boys, but it was all they had out here on the open plain. Nestor made sure that his companions were out of the line of fire, then spurred forward to see what was happening.

It was a massacre, he saw immediately. Even though Beaver-Tail's band outnumbered the attackers more than three to one, many of the Arapaho were squaws and children. Not all of the warriors were armed with rifles, and those that were had only old single-shot weapons. The eight men who were sweeping down on them had repeaters, and they seemed to be good with the Winchesters.

Nestor lifted his own Sharps, then hesitated. He had thought at first that the attackers were probably Claw and his renegades, but now he saw that they were white men. Still unsure what to do, Nestor had that problem solved for him when Michael Hirsch pounded by on his horse, crying, "No! Stop! They're friendly!"

None of the raiders were paying any attention to the boy, but Nestor saw that Michael was about to ride right into the flying lead. He spurred forward, his horse giving a great leap that brought him even with Michael. Nestor reached out, wrapped an arm around the youngster, and hauled him out of his saddle. Michael kicked and yelled, but there was nothing he could do to stop Nestor from turning around and galloping back to the relative safety of the buggy.

Nestor found Sister Laurel, Lucinda Broderick, and Wesley huddled behind the vehicle. He dropped out of the saddle, moving lithely for such a big man, and took Michael with him. Thrusting Michael to the ground, he growled, "Do what I tell you, boy! Stay there!"

Sister Laurel clutched at Nestor's arm. "Mr. Gilworth, you have to stop them!" she exclaimed. "They're killing all those Indians!"

"I know, Sister," he told her bleakly. "And there ain't a damn thing I can do about it."

"But why?" Wesley wailed. "Beaver-Tail and his people didn't do anything wrong!"

"Nothin' but have red skins," Nestor muttered.

Suddenly Lucinda cried out, "My God! That's Owen! That's my husband out there!"

She was peering around a corner of the buggy. Nestor followed her gaze and saw a big, florid-faced, fair-haired man charging through the remaining Indians. There was a Colt in his hand, and he was pulling the trigger as fast as he could. He mowed down several Indians as he came to them. He did not pause to reload but pounded on toward the buggy instead, evidently looking for Lucinda.

Nestor had the Sharps up and ready as Owen Broderick brought his horse to a sliding halt near the buggy. "Hold it, mister!" Nestor called out, his voice booming as he tried to get through to Owen. He was afraid that the killing rage might have gripped the other man, that Owen would grab another gun and start shooting at anyone close to Lucinda.

Instead, Owen flung himself out of the saddle and ran toward them, shouting Lucinda's name. She broke away from Sister Laurel and ran to meet him. She threw herself into his arms and buried her face against his chest as he embraced her. "Oh, God, Owen," she sobbed. "I didn't think I'd ever see you again!"

The guns were firing sporadically now. Michael and Wesley moved up beside Nestor to watch the last of the Indians fall. A sob wrenched from Michael's throat, and Nestor put a hand on his shoulder to hold him back, just in case he tried to lunge out onto the battlefield again. The snow-covered plain was dotted with bodies and stained by great splashes of crimson.

A couple of the white men dismounted, guns held ready, and began checking the fallen Indians to make sure they were dead. Five men rode toward the buggy, three of them at a rather nonchalant pace. But the other two hurried to the vehicle. Nestor could see how agitated and upset they were as they dismounted and came over to Owen, who was still holding Lucinda and stroking her hair.

"Dammit, Owen!" one of them said angrily. "We did it again! These aren't the Indians who hit our ranch. Most of them are women and children, for Christ's sake!"

"Driscoll shouldn't have started shooting," the other man added. "I got no love for redskins, but this was just plain murder!"

Owen Broderick looked up. "What the hell are you talking about?" he demanded. "What women and children?"

Nestor's mouth tightened. Clearly, in his rage at what he thought were the savages who had kidnapped his wife, Owen had not even noticed whom he was killing.

Lucinda looked up at her husband. "Max and Al are right, Owen," she said. "These Indians helped me. They aren't the ones who raided our ranch!" She looked past him at the sprawled bodies, and fresh tears sprang to her eyes. "And now they're all dead . . . !"

The other three white men cantered up. The one in the lead had long, lank brown hair and a drooping mustache. He touched the brim of his battered hat and said, "Howdy, ma'am. Reckon you're Miz Broderick. Now you don't have to thank us for savin' you from these here savages. It was the least we could do."

Owen was looking at the results of the attack, and his florid skin began to grow pale. "Shut up, Driscoll!" he snapped. "These were the wrong Indians. There was no need to kill them."

Driscoll shrugged. "We been over that before, Owen. Ain't none of these heathens worth sheddin' any tears over."

"You son of a bitch!" Michael shouted. The boy leapt forward, his face wild with rage.

Nestor lunged, grabbed the collar of his coat, and jerked him back. "Hold on, boy," he said in a low voice. "We'll get to the bottom of this."

Owen passed a hand in front of his face. He was clearly shaken by the discovery that he and his brothers had been part of an atrocity. "What's done is done," he said harshly. "I'm sorry if some innocent people got hurt. But I had to get my wife back."

"At the cost of dozens of lives, sir?" Sister Laurel demanded. Her features were set in hard, angry lines. "I intend to report this to the authorities when we get back to Abilene!"

Nestor grimaced. He wished she had not said that. He saw the looks that flashed across the faces of Driscoll and his men. He started to tip up the barrel of the Sharps when Driscoll suddenly palmed out his holstered Colt.

"Hold it right there, big feller," Driscoll growled. "You best put that buffalo gun down before somebody gets hurt."

One of the other men—one of the Broderick brothers, Nestor figured—said, "Driscoll, what the hell are you doing? These folks are—"

"These folks are confused," Driscoll said in a hard voice. "We saved 'em from some murderin' redskins, but they don't seem to understand that."

"That's a damned lie!" Wesley burst out. "Those Indians helped us, maybe saved our lives."

Driscoll ignored the blond boy. He eared back the hammer of his Colt and looked meaningfully at Nestor. "I told you to put down that carbine."

Slowly, Nestor stooped and laid the Sharps on the snow-covered ground. He was seething, but he took control of that fiery emotion. He would have to let this situation play out a little longer before he decided what he would do.

Owen Broderick put his hands on Lucinda's shoulders. "Listen, if these aren't the Indians who raided the ranch, what happened to them?"

"I . . . I escaped from them early this morning, right after sunup," Lucinda explained. "I was running away when these people found me and helped me."

"Are you . . . all right?"

Lucinda shuddered. "I don't know if I'll ever be all right again, Owen. But I'm not hurt, just cold. I can travel."

"Good." Owen's voice was flat. "Because we're going to go find those other savages."

Driscoll grinned, while Lucinda and the others looked astounded. "Reckon that's just what I wanted to hear you say, Owen," he said dryly.

Lucinda stared up at her husband in disbelief. "But, Owen, why? Why can't we go somewhere safe—"

"Did the Indians take that little chest from my study?"

Lucinda took a deep breath, then nodded. Understanding dawned on her haggard features. "Claw had it," she said.

"Claw?"

"The war chief. The leader of that band of renegades. The man who . . . Oh, God—"

Owen folded her into his arms again. "Never mind. Don't even think about that, not ever again. Just take me back to where you left them. Can you do that?"

She nodded weakly. "I . . . I suppose so. It shouldn't be too hard to backtrack."

Nestor had been watching the exchange closely. He saw the glance that passed between Driscoll and his men, when Owen Broderick mentioned the chest. Nestor had no idea what that meant, but evidently it was important. Owen and the others were paying no attention to Sister Laurel and the two boys and him, now that Driscoll was covering them. Nestor had a feeling that they had stumbled into something that had plenty of strong currents under the surface.

"Well," he said, "I don't reckon you folks need us anymore. We'll just mosey on back to Abilene—"

"I don't think so," Driscoll drawled. "You heard what Miz Broderick said, mister. There's still some maraudin' Injuns in the area. No, I reckon you and the sister and them young'uns will be safer if you stick with us."

Nestor met the man's gaze and read the cold menace in his eyes. He figured that he could pull his old Dragoon, get off a shot or two, and maybe even snag the Sharps off the ground. But even if he downed one or two of the hardcases, the ones who were left would get him. And there was a better than even chance that Sister Laurel or Michael or Wesley would catch some lead in the fracas.

He had no choice. He had to wait.

"All right," he said. "We'll ride with you. Mighty nice of you to offer the company, friend."

Driscoll grinned mockingly. Clearly he did not believe Nestor, any more than Nestor believed him. "You're mighty welcome, mister."

"Gilworth's the name," Nestor said softly. "Nestor Gilworth."

One of the other hardcases frowned. "Gilworth? I heard of a feller named Gilworth, used to scout for the Army. Supposed to be hell on wheels—"

A faint grin played around Nestor's mouth. "That's me, son," he said quietly.

Driscoll and his men glanced at each other, and Nestor could see worry in their eyes. That was good; let them stew on it for a while. They knew his reputation. Now let them wonder what he was planning.

He just hoped that he could come up with a plan before all of them got killed.

All of the Indians were dead. Pearson and Mitchell checked the bodies, then rode up to Driscoll and with a nod confirmed it. Driscoll turned to Owen and grinned. "If we're goin' to find them other heathens, we'd better get a move on," he declared. "If they're around here, they might've heard the shootin'."

"That's right," Owen agreed. "Come along, Lucinda. I want you to ride with me."

A few minutes later the group moved out, heading back along the trail to the spot where Lucinda had been found by Michael, Wesley, and the Arapaho. Driscoll quietly spoke to his men, and they ranged around the company, making sure that they could cover Nestor Gilworth, the nun, the two boys, and the Brodericks. Now that they were this close to a fortune, they were not going to let anything spoil the chances of getting their hands on it.

Driscoll felt sure that the chest Owen had asked about contained the loot Max and Al had mentioned back in the line shack. Fifty thousand dollars, they had said. That was more money than Driscoll had ever seen in his life, let alone held in his hands. When he thought about having that much money, he did not even feel the cold.

Once they found the other Indians, it would be simple to grab the chest, he thought. This war chief called Claw and his men would put up more of a fight than the other groups they had encountered, but Driscoll did not doubt for a second that he and his partners would come out on top in the battle. When that was finished, he would no longer need the Brodericks and those folks from Abilene.

A grim smile tugged at his mouth. His men knew what to do. Before this day was over, they would be fifty grand richer. And there would be no witnesses left alive to connect any of them with the killings.

Yes, sir, Tate Driscoll thought, *everything's working out just fine.*

"Goddamn it!" Owen Broderick raged as he looked down into the dry wash where Claw's camp had been. It was empty now, the disturbed snow the only sign that anyone had been there during the last twenty-four hours. Sore Toe's body was gone, but the snow was still bloody.

"What did you expect?" Lucinda asked. "I told you they probably came after me when they found out I was gone."

"Why didn't they catch up to you, then?" Owen wanted to know. "You said you were on foot."

"Only part of the time. I had ridden quite a ways before my horse fell."

Driscoll frowned. "Still they should've caught up to you, ma'am. Reckon you had plenty of luck on your side."

Maybe that was true, Nestor thought as he looked

over the campsite, but maybe not. He agreed with Driscoll's assessment. Something was wrong.

Driscoll's men were still unobtrusively maintaining positions where they could cut down anyone who started any trouble. Nestor had known what they were doing when he first noticed them moving to the flanks of the party. One of them had gone ahead to scout the wash as they drew near it, and that man had signaled that all was clear. Nestor was not surprised Claw was gone. It would have been a shock to find a clever savage like him in the same place for very long.

"What now?" Nestor asked. "How long do you intend to stay out here, Broderick? It's the middle of the afternoon now. We'd best try to find a settlement 'fore nightfall. Goin' to be mighty cold again tonight."

"I know that," Owen snapped. "Just shut up and let me think."

Max moved his horse up next to his brother's. "Give it up, Owen," he urged. "We've got Lucinda back. That's what's really important."

"I don't want that savage thinking he can raid our place and kill our families and get away with it," Owen grated. "He's got to pay!"

"Damn right!" Driscoll said. He pointed at the tracks left by Claw's men when they broke camp. "We can follow the bastards, Owen. Now that we're this close, we can't let 'em go."

"Driscoll's right," Owen said. He slid his hand to his hip, pushed aside his coat, and caressed the butt of his Colt. "We're going to find Claw and his men, then we're going to kill them."

Sister Laurel spoke up. "The Lord says that vengeance belongs to Him, Mr. Broderick."

Owen turned toward her, and the look of a man gone over the edge was plain in his eyes. "Then He's just going to have to wait in line, Sister."

Chapter Sixteen

EVERY HAIR ON THE BACK OF NESTOR GILWORTH'S SHAG-gy head prickled with warning. Something was badly wrong, and he thought he knew what it was. They were riding into a trap.

They had been tracking Claw's band for an hour. The renegades had struck out from their camp and followed Lucinda's trail. But they had inexplicably veered off before catching up with her.

Tate Driscoll had studied the welter of tracks for several minutes. Then he said to Lucinda, "No offense, ma'am, but I reckon ol' Claw decided it weren't worth the trouble to go after you anymore."

Lucinda said nothing. She was riding behind Owen, and she tightened her arms around him. But Nestor could see the loathing in her eyes as she looked at Driscoll.

Owen had not seemed to hear the comment. He had

only grunted, "Come on," and heeled his horse into motion.

They traveled a few more miles and still did not sight the Indians. They were heading north toward the Smoky Hills, and the terrain was becoming slightly more rugged as they drew closer to the low line of hills.

Nestor grew more nervous with each passing minute. The little hills and valleys made it more difficult to spot anything—especially renegade Indians.

Driscoll was riding beside Owen and Lucinda. Max and Al Broderick were right behind their brother and sister-in-law. Michael and Wesley were next, flanking the horse that was pulling Sister Laurel's buggy. Nestor rode alongside the buggy itself. He could tell from Sister Laurel's expression that the nun was as worried as he was. Driscoll's men flanked the group, two on each side.

Somebody had to try to get through to Owen Broderick and talk some sense into him before it was too late. Nestor figured he was elected. Max and Al had had no luck in persuading him to turn back.

Nestor urged his horse past the boys and pushed closer to the Brodericks. He noticed the way Driscoll's men tensed and put their hands closer to their guns, but he chose to ignore it. They had not disarmed him; he still had his Dragoon and his bowie and had slid the Sharps back into its boot. These hardcases seemed to believe they could handle him if he started anything.

He pulled up even with Owen Broderick, on the other side of the man's horse from Driscoll. "I want a word with you, Broderick," Nestor said.

Owen barely glanced at him. "What is it?"

"You may not know it, mister, but you're chasin' a

pretty smart man. Claw ain't lived this long by bein' easy to catch."

"He left a plain enough trail to follow," Owen snorted.

"Maybe that's just what he wanted you to do," Nestor pointed out.

Driscoll laughed. "You sound as scared as an old woman, Gilworth. I thought you'd fought Injuns before."

Nestor's eyes narrowed. "I've tangled with more Injuns than a varmint like you's got fleas, Driscoll. That's why I reckon we're ridin' right into a heap of trouble."

"Nothin' we can't handle," Driscoll scoffed.

Max Broderick rode up beside Nestor. "What do you think we should do, Mr. Gilworth?"

Nestor eyed the ridge that rose in front of them. The trail led up the slope and disappeared over the top of it. He grunted. "For one thing I wouldn't ride blind into what might be a trap. We need a scout."

"You volunteerin', Gilworth?" Driscoll jeered. "How do we know you wouldn't just keep on ridin'?"

"I ain't goin' to abandon Sister Laurel and them boys," Nestor replied. "But I'm willin' to do a little reconnoiterin'."

"Forget it," Driscoll snapped. "We know what we're doin', don't we, Owen?"

Owen nodded curtly. "We're going to pay that bastard back—"

The crack of a gunshot and a strangled cry from Max cut him off.

Nestor spun around and saw blood pouring from Max Broderick's throat. Max's fingers scrabbled at his saddlehorn but failed to grasp it. He tumbled from the back of his horse, dying as he hit the snowy ground.

"Look out!" Driscoll yelled. He pulled his Winchester out of its boot and looked around wildly, trying to discover where the shot had come from.

Lucinda twisted and, as she saw Max's sprawled body, let out a scream. Uttering bitter curses, Owen and Al drew their own guns. Driscoll's men also had their hardware out, but there was nothing to shoot at, no targets to be seen on the snow-covered landscape.

Nestor hauled out his Sharps as he reined in. "Get in the buggy, boys!" he rapped to Michael and Wesley, who quickly dismounted and scurried to obey him. He looked at the ridge they had been approaching, at the spot where the tracks of Claw and his warriors disappeared. But suddenly instinct told him that the threat was not coming from there. Claw was too cunning for that.

The Indians charged up out of a depression to the left, firing their rifles and whooping blood-curdling war cries. Asa Mitchell was torn from his saddle by a couple of slugs, and Lee Roy Johnson let out an agonized cry as lead ripped through his midsection. He sagged but managed to stay on his horse. Driscoll's two other men whipped up their guns and started returning the fire.

Driscoll began to fire his Winchester. Owen and Al had no time to deal with their brother's death. Grimly the two Brodericks started shooting. Owen wheeled his horse to turn it, so his body would shield Lucinda from the onslaught. Lucinda buried her face in his back and clung tightly to him.

Nestor brought the Sharps to his shoulder and, taking careful aim, sighted in on one of the charging Indians. When he pressed the trigger a second later, the big gun boomed heavily and recoiled against his shoulder. He saw his target lift from the back of his horse and tumble to the ground. The .50 caliber slug had gone home. The distance was too great to use his Dragoon; the pistol was not accurate over a dozen feet. Calmly he started to reload the Sharps.

Nestor knew these Indians were not like Beaver-Tail's band. They were hardened killers, and they outnumbered the whites. Owen Broderick's stubbornness and Tate Driscoll's greed had led them into a trap that would get all of them killed. But Nestor intended to postpone that for as long as he could. He fired again and saw another Indian go down.

Suddenly in the confusion and spraying snow, Nestor noticed that the buggy was careening wildly. The little mare was rearing and plunging in fright at the bullets that were booming around her, and Sister Laurel was desperately trying to control her. Swinging his horse around, he raced toward the buggy. Nestor slid his bowie from its sheath and leaned forward. As he drew up to the vehicle, he reached over and slashed the lines. The terrified mare bolted; the buggy rolled to a halt in her snowy wake.

Sister Laurel stared in shock at Nestor. "Dear Lord, why did you do that?" she cried.

"Runnin' ain't goin' to do us no good," Nestor called over the crackle of gunfire. "But we can use the buggy for cover. Get down and crawl behind it!"

Forting up was the only chance they had, and it was a slim one. Nestor slid out of the saddle and slapped his horse on the rump to send it running after the mare. Sister Laurel, Michael, and Wesley scrambled out of the buggy and crouched behind it. Nestor joined them and grimaced as he saw that the light frame provided only scant cover. Nevertheless, he gritted his teeth and edged out from the corner of the buggy to fire the Sharps again. He saw Al Broderick go down, his coat torn and bloody in several places.

From the way Al hit the ground, Nestor knew he was dead.

Suddenly Owen yanked his mount around and galloped toward the buggy. Nestor realized that Owen had noticed what they had done and was joining them. Driscoll, Pearson, and Dunn tried the same thing. Johnson was still on his horse, curled over the pommel, more dead than alive.

The Indians were closing in now. Several of them had been killed, but the survivors still outnumbered them. Nestor saw the savage face of the warrior who was leading the charge and knew that he was looking at Claw. He was starting to settle the sights of his Sharps on the man's chest when Owen Broderick vaulted off his horse, dragged Lucinda with him, and bumped into Nestor. The Sharps boomed, but the shot went wild.

A moment later Driscoll and his men approached the buggy. They did not wait until they were behind it before they flung themselves out of their saddles and ran toward the vehicle. *It's gonna get mighty crowded back here,* Nestor thought. But Dunn and Pearson never made it to the buggy. Both men stumbled and went down as Indian bullets tore through them.

Lucinda Broderick was still screaming. Her husband grabbed her arm and thrust her to the ground next to Sister Laurel, who was crouched behind the buggy wheel. Michael and Wesley were there, too, their eyes wide with fear. Suddenly Michael cried, "Give me a gun!"

Nestor shook his head. There was a chance Claw would not kill the boys if they did not fight back. Indians had been known to take white youngsters captive. But given what he knew of Claw, Nestor realized that was not very likely.

He was about to pull the Dragoon and give it to

Michael when a slug clipped his left shoulder, ripped through the buffalo coat, and burned a crease in his flesh. Nestor winced and staggered back a step. Then the Indians were swarming around them before he had a chance to do anything. One of them was using his rifle as a club. He lashed out with the weapon and hit Nestor's good shoulder, making his arm go numb. The Sharps slipped out of his fingers.

Owen Broderick caught a bullet in the side. The impact threw him against the buggy, and the light frame rocked wildly. Next to him, Driscoll dropped his Colt and suddenly thrust his arms into the air. "Don't shoot!" he yelled. "For God's sake, don't kill us!"

Nestor glanced scornfully at Driscoll. *Now he shows his true colors,* he thought. As was the case with a lot of men who thought they were tough, Driscoll was really a coward.

But the fight was over, that much was obvious.

Nestor rose, positioned his massive body between the Indians and Sister Laurel, Lucinda, Michael, and Wesley, and planted his feet. Claw and his men surrounded the buggy. The war chief glared at all of them; slowly his expression changed until he had an unpleasant smile on his face. He looked past Nestor at Lucinda and said, "So, Yellowhair, you have come back to me. You must have missed what I brought you in the night."

Owen was clutching his bloody side. He stared at the arrogant Indian, his face crimson with rage, and gasped, "You . . . you son of a bitch! You keep your filthy hands off my wife!"

Slowly Claw slid off the back of his horse. As his men kept their guns trained on the survivors, he ambled up to the buggy. He fixed his gaze on Owen and said, "So, you are Yellowhair's husband. I understand why you wanted her back." Claw laughed crudely. "She drains a man's seed very well. Even the coldest nights are warm in her blankets."

Owen trembled; his face was a mask of pain and rage. "You're nothing but an animal!" he roared.

Claw's mouth twisted in a hard, ugly sneer. "And your woman is nothing but a slut! Is that what you wish to die for, white man?"

"Damn you," Owen hissed. "Where's my money?"

The Sioux chieftain laughed. Then he turned and spoke harshly to one of his men. The brave reached into a bag that was slung on his horse's back and pulled out a small wooden chest. He tossed it to Claw, who caught it deftly despite his malformed hand.

"Is this what you mean, white man?" the war chief demanded as he thrust the chest toward Owen.

His eyes burning, Owen straightened and, evidently forgetting the bullet wound in his side, lurched forward to rip the chest out of Claw's fingers. Claw raised his other hand in a gesture to his men not to shoot. Clearly, he no longer considered Owen or any of the whites a threat.

Let him believe that, Nestor thought as he watched. He was beginning to regain the feeling in his left arm, and he was willing to bet that he could get out his Dragoon and put a ball in Claw's head before any of the renegades could stop him. He just had to wait for the right moment.

They were all going to die, but Claw was going with them, Nestor vowed silently.

Owen Broderick's bloodstained fingers had been fumbling anxiously with the catch on the chest. At last it swung free. Then he threw back the lid and peered inside it.

An insane howl tore from his throat. He dropped the chest; its contents spilled onto the snow. It was a store of buffalo jerky.

Claw was laughing again. "What good is white man's money to me?" he taunted the stunned prisoners. "Nothing! I used the paper for kindling and threw away the rest. But that chest is very good for storing jerky."

Owen was still staring into the empty chest. Slowly he raised his eyes and looked around wildly. "All for nothing," he muttered. "All of us dead for nothing . . ."

Then, with a berserk cry, he leapt at Claw. His bloodied hands reached for the Indian's throat.

"No!" Claw shouted to his men. His good hand flashed to his waist and brought out the knife sheathed there. He flung up his other arm to block Owen's move and drove the blade toward the white man's belly.

Lucinda screamed. Owen grunted in pain as the knife plunged into his flesh. Claw ripped the cold steel from side to side with all of his wiry strength, then stepped back and watched as Owen's fingers pawed weakly at his middle. Owen opened his mouth, and blood bubbled out between his lips, but he made no sound. Then he pitched facedown in the snow. Lucinda sobbed wildly as she stared in horror at his body.

Suddenly Tate Driscoll darted to the side. He ignored the gun that lay at his feet. Nestor realized he was trying to use Owen's death as a distraction and that he hoped to escape. One of the Indians let out a yell of surprise as Driscoll shot by him and ran frantically toward the ridge.

What happened next was no surprise to Nestor.

Claw barked a command, and half a dozen Winchesters cracked. The bullets slammed into Driscoll's back. The outlaw shrieked, arched his back, and tried to reach behind him to grasp the wounds. He stumbled a few more steps, then collapsed into a snowdrift.

All the Indians were looking at Driscoll. Nestor knew this was his only chance.

His hand slid under the buffalo coat, gripped the butt of the Dragoon, and hauled the heavy pistol free. He was squeezing the trigger even as he brought it up into line. The weapon exploded with a thunderous roar, and a puff of black powder floated over the brilliant white snow.

But Claw had seen Nestor's movement out of the corner of his eye, and he threw himself to the side. The ball whined past his ear in a rising arc. It smashed into the chest of one of the mounted Indians and drove him from the back of his horse, killing him instantly. Nestor pulled the trigger again and saw another renegade fall. He kept firing, and the Indians wheeled their horses wildly as they tried to save their own skins.

"Run!" Nestor boomed. He grabbed Wesley's shoulder and shoved him away from the buggy. "Go!" He triggered off his last two shots as Michael, Sister Laurel, and Lucinda sprinted behind Wesley out of the circle of distracted Indians.

But the Indians recovered quickly from their shock. Uttering angry cries, they began to close in on Nestor. He dropped the Dragoon and stooped to snatch up the Sharps. One of the warriors leapt from the back of his horse only feet from where Nestor was crouching and lunged with the knife he was brandishing. Nestor tipped the barrel of the buffalo gun up and squeezed the trigger. The renegade's head disappeared in a shower of blood and brains. The knife fell from his nerveless fingers, and Nestor grasped the hilt before it hit the ground.

"Kill him!" Claw shrieked.

The Sioux warriors, their knives held lethally, swarmed over him on foot. He met their charge by lashing out with the knife in one hand and swinging the empty Sharps like a club with the other.

As Wesley led the others in their desperate flight from the battle, he looked over his shoulder and saw the Indians close ranks around Nestor. The boy sobbed as Nestor went down in a knot of savages. But he kept running. He had hold of Lucinda Broderick's arm, and he urged her on. He could hear Michael breathlessly encouraging Sister Laurel a few feet behind him. Nestor was selling his life dearly to give them this slim chance to escape. Wesley felt the tears freeze on his cheeks in the cold air.

Claw watched what was left of his band drag Nestor down like a pack of dogs attacking a grizzly bear. Then he realized that the others had slipped away, and he jerked his head around. He spotted them running frantically through the snow about seventy yards away and grinned. Hurrying to his horse, Claw vaulted onto its back and leaned over to pick up a war lance that one of his men had driven into the ground when they surrounded the buggy. He banged his heels against the pony's side and kicked it into a gallop.

He would ride them down, gut them on the lance, he thought triumphantly. The two boys and the nun would die quickly, but Lucinda . . .

Lucinda he would give to his men. When they were

through with her, if she still lived, he would flay every inch of skin from her body until she begged for death.

Suddenly, gunshots blasted behind him. Claw twisted and saw at least two dozen white men galloping toward the buggy. All of them carried rifles, and they were using the weapons with deadly effect. His warriors were spinning and falling as the hail of bullets rained down on them.

A vicious grimace twisted Claw's face. He had no idea who the newcomers were, but it was clear that all of his men were going to die. Perhaps he would, too, but before he did, he would kill those four whites. His plans for Lucinda would have to be abandoned, but that was all right. At least he would be able to see her writhing on the end of his lance.

Luke Travis and Cody Fisher led the search party from Abilene straight toward the knot of fighting warriors. They swarmed around the Indians. As the first shots were fired, the Indians turned to face the new threat. The renegades shouted their defiance and tried to fight, but they were too slow. Within moments all the Indians lay dead.

Travis reined in and dropped out of his saddle. Beside him, Cody Fisher dismounted and cautiously approached the bloodied bodies heaped on the reddening snow a few feet away from Sister Laurel's horseless buggy. The marshal, his Peacemaker at the ready, scanned the surrounding area. Suddenly the pile of bodies quivered and began to move, and Travis snapped his revolver up.

A shaggy form abruptly surged up from the snow and cast aside the corpses that buried him. His bearded face a mass of cuts and scratches, a grinning Nestor Gilworth said, "Howdy, Marshal."

Travis gaped at Nestor, as the big buffalo hunter stepped over several bodies and strode toward him. Orion McCarthy, who was sitting on horseback behind the marshal, uttered an incredulous curse.

The grin on Nestor's face was suddenly replaced by a look of alarm. The big man turned, looked around wildly, and cried, "Marshal, where're Sister Laurel, Wesley, and Michael?"

One hundred yards from the buggy, Claw was closing in on the fleeing whites. He swooped in and, guiding the horse with his knees, lifted the lance. He saw Lucinda glance over her shoulder, saw the terror in her eyes, and laughed. No one could stop him now, he thought and smiled savagely.

Nestor spotted the distant figures and whirled to the rescue party. One of the men was carrying a Sharps Big Fifty, just like the one Nestor had broken over the heads of several Indians. "Toss me that Sharps, mister!" he snapped, and Travis echoed the command. The townsman threw the heavy rifle toward Nestor.

The tracker's big hands deftly caught the weapon. In one sweeping motion he turned, brought it to his shoulder, and squinted down the long blue barrel. Through the notch in the sight, Nestor saw Claw raise his lance to thrust it at Lucinda's back. The big man squeezed the trigger—and uttered a silent prayer that the gun was loaded.

A .50 caliber slug smashed into the Sioux, blew a fist-sized hole through him, and lifted him off the galloping pony. He flew through the air and crashed to the ground. The lance fell harmlessly from his hand.

Slowly Nestor Gilworth lowered the Sharps, a grim smile on his grizzled face. Then he turned around and saw the men from Abilene gaping at him. He handed the rifle back to its astonished owner and said calmly, "Your sight's a mite off, son, but I figgered as much and allowed for it."

Chapter Seventeen

—◆—

It was an hour after dark when the tired group reached Abilene. The temperature was dropping, and it promised to be another very cold night. But for some reason Nestor Gilworth felt warm.

Luke Travis had patched up his wounds as best he could. None of them appeared to be too serious, but he would still need some attention from Dr. Aileen Bloom. A few of the gashes he had suffered during the hand-to-hand battle with Claw's men would need sewing up. Some hot, strong coffee had gone a long way toward restoring Nestor's strength.

He had shaken hands with Travis and Cody and said, "Reckon I owe you and these other fellers my life, Marshal. If'n you hadn't heard the shootin' and come runnin' like you did, those redskins would've killed us all."

"I'm just glad we came out to look for you and were able to lend a hand," Travis had replied.

"Looked like you were giving a pretty good account of yourself," Cody added with a grin.

"I was just tryin' to keep 'em busy for a few minutes, so Sister Laurel and the boys and that other lady would have a chance to get away." They were riding back toward Abilene, the sun dipping below the horizon behind them, as Nestor spoke. He turned and glanced at the figures draped over several of the horses. Lucinda Broderick rode alongside the bodies of her husband and brothers-in-law. Nestor went on, "What do you reckon Miz Broderick's goin' to do now?"

"I asked about that," Travis replied. "The family had a ranch west of here, and it'll go to her now that everyone else is dead. But she doesn't want to go back there. She asked if I'd see to the details of selling it for her. Said something about going to live with some relatives in Missouri." The marshal shook his head grimly. "After all she's gone through, I can see why she wouldn't want to go back to that ranch."

Nestor nodded. "That feller Claw was one mean son of a bitch, all right."

On the other side of Travis, Cody leaned forward in his saddle and asked, "Why didn't he just grab Mrs. Broderick earlier, before she ever hooked up with you and the others, Nestor?"

"I've done some thinkin' on that, Deputy. Ain't no way of bein' sure, but I figure he was sort of playin' with her, lettin' her think she might have some hope of gettin' away. Then, after we found her, ol' Claw probably kept an eye on us, just waitin' for the right time to jump us. The Brodericks and Driscoll and them others beat 'em to it. Once Claw saw that Broderick had his mind set on trackin' him down, it was just a matter of leadin' us on and watchin' for a good place to spring the trap."

"That makes sense, all right," Travis agreed. The look he gave Nestor made it plain that he was not accustomed to hearing such logic from the big man.

But a great deal had changed since the Stillmans rode into town two weeks ago. Nestor had given up the bottle, and Michael Hirsch and Wesley Stillman were well on their way to becoming friends. Sharing a common danger would do that. Both boys were riding in the buggy with Sister Laurel. Nestor had heard part of their conversation and knew that Wesley was more than willing to stay on at the orphanage now that he had endured the nightmare on the snow-covered plains. But someday, he had told Sister Laurel and Michael, he intended to head on to California, just the way his father had wanted.

Now, as the large party of riders entered Abilene, Nestor felt as if they were his family. Travis and Cody were affording him some respect, and Wesley and Michael seemed to look up to him as if he were some sort of hero. He would have to straighten them out on that. He was no hero—just a man doing his best.

As they rolled down Texas Street, Judah Fisher pushed open the door of the Sunrise Café and raced into the street. A crowd of townsfolk streamed out of the door behind him. Down the block, Augie, Orion McCarthy's assistant, led another group of citizens out of Orion's Tavern.

Travis lifted his hand and brought the procession to a halt in front of the café.

The pastor hurried to the buggy and embraced Sister Laurel as she climbed down. Then he turned to the two boys and hugged them, too. "Thank the Lord," he said fervently. "I wasn't sure I'd ever see any of you again."

"God was indeed merciful to us," Sister Laurel said. She smiled up at Nestor, who had reined in beside them. "The Lord in His wisdom provided a means for our salvation from the weather and the Indians."

"Indians?" Judah cried in surprise.

"It's a long story. Let's get these two boys back to the orphanage. They need a hot meal and some sleep. I'll tell you all about it, Judah."

"All right." Judah started away with Sister Laurel, Michael, and Wesley. Suddenly, he looked over his shoulder at Nestor. "Are you coming, Nestor?"

The big man grinned. "I'll be along as soon as the doc is through with me."

The street was full of noise as the people who had remained in town questioned the members of the rescue party. Citizens were crowding around Nestor and slapping him on the back and congratulating him, as the story of his part in the adventure spread. He was starting to feel downright uncomfortable, and it was not from the wounds he had sustained in the fighting. He looked around and caught Travis's eye.

"Here now, let us through," the marshal said in a loud voice as he took Nestor's arm. "This man's got to go see the doctor. I'm sure Nestor will be glad to tell you all about it later."

The crowd parted, allowing Nestor, Travis, and Cody to pass through to the boardwalk. The trio started toward Aileen Bloom's office with the two lawmen flanking the massive former buffalo hunter.

"So you'll be staying on at the orphanage as their handyman?" Cody asked as he walked beside Nestor.

"As long as they'll have me," he replied.

Travis said, "I've been thinking, Nestor. How would you feel about doing some work for me from time to time? I could use a jailer and another deputy every now and then."

Nestor stopped in his tracks and frowned. "Me, a lawman?" he asked in disbelief.

Travis shrugged. "You've seen the place from the wrong side of the bars enough times. How about being on the right side for a change?"

A smile spread slowly across Nestor's bearded face. He reached up and tugged his disreputable black hat down tighter. "Nestor Gilworth, deputy marshal," he rumbled. "Durned if it ain't got a nice ring to it."

Travis laughed and slapped him on the back, and the trio continued down the boardwalk.